Forty-Seven Hours to Hurricane Harvey is historical fiction based on a real town and events, drawn from a variety of sources, including personal, published materials and interviews. For dramatic and narrative purposes, the story contains fictionalized scenes, characters and dialogue. All the characters, with the exception of Texas Governor Greg Abbott, Tony Amos, Guy Harvey and Dale Nelson, are fictitious. Any similarity to any person living or dead is merely coincidental.

The picture on the cover of this book is of the Lydia Ann Lighthouse in Port Aransas. It was taken at sundown by the Author in August of 2016, one year prior to Hurricane Harvey's arrival.

Dedication

This Book is dedicated to all the First Responders and the families who support them. From the Coast Guard and National Guard to the Police, Firefighters, EMT's. To the City, County and State workers who worked long hours under difficult circumstances to help those in need.

It is also dedicated to the teams of Utility repairmen and women who came from all over the country to get our power back up and running again, many bringing their own poles with them.

And finally, to the unsung heroes; the average 'joes' who set up tables, giving away free bottles of water or a sandwich to a needy passer-by. Whether it was one person in front of their home or "Cowboy Camp David" in Port Aransas feeding hundreds, (with their awesome sign: Free Food, Free Water, Free Hugs) -your compassion for others will not be forgotten.

Thank you and God bless-

Introduction

Tropical storm Harvey waxed and waned over the course of several days in mid-August of 2017 leaving the inhabitants of the Gulf of Mexico coastline cautious, but not overly concerned. At least not yet. Many tropical storms and hurricanes had come and gone over the years to either die off before making landfall, or take a sudden turn, leaving all the anxious souls wondering why they were nervous to begin with. Hurricane Harvey became a Category 4 hurricane that made landfall causing catastrophic flooding and many deaths. It is tied with 2005's Hurricane Katrina as the costliest tropical cyclone on record, inflicting $125 billion in damage. In a four-day period, many areas received more than 40 inches of rain as the system slowly wandered over eastern Texas, causing unprecedented flooding. With peak accumulations of 60.58 in Nederland, Texas, Harvey was the wettest tropical cyclone on record in the United States. The resulting floods inundated hundreds of thousands of homes, displacing more than 30,000 people and prompting more than 17,000 rescues.

As seen in the first NOAA report dated August 19th, Harvey had degenerated from a tropical storm back into a tropical wave. Despite the downgrade, this was the year for Port Aransas, Aransas Pass and Rockport/Fulton to be hit head-on by a major hurricane. It's worth noting that it took Harvey only 47 hours to go from being *re-declared* a Tropical Storm, to a

Category 4 Hurricane as it made landfall. The NOAA weather bulletins incorporated into this book were taken directly from the online archives, some being shortened for the sake of brevity. They can be a little tedious, but there is much useful information there for those interested in the details. The important parts of the bulletins have been underlined for those who don't care for so much information.

Enjoy-

Forty-Seven Hours to
Hurricane Harvey

Part One-The Storm

Chapter 1

NOAA Hurricane Center: BULLETIN
Remnants Of Harvey Advisory Number 11
NWS National Hurricane Center Miami FL
AL092017
1100 PM EDT Sat Aug 19 2017
...HARVEY DEGENERATES INTO A
TROPICAL WAVE...
SUMMARY OF 1100 PM EDT...0300
UTC...INFORMATION

LOCATION...14.3N 71.8W
ABOUT 135 MI...215 KM N OF NTHRN TIP OF
GUAJIRA PNSULA COLOMBIA
ABOUT 765 MI...1230 KM E OF CABO
GRACIAS A DIOS ON NIC/HON BORDER
MAXIMUM SUSTAINED WINDS...35 MPH...55
KM/H
PRESENT MOVEMENT...W OR 275 DEGREES
AT 22 MPH...35 KM/H
MINIMUM CENTRAL PRESSURE...1007
MB...29.74 INCHES

WATCHES AND WARNINGS

There are no coastal watches or warnings in
effect.
Interests in northern Nicaragua, northern

Honduras, Belize, and the
Yucatan Peninsula of Mexico should monitor the
progress of the
remnants of Harvey.

DISCUSSION AND 48-HOUR OUTLOOK

At 1100 PM EDT (0300 UTC), the remnants of
Harvey were located near latitude 14.3 North,
longitude 71.8 West. The tropical wave
associated with Harvey's remnants is moving
quickly toward the west near 22 mph (35 km/h), and
this general motion will continue for the
next day or two. The remnants are expected to
move westward across the central Caribbean Sea on
Sunday and across the western Caribbean Sea toward
Central America on Monday.

Maximum sustained winds are near 35 mph (55
km/h) with higher gusts.
The estimated minimum central pressure is 1007
mb (29.74 inches).

HAZARDS AFFECTING LAND

None.

NEXT ADVISORY

This is the last public advisory issued by the
National Hurricane
Center on this system unless regeneration occurs
or if tropical

cyclone watches or warnings are required for
land areas.   Additional information on this system can
be found in High Seas Forecasts
issued by the National Weather Service, under
AWIPS header
NFDHSFAT1, WMO header FZNT01 KWBC,
and available on the Web at
http://www.opc.ncep.noaa.gov/shtml/NFDHSFAT1.sht
ml.

Tuesday-- August 22nd 6:45 AM

Aransas Pass, Texas

Needing some coffee, I walk into my usual morning destination, CBC otherwise known as Coastal Bend Coffee. 'I'm in luck!' I think as I spot my favorite Barista—Emily who's on the bar preparing a couple of drinks. She's the only one I trust to get my double tall hazelnut latte just right. You wouldn't think it would be so hard, but as I've come to learn, the process of making a latte is as much an art as it is following a recipe.

Perusing the pastry case to my left, waiting my turn in line, I decide to order one of their bear claws. CBC is one of the few coffee shops in the area that makes their own offerings. It's best one of the reasons for coming here, if only to enjoy the smells. Coffee and pastries, a great way to start the day. Another thing that makes this place special are all the paintings and framed photographs by local artists. There's a wide variety from birds, to beach scenes; even a few of the Lydia Ann Lighthouse in Port Aransas not far from here.

"Good morning Juan, my usual please. And add a bear claw, thanks."

"You got it; Emily's already got your coffee started Paul." Looking up at me, he adds, "How's your morning going so far?"

Holding my iPhone up to the pay station where you would normally swipe your credit/debit card, it instantly deducts $6.79 using my Apple Pay App. "No complaints here, just heading to work to make a little money, so I can support my coffee habit. I'm looking forward to surfing some decent waves tomorrow in Port A (Port Aransas) coming in from what is left of the tropical storm in the gulf."

Dropping a buck in the tip jar I tell Juan to have a great day and move along the counter to my left, waiting for my morning pick-me-up to be finished.

"How's it going Emily?" I call out above the noise of the milk steaming in the stainless-steel pitcher.

She glances my way with a smile, then turns her head towards the counter near the windows to her left. It's where all the condiments sit to put that final touch on your steaming brew. "I'm doing great . . . how about you?"

Turning to see what she's looking at; I see an older man at the condiment stand, trying to hide the fact that he's stuffing sugar packets and napkins into his jean pockets. His long silver hair and shaggy beard somewhat hiding his face.

Catching my eye, she leans in towards me saying, "That's Eliot. A homeless man who comes in frequently and scrounges what he can. Usually he comes over and asks me to add hot water to his bowl of instant oatmeal or ramen noodles. Some of the others here get upset, but as long as he doesn't cause trouble, I don't care. He's always been nice to me, besides he's a Vet; my Dad was one too."

Eliot looks in our direction, catches us watching

him, then turns and quickly walks out the door.

Facing back my way, she sets the cup on the counter, "Here you go Paul, enjoy!

"Thanks Emily." I pick up my 'elixir of life' and head out the front door towards my Jeep. Taking a careful sip, I get behind the wheel and drive off to work.

Today is one of those days I'm truly glad for air conditioning. It's not only hot outside it's very humid too. By noon it'll be in the 90's (it's in the 80's now). And the humidity 70% or more. I don't mind it so much at the beach, just not when I'm fully dressed and heading for the grocery store where I work. But that's life when you choose to live this close to the water. Through the windshield I spot a dozen pelicans flying overhead in a 'V' formation heading for the gulf. I never gave it a second thought until my former girlfriend introduced me to bird watching. It's still not my 'thing' as much as it was hers, but I must admit that finding out brown pelicans have a seven-foot wingspan, and the white pelicans (when they show up during the winter months) have a nine-foot wingspan, is impressive. One amazing part is that I can be driving down the freeway (Highway 181 near the Harbor Bridge) heading toward Corpus Christi at fifty-five mph, and they keep up with me without much effort at all. Pretty good for what many would consider an ugly bird.

Pulling into the store parking lot I find a spot along the outer edge where no one likes to park. For one reason it's company policy. Secondly; I'm trying to avoid anyone scratching my paint job. Besides enjoying the beach in Port Aransas and my Xbox, this Jeep is my life.

Heading inside I beeline for the time clock and then check in with the head clerk.

"Good morning Alex, where do you want me today?"

"First Paul, you're five minutes late, let's not ruin your good record." Looking up from his 'day sheet', he points me in the direction of a cash register. "Please go relieve Sylvia over on number seven, let her know it's break time."

Replying, "You got it," I tuck tail, check my nametag and head for the register. Waiting until she finishes with the customer in front of her, I slide into her spot, "Break time Sylvia."

"Thanks Paul," she responds as she walks off to the break room.

Keying in my code, the register is now open for business. As I begin to check customers through, I notice that a lot of my usual's are buying up extra batteries, water and candles. The kind of stuff you get when bad weather is coming. Don't they know Harvey's been downgraded? Not even a tropical storm anymore? Besides, Dale Nelson on KRIS TV news (our longtime Meteorologist) has said more than once that only the first few hurricanes of the season have ever hit the Corpus Christi area. Hurricanes are named in alphabetical order and no hurricane after the letter C has ever hit us. Which ones did he mention? Carla in 1961, Celia in 1970 and Amelia in 1978? And Harvey, starting with the letter H, is way down the alphabetical list already—I see no reason to worry. Besides, I love stormy weather! I was hoping that a tropical storm might come our way this summer- we could use the rain.

One of my favorite customers is just reaching the front of the line, Mrs. Henry, a gray-haired soul. "Good morning," I greet her, "how are you today?"

"I'm fine Paul, but I just wanted to tell you how sorry I am about your parents, I just found out yesterday. I wish you would have let me know. I feel just   horrible!"

"Thank you, Mrs. Henry, it was six months ago now, so I just don't talk about it much. They were killed by a drunk driver coming back from San Antonio one night on Highway 37."

"Well I know it's been a long time, but I just want you to know I'm thinking about you and hope you're doing alright."

"I'm managing ok, thank you."

Truth be told I was still mourning them although we'd been distant since I was in high school. I'd just graduated three years ago, and I remember how I thought I had so many things figured out; smarter than my parents and all that. Funny how quickly life catches up to you when you must pay your own rent, buy your own car insurance, well, you know what I mean. Electricity's not cheap either. And I don't think you realize how much you love your mom and dad until they're gone. We argued a lot before I moved out. Now I wish I could have even the arguments back. I would even be alright with how much they tried to get me to go to church-- just to have them around again. I'm starting to realize that maybe they were trying to look out for me, not just being pushy Christians; I just never got it is all. I always wanted to be the captain of my own ship, and now I am.

"Have a nice day Mrs. Henry, I'll get Christy to help you out with your groceries."

"Thank you, Paul, God bless you."

I cringe at that, but I recognize she means no harm. She unknowingly hit a sore spot with me. If there is a God—where was he when my parents got killed? Doesn't he look after his "children?" What's the use of going to church if he lets things like that happen? Not for me. No thanks. I only believe in things I can see.

Before you know it, the day is over, and I walk out to the parking lot. I can't help but admire my Jeep, a White Wrangler Rubicon, it's been so much fun! Driving down Port A beaches, trips to San Antonio, I especially like taking the soft top off and feeling the wind in my hair. It was the one thing I decided to do with my inheritance when my folks passed away. Friends told me to invest it for the future, but hey, live for today I say. You only live once right?

I walk out to the jeep, intent on hitting the gym on the way home. It's my newest diversion now that I'm a bachelor again. No, I wasn't married, but my old girlfriend sure made me feel that way. Texting me every 5 minutes to see what I was doing, constant hints about looking for rings and setting a date. No thanks, captain of my own ship, remember? And there are plenty of good-looking women to ask out at the gym, at work too for that matter. But I'm just enjoying being free for a while, and a little richer as well. Women can be sooo expensive. Being twenty-one gives me lots of options and I don't want to miss any of them.

Not feeling like dropping by CBC for coffee, (I've given up beer since my parents got killed by a drunk) I head home for another round of gaming on my Xbox. Trying to decide between Gears of War 4 and Forza Horizon 3. I feel like killing something tonight. Gears of War it is.

Chapter 2

BULLETIN

Tropical Depression Harvey Advisory Number 12
NWS National Hurricane Center Miami FL
AL092017
1000 AM CDT Wed Aug 23, 2017

...HARVEY REGENERATES INTO A TROPICAL DEPRESSION...
...HURRICANE AND STORM SURGE WATCHES ISSUED FOR PORTIONS OF THE TEXAS COAST...

SUMMARY OF 1000 AM CDT...1500 UTC...INFORMATION

LOCATION...21.5N 92.5W
ABOUT 535 MI...860 KM SSE OF PORT OCONNOR TEXAS
ABOUT 470 MI...755 KM SE OF PORT MANSFIELD TEXAS
MAXIMUM SUSTAINED WINDS...35 MPH...55 KM/H
PRESENT MOVEMENT...NW OR 310 DEGREES AT 9 MPH...15 KM/H MINIMUM CENTRAL PRESSURE...1006 MB...29.71 INCHES

WATCHES AND WARNINGS

CHANGES WITH THIS ADVISORY:

A Storm Surge Watch has been issued for the coast of Texas from Port Mansfield to High Island.

A Hurricane Watch has been issued for the coast of Texas from north of Port Mansfield to San Luis Pass.
A Tropical Storm Watch has been issued for the coast of Texas from the Mouth of the Rio Grande to Port Mansfield and from north of San Luis Pass to High Island.
The government of Mexico has issued a Tropical Storm Watch for the coast of Mexico from Boca De Catan to the Mouth of the Rio Grande.

SUMMARY OF WATCHES AND WARNINGS IN EFFECT:

A Storm Surge Watch is in effect for...
* Port Mansfield to High Island
A Hurricane Watch is in effect for...
* North of Port Mansfield to San Luis Pass
A Tropical Storm Watch is in effect for...
* Boca De Catan Mexico to Port Mansfield Texas
* North of San Luis Pass to High Island

DISCUSSION AND 48-HOUR OUTLOOK

At 1000 AM CDT (1500 UTC), the center of

Tropical Depression Harvey was located near latitude 21.5 North, longitude 92.5 West. The depression is moving toward the northwest near 9 mph (15 km/h) and a track toward the northwest or north-northwest is expected for the next 48 hours. <u>On the forecast track, Harvey should be approaching the Texas coast late Friday.</u>

<u>Maximum sustained winds are near 35 mph (55 km/h) with higher gusts. Some strengthening is forecast during the next 48 hours, and Harvey could become a hurricane on Friday.</u>

An Air Force Reserve Hurricane Hunter aircraft recently reported a minimum central pressure of 1006 mb (29.71 inches).

HAZARDS AFFECTING LAND

<u>RAINFALL: Harvey is expected to produce total rain accumulations of 10 to 15 inches with isolated maximum amounts of 20 inches over the middle and upper Texas coast and southwest Louisiana through next Tuesday, with heavy rainfall beginning as early as Friday morning.</u> Harvey is also expected to produce total rain accumulations of 3 to 9 inches in portions of south, central, and northeast Texas and the rest of the lower Mississippi Valley. Rainfall from Harvey could cause life-threatening flooding.

STORM SURGE: The combination of a dangerous storm surge and the tide will cause normally dry areas near the coast to be flooded by rising waters moving inland from the shoreline. The water is expected to reach the following heights above ground if

the peak surge occurs at the time of high tide...
Port Mansfield to High Island...4 to 6 ft

The deepest water will occur along the
immediate coast near and to
the northeast of the landfall location, where the
surge will be
accompanied by large and destructive waves.
Surge-related
flooding depends on the relative timing of the
surge and the tidal
cycle, and can vary greatly over short distances.
For information
specific to your area, please see products issued
by your local
National Weather Service forecast office.

WIND: Hurricane conditions are possible
within the hurricane watch area by late Friday, with
tropical storm conditions possible by early Friday.
SURF: Swells generated by Harvey are likely to
affect the Texas,
Louisiana, and northeast Mexico coasts by
Friday.   These swells are
likely to cause life-threatening surf and rip
current conditions.
Please consult products from your local weather
office.

NEXT ADVISORY

Next intermediate advisory at 100 PM CDT.
Next complete advisory at 400 PM CDT.

<<<<<<<   >>>>>>>

Chapter 3

Tropical Storm Harvey Tropical Cyclone Update
NWS National Hurricane Center Miami FL
AL092017
1100 PM CDT Wed Aug 23 2017

...AIR FORCE PLANE FINDS TROPICAL
STORM FORCE WINDS...

An Air Force Reserve hurricane hunter aircraft
just measured
tropical storm force winds in Harvey. The
maximum winds are
estimated to be 40 mph (65 km/h) with higher
gusts.

SUMMARY OF 1100 PM CDT...0400
UTC...INFORMATION

LOCATION...22.0N 92.6W
ABOUT 500 MI...810 KM SSE OF PORT
OCONNOR TEXAS
ABOUT 440 MI...705 KM SE OF PORT
MANSFIELD TEXAS
MAXIMUM SUSTAINED WINDS...40 MPH...65
KM/H
PRESENT MOVEMENT...NW OR 325 DEGREES

AT 2 MPH...4 KM/H
MINIMUM CENTRAL PRESSURE...1002
MB...29.59 INCHES

<<<<<<<   >>>>>>>

Wednesday-- August 23rd, 2017

My phone wakes me up from a dead sleep. I was gaming until 4 o'clock this morning and now I'm paying for it.

"Paul, it's Alex down at the store. Is there any way you can come in to work this morning, we're getting slammed."

"What?" I sputter.

"Did I wake you up? It's almost 11am!"

"Yeah—yeah Alex, just had a late night. So, give me some time to get dressed, a cup of coffee and I'll be down in about 30 minutes."

"Ok Paul, thanks." I can hear the grin on his face as Alex says, "I hope she was worth it."

"Nope, just me and my Xbox. See you in a bit."

Having showered last night after my workout I feel good enough to just throw on some clean work clothes and head out the door to the coffee shop. Walking into CBC it's Emily on the till this time and Pablo working through the line of the marked cups at the bar.

"Hey Emily, I need a large drip coffee of the day with a splash of breve, I'm in a hurry."

"Pablo, did you get that? "She looks over to the espresso bar and Pablo nods his head, replying, "got it."

"So, Paul, why the big hurry?"

"I got called into work today, something about being busy."

"That's $2.98 Paul, and I'm not surprised with the storm and all."

"What are you talking about Emily, is there another storm coming in now?" I have my phone out paying with Apple Pay once again.

"No—same one. Harvey has regenerated into a tropical storm and they think it might come this way. Everyone this morning has been talking about it, but who knows what will happen, right?"

"Wow, wish I could talk more but I gotta run. Thanks Emily, Pablo."

It's no wonder I got called in. Being the only major grocery store in Aransas Pass (besides Wal-Mart) we get our fair share of business. A lot of people in Port Aransas even take the short ferry ride across the channel and drive the fifteen minutes over to us, instead of driving the thirty minutes into Corpus Christi on highway 361. I don't think there's anything to worry about, but it doesn't matter what I believe; if people get it in their heads this storm is coming, even if it's just close, well, no surprise the store's getting super busy.

Heading towards work the weather looks fine to me; sunny, hot, a light breeze--the usual. Even the laughing gulls in the parking lot seem happy as they eat food scraps tossed out of car windows (there's no such thing as a 'sea' gull by the way, something else my old girlfriend taught me). Feeding the laughing gulls (the most common of the gulls around here) is something visitors get a kick out of doing. The problem is, we end up with a parking lot full of hungry birds who like to poop on everything. Not so cute after all. They'll grab their snacks and drinks and then head from our store to Port Aransas just fifteen minutes away if the ferries are not backed up. An hour or more if they are.

Sure enough, the store's so busy I have a hard time finding an empty parking spot, so I park across the street and walk in to find Alex and get started.

"Clock in and take over on register twelve Paul, and thanks for coming in."

"You're welcome Alex, has it been this busy all morning?" I query as I pan around and see all the people.

"It happened just after ten when the newest weather forecast about Harvey came out, I guess everyone just started calling each other and now we have this," he follows my gaze at the crowds in the building.

"Ok, I'll get going."

No surprise the type of shopper coming through my line is preparing for serious weather. The kind who try to think ahead, 'just in case'. As I'm ringing all this stuff up, it occurs to me that I don't have much back at the apartment other than a couple of candles that Sharon (old girlfriend) left behind, a gallon of distilled water (for ironing work clothes) and an empty fridge. Think I'll buy a few things when I get off. Maybe a flashlight, extra batteries, bread, peanut butter and jelly (you know, easy to fix foods, no cooking necessary), bottled water, stuff like what I've seen coming through the line. This many people can't all be wrong, can they? I check my cell phone for weather updates on my lunch break but nothing I haven't already heard.

After clocking out at six pm my personal shopping begins. The store is as busy as I have ever seen it, including holidays, so it takes me five minutes just to locate a shopping cart. It never occurred to me that I might not find much to buy, but that's exactly what happened. Walking down the semi-empty aisles I end up with a few tuna pouches, some canned pasta, soups, and a bag of tea light candles (the rest of the candles and even the flashlights are gone, batteries too). I figure I'll just use the light on my cell phone if needed. All the inexpensive store brand water is cleared out, but I pick up two 24 count packages of Dasani and count myself lucky. No peanut butter, jelly or bread to be had. And I'm not surprised to see the wine and beer coolers cleared out, but all the toilet paper too? Really? I check out and beeline for my ever-trusty jeep.

Driving home, feeling tired, I decide to drop by my favorite coffee shop and see if they have any sandwiches left. A little caffeine wouldn't be too bad either. They make the best chicken-salad sandwiches in Aransas Pass.

The CBC lot is half full, unusual for evening time. I spot Eliot sitting at a table outside the front door on the patio, enjoying the shade from a large blue umbrella. It's still hot despite the light breeze so he has to be miserable, but it doesn't seem to bother him. He's got his backpack next him on the ground and is staring off into the distance. What is a homeless person's life like I wonder? *Why* is he homeless? Is it something he chose? With no easy answer in sight I clear my thoughts and walk inside.

Susan is at the register as I walk in enter; a pretty brunette in her early 20's. I know she has a 2-year-old daughter from previous conversations, her pride and joy, and her reason for getting out of bed in the morning.

"Hey Susan, how's it going this afternoon?"

"Good Paul, what'll it be today?"

"Do you have any iced coffee left?"

"You're in luck. What size would you like?"

"How about a large with 5 pumps of hazelnut and some breve on top? And do you have any chicken salad sandwiches left?"

"Sorry, ran out earlier today, but if I remember right you like our smoked turkey, and I still have some of that."

"Great, with mayo and lettuce please. By the way, have you heard anything else about the storm coming in?"

"Nothing since this morning Paul, but I'm planning on heading to Austin where my folks are if it gets worse."

"You really think there's a chance it will?"

"I don't know but once you have a kid, you stop taking so many chances and you consider what's best for them. She's my life now."

Glancing to my left there's a mid-20's man standing next to me, his height--6 feet, making him a few inches taller than me.

Susan looks in his direction and says, "Hi Matt,

I'd like you to meet Paul— a friend of mine, Paul, this is Matt."

Matt looks at me and gives me a firm handshake, the kind that tells you he's no stranger to working hard. His size is somewhat intimidating, broad shouldered but trim, with chestnut brown hair.

"Pleased to meet you Paul."

"Likewise, Matt."

I'd seen the bible study group he leads here in the evening from time to time but always managed to avoid them until now.

Nodding towards the back corner where a large table with five or six people are sitting, he says, "My church group over there is discussing how to prepare for the storm that may hit us. You're welcome to join us if you like."

"Thanks, but no thanks," I respond just a little too quickly, hoping I didn't reveal just how anxious I was to get away from them. He seems like a nice guy, but I just don't want to get roped into any religious discussions.

"Well, if you change your mind, you're always welcome to join us, just good people getting together to share the Word." Then he looks at me with a smile and says, "Don't forget, God loves you!"

I pay for my coffee and sandwich then head to the other end of the counter to wait for my order. The iced coffee comes up quickly, so I put a straw in it and take a sip. The longer I stand here the madder I get. There it is again; this 'thing' I have with Christians. What is it with these people? So, if you get religion then all of a sudden no more problems? No more worries? You go around with a stupid smile on your face every day? I don't buy it. My internal pressure cooker has been simmering for a long time now and Matt has just turned the flame up. He takes the drinks he has ordered for his group and walks past me to his table. A moment later my sandwich is ready, so I grab the bag and move towards the door. Welling up inside of me is all the frustration and anger of losing my parents. Parents who called themselves Christians too and here is some guy telling me God loves me? Well if God loves me so much why did mom and dad have to die?

Just as I'm about to reach the door my emotions get the better of me and I turn to the right and go straight to Matt's table. He's facing me with his back against the wall. The smile he has when he first sees me coming towards him melts into concern as he recognizes the anger building on my face.

"Hi Paul. Is something wrong?"

I approach the table as my eyes attempt to drill holes through his. "You're damn right, I'm tired of people telling me how much God loves me when He let my parents die in a car wreck almost six months ago."

"I'm sorry--" Matt starts to reply, but I am not about to give him the chance to respond.

Cutting him off I shout, "Don't tell me you're sorry! What the hell do you know about losing your parents like that?"

Matt breathes for a moment, then looks at me with a quiet resolve, and calmly replies, "I don't."

By this time the whole table is looking at me, waiting for me to explode, unsure how to react. Yet Matt doesn't try to jump in with some polished words of biblical wisdom, nothing to try to sugar coat things. In a calm voice he simply says, "What happened Paul?"

I was taken aback, not expecting his placating attitude. Taking it down a notch I bark, "They were killed by a drunk driver going the wrong way on the freeway, on their way home to San Antonio one night." I could feel the emotion welling up inside, the tears threatening to reveal themselves and run down my face, but I refuse to let them. Yelling a little louder, "Where was your God when that jerk got behind the wheel? Where was your God when he turned the wrong way onto the freeway? Where was your God when my parents hit him head on? I'm sick of people telling me God loves me!!"

My pain and anger overwhelm me as I turn and walk swiftly for the exit. It was leave or completely lose it. Fight or flight. Getting behind the wheel I just sit in my jeep for a couple of minutes to try to get control of the adrenaline racing through me. The shaking in my hands is just beginning to subside when I see Matt approaching my window. He has his hands palms-out in front of him as if to say, "I'm not going to do anything . . . give me a chance to speak." I wanted to go off on him again, and yet I was beginning to feel a little guilty for the way I screamed at him in front of his friends. I decide to give him a chance to talk. I did kind of owe it to him after venting like that.

Rolling down the window Matt firmly but quietly speaks to me saying, "Paul, I don't pretend to know how you feel. I also know you're very mad at God right now," he pauses, "and not at me. I just want to say one thing and then I'll leave you alone. I *do* know something of the *kind of pain* you're going through. When I was fifteen my father, who was drunk, flew into a rage and shot my mother over some stupid argument. That was eleven years ago. She's buried in Rockport and my dad died in prison five years back." Matt paused for a moment letting me take it all in. "If you want someone to talk to, you know where I am-- here at the coffee shop two nights a week. If not, know that I'm praying for you whether you believe in God or not."

With that Matt turns around and walks back into the shop. I tell myself that I don't care. This is my pain, I own it. Who the heck is *he* to tell me he might understand what I'm feeling? But my cold broken heart begins to warm ever so slightly just the same. What he did took guts. Whether I agree with him or not, I can respect that.

I head home to eat my sandwich and then try to get a little game time in, but I can't focus on what I'm doing. Despite how mad I am at Matt; he has given me something to think about. For the first time since my parent's death, I consider the possibility that I'm not the only one to have their parents die on them in a tragedy. With that thought I decide to go to bed and get some rest since I start work tomorrow at 7am. And after today I'm sure it's going to be busy, especially if Harvey really is coming our way. A quick shower and a peanut butter bar prepares me for catching some Z's, but those Z's are a long time coming.

Thursday-- August 24th, 2017

I awaken to my phone alarm, six am comes *so* early in the morning. I didn't get much sleep last night, but you know what? It's ok, I figure I'll get all the sleep I need when I'm dead. Climbing out of bed I get on Facebook, Snapchat and Twitter to see what's going on with my friends. After that I check my bank account balance, the news, and then quickly get off my laptop, being reminded just how much I hate the news media—it's always so negative. Anyway, I was only looking for something new about Harvey.

Heading towards CBC for my morning coffee I note that the weather seems normal; sunny, hot and very humid. Ninety percent already, yikes. If you don't like to sweat 24/7, don't live on the Texas coast during the summer.

Looking at the hood, I decide my jeep could use a wash (the gulls love me, the terns too for that matter) but I think I'll wait until after the storm blows through. No use wasting good money, right?

As I walk in to Coastal Bend Coffee, I see my "fave," Emily is there at the bar making espresso drinks. Pablo spots me in line and is quick to mark my cup, getting it in the queue while I wait my turn to pay. I wish they had the app like some coffee shops where you order with your phone, pay with the app, and then just go straight to the Barista and pick up your drink. No waiting in line, no hassle, just "bing-bang-bong," as my ex-girlfriend used to say. Oh well, maybe one of these days. I just love technology.

Soon, it's my turn to pay and I have my iPhone ready to go. Passing my phone over the receiver I say, "Hi Pablo, how's your morning?"

"Good Paul, just worried about Hurricane Harvey, it's not looking good."

"What have you heard?"

"The storm is growing a little stronger and it looks like if nothing else, we'll get a ton of rain out of this. Some estimates as high as fifteen to twenty inches."

"I didn't know that, and I hope they're wrong. I remember the last time it flooded here, and it wasn't that long ago. And it wasn't fifteen to twenty inches, only five or six—that was bad enough."

"Well, let's just hope it doesn't turn into a hurricane, a tropical storm's enough for me."

"I'm with you there, thanks Pablo. See you tomorrow."

Grabbing my drink from the bar, I call out, "Thanks Emily, have an awesome day!" adding, "Stay dry!"

"You too Paul!" Her big smile sending me on my way to work.

I arrive at the store five minutes early for the first time in forever, but sadly no one seems to notice. There's a buzz going through the place; a heightened tension amongst my co-workers here, and not just because of all the customers. Alex is even working today, standing next to another head clerk surprised because I know he's usually off on Thursdays.

"Hey Alex, where to," as I check in with the 'boss,' my immediate boss anyway.

"Paul, go relieve John on register three, he's due

for a break."

"Sure Alex, by the way, why are you here?"

"Management thinks the storm is coming, so they asked me last night to come in, and by the level of customers in the store, they definitely needed me. We've been busy since 5:30 this morning."

"I'll guess we'll see soon enough if Harvey comes our way," although I'm not 100% convinced.

I notice as the customers come through my line, a lot of what we ran out of yesterday has been restocked already. That's one of the things I like about my company; they react quickly and were able to get a couple of trucks in last night from San Antonio. I'm proud of where I work.

Just chatting with my regulars, it seems that I must be one of the few that thinks this weather thing is no big deal. I believe something will happen to cause this storm to bypass us or fizzle out altogether—time will tell. A couple of hours into my shift I get my first break, and then head back to the registers. It was just before lunchtime, that we all get a message over the intercom that I've never heard before. My life was about to change and although I didn't know it at the time, I was very unprepared.

Chapter 4

BULLETIN

Tropical Storm Harvey Advisory Number 16
NWS National Hurricane Center Miami FL
AL092017

1000 AM CDT Thu Aug 24, 2017

...HARVEY QUICKLY STRENGTHENING AND
FORECAST TO BE A MAJOR HURRICANE WHEN IT
APPROACHES THE MIDDLE TEXAS
COAST...LIFE-THREATENING STORM SURGE AND
FRESHWATER FLOODING EXPECTED...

SUMMARY OF 1000 AM CDT...1500
UTC...INFORMATION

LOCATION...24.0N 93.3W
ABOUT 365 MI...590 KM SE OF CORPUS
CHRISTI TEXAS
ABOUT 360 MI...580 KM SSE OF PORT
OCONNOR TEXAS
MAXIMUM SUSTAINED WINDS...65
MPH...100 KM/H
PRESENT MOVEMENT...NNW OR 340
DEGREES AT 10 MPH...17 KM/H
MINIMUM CENTRAL PRESSURE...982
MB...29.00 INCHES

WATCHES AND WARNINGS--------------------

CHANGES WITH THIS ADVISORY:
None.

<<<<<<<   >>>>>>>

The announcement comes over the stores PA system: "Attention everyone, we have just received two very important pieces of information. Can everyone please stop what they're doing for just a moment." After a short pause, Joanne the Assistant Manager continues, "Please listen carefully: as of 10am the National Weather Service has announced that even though Harvey is still classified as a tropical storm, it is now forecast to quickly become a hurricane and is tracking towards the Texas coastline. Secondly, Port Aransas, our island neighbors five miles to the East have just announced a mandatory evacuation for all residents and visitors. It has been decided that we will close as well, effective immediately giving everyone in the store the opportunity to finish their shopping and go home. So, please complete your shopping and head for a cash register. We regret the trouble this may cause you and thank you for your understanding."

Feeling a bit of a shock at the words I've just heard; I quickly regain my focus and continue to scan the items in the cart before me. From where I stand I can see through the glass exit doors and marvel at the sun shining outside--the weather appearing normal. It's hard to believe Harvey is any real threat to us when it looks so nice out there. A couple of department heads beeline for the two entrances/exits to prevent new customers from coming in. I thank each customer and wish them well as they proceed to leave with their purchases. Forty-five minutes later the lines begin to empty, and I'm asked to bring my cash drawer to the office, then clock out and call it a day.

On my way to the door I find Alex, "What's the plan boss, should I show up tomorrow for my normal shift just in case?"

"No Paul, just call me in the morning, and we'll take it one day at a time. You have my cell number, right?"

"I do. Ok Alex, talk to you tomorrow."

Walking through the parking lot I spot my favorite gull on the edge of the flock, looking for crumbs near one of the shopping cart return areas. 'One legged Willie' as we call him seems to look my way as if he (or she) recognizes me.

"Sorry I don't have anything for you today Willie," I announce, wishing I had something left over from my usual lunch sandwich to give him (he loves the bread crumbs). Willie glances my way once more and then continues to hop around on one foot looking for food, oblivious to the idea that he would be considered 'handicapped' in the human world. He's a reminder to me you're only as handicapped as you perceive yourself to be.

As I climb into the jeep, I notice there's still no real wind to speak of and it's partly cloudy. Here's hoping the weather people have it wrong and that this is all going to turn out to be no big deal. A little storm would be nice, and some rain too; just not another Katrina.

Driving towards home I decide to pull into the coffee shop since they'll probably be closed tomorrow. Lucky for me they're still open!

Walking in I find Pablo at the register, "Hey Pablo, you all alone? Where's your sidekick?"

"Emily's getting things squared away in the back, we're going be closing in about 30 minutes."

"You must have heard about the mandatory evacuation in Port Aransas."

"We did, but ten minutes ago a customer came in and told us there's also a mandatory evacuation for Aransas Pass. Time to 'baton down the hatches' and 'get out of Dodge'. Or as my mom would say, it's time to 'Vamonos.' Emily called and confirmed the evacuation orders, so we're open just long enough to get the food put away, clean things up a little, and leave." Changing gears, he asks, "What'll you have?"

At this point my head's swimming; I thought Port Aransas was being overly cautious, but this changes things. Should I now try to get out of town too?

"I'll take any sandwich you might have left, and a half pound of coffee; that Columbia blend I like so much. I need something to last for a few days in case you're not open right away."

Emily pops out of the back room and spots me, gives Pablo a hand having overheard our conversation, and rings me up. "It looks like we've got a tuna salad sandwich ready Paul, and Pablo will grind up that coffee for you, $14.83 including tax."

I pay with my iPhone and glance up, "So Emily, do you believe this is going to get serious?"

"No way of telling but my folks called two

minutes ago and told me I could bring my cat and come stay with them in San Antonio, so I think I will. Better safe than sorry right?"

"Yeah, I guess so," responding deep in thought. Now I'm *really* wondering what I should do.

As I head down to the end of the counter where Pablo's grinding the beans, I spot Matt at a small table with a blonde woman. They seem to be going over some notes in front of them. She's a 'cowgirl' kind of pretty; long blond hair in a pony tail, with bright blue eyes to match. I notice they're both wearing the same style western shirts and Lee jeans, I'll bet they're married.

It begins to gnaw at me that I should say something to Matt, as much as I hate to admit it, I screwed up. I shouldn't have yelled at him the other evening like I did. He just pushed the wrong button on the wrong night. Time to eat some crow and do what I believe would make mom and dad happy.

Pablo hands me the bag with my purchase.

"Thanks Pablo, take care of yourself, you and Emily be safe," shouting the last part out.

"You too, Paul," they call out together.

I sheepishly head for Matt's table as he and the woman look up.

"Hi Matt, I hate to bother you, but I've thought a lot about what you said to me, and I wanted to apologize for going off on you the way I did."

Matt considers my words for a moment, then slowly extends his hand and says, "Apology accepted."

I shake his hand, continuing, "You just said the wrong thing even though there was no way for you to know. Religion is a very touchy subject with me. I'm sorry."

"Like I said Paul, we've both lost our parents but in different ways; we have more in common than you might know. By the way, I'd like you to meet my wife Jennifer, Jen this is Paul."

"Hi Paul, glad to meet you. After hearing about what happened, it's good to see you're feeling differently about things."

For a second or two we just look at each other and then Matt breaks the uneasy silence with, "By the way, you know about the evacuation orders, right?"

"I just heard it from the gang here, and I'm hoping it turns out to be nothing. I don't have the money to go someplace like San Antonio or Austin and hang out for a couple of days."

Jennifer responds by saying, "Well, we were just talking about our own plans. I'm going up to San Marcos with our dogs, but Matt's planning to stay here and watch over the horses. We're trying to reach friends now with a horse trailer to get them moved, but they haven't called back yet and may not even be in town at this point." Pausing, she appears to have a light go off over her head, saying, "We've got a solid brick house over on Armstrong road, why don't you come stay with Matt if it gets crazy here?"

Matt stares at Jen with one of those, "Are you insane!?" looks.

Jennifer continues despite Matt's glare, "If it gets bad you could use the help, Matt. Besides, it sounds like Paul has no place else to go." Glancing back my way, "Where are you staying now Paul?"

"I'm in a two-story apartment complex off Wheeler Road."

"If it's the one I'm thinking of, it couldn't take a serious storm."

"You're probably right, but the last thing I want to do is impose. I'm sure we'll get rain, but I'm not convinced it's going to get 'bad-bad'. I think it might actually be fun!"

Jennifer reaches over and pulls a business card out of Matt's shirt pocket and begins writing on the back. Finishing she hands it to me saying, "Here's our address on Armstrong Road. If you do come over, please close the gate behind you to keep the horses in."

"Thanks, you all. Let's hope it doesn't get that bad. Well, I've got to run, stay safe."

"You too Paul," Matt responds, "We'll keep you in our thoughts and prayers."

They seem to believe this stuff I think, so I guess it couldn't hurt— they mean well.

Arriving at my apartment I take some time to assemble anything that might be useful on the kitchen counter; candles, matches, spare cell phone battery charger, the coffee, a flashlight I found, some other items. I ignore the parade of families and suitcases passing by my window and into the parking lot, packing up their cars and leaving. No sense of adventure I tell myself, they're going to miss all the excitement! Now it's time to catch up with my Xbox; Gears of War is calling my name.

Chapter 5

BULLETIN
Hurricane Harvey Advisory Number
19...Corrected
NWS National Hurricane Center Miami FL
AL092017
1000 PM CDT Thu Aug 24, 2017

Corrected for time of next intermediate advisory

...HARVEY EXPECTED TO STRENGTHEN AS
IT MOVES TOWARDS THE
TEXASCOAST...LIFE-THREATENING AND
DEVASTATING FLOODING EXPECTED NEAR THE
COAST DUE TO HEAVY RAINFALL AND STORM
SURGE...

SUMMARY OF 1000 PM CDT...0300
UTC...INFORMATION

LOCATION...25.2N 94.6W
ABOUT 250 MI...400 KM SE OF CORPUS
CHRISTI TEXAS
ABOUT 245 MI...400 KM SSE OF PORT
OCONNOR TEXAS
MAXIMUM SUSTAINED WINDS...85
MPH...140 KM/H

PRESENT MOVEMENT...NW OR 315 DEGREES AT 10 MPH...17 KM/H
MINIMUM CENTRAL PRESSURE...973 MB...28.74 INCHES

WATCHES AND WARNINGS

CHANGES WITH THIS ADVISORY:
None.

DISCUSSION AND 48-HOUR OUTLOOK

At 1000 PM CDT (0300 UTC), the center of Hurricane Harvey was
located near latitude 25.2 North, longitude 94.6 West. Harvey is
moving toward the northwest near 10 mph (17 km/h). This general
motion is expected to continue with a decrease in forward speed
during the next couple of days. On the forecast track, Harvey will
approach the middle Texas coast on Friday and make landfall Friday
night or early Saturday.   Harvey is then likely to stall near or
just inland of the middle Texas coast through the weekend.

Reports from an Air Force Reserve Hurricane Hunter aircraft
indicate that maximum sustained winds remain near 85 mph (140 km/h) with higher gusts.   While

Harvey has changed little in strength over
the past several hours, strengthening is expected
to resume later
tonight, and Harvey is expected to become a
major hurricane by
Friday before it reaches the middle Texas coast.

Hurricane-force winds extend outward up to 25
miles (35 km) from the center and tropical-storm-force
winds extend outward up to 105 miles
(165 km).
The latest minimum central pressure reported by
the Hurricane
Hunter aircraft is 973 mb (28.74 inches).

HAZARDS AFFECTING LAND

RAINFALL: Harvey is expected to produce
total rain accumulations
of 15 to 25 inches and isolated maximum
amounts of 35 inches over
the middle and upper Texas coast through next
Wednesday.   During
the same time period Harvey is expected to
produce total rain
accumulations of 7 to 15 inches in far south
Texas and the Texas
Hill Country eastward through central and
southwest Louisiana, with
accumulations of up to 7 inches extending into
other parts of Texas
and the lower Mississippi Valley. Rainfall from
Harvey will cause

devastating and life-threatening flooding.

STORM SURGE: The combination of a dangerous storm surge and the tide will cause normally dry areas near the coast to be flooded by rising waters moving inland from the shoreline. The water is expected to reach the following heights above ground if the peak surge occurs at the time of high tide...

N Entrance Padre Island Natl Seashore to Sargent...6 to 12 ft

Sargent to Jamaica Beach...5 to 8 ft

Port Mansfield to N Entrance Padre Island Natl Seashore...5 to 7 ft

Jamaica Beach to High Island...2 to 4 ft

Mouth of the Rio Grande to Port Mansfield...2 to 4 ft

High Island to Morgan City...1 to 3 ft

WIND: Hurricane conditions are likely within the hurricane warning area late Friday and Friday night, with tropical storm conditions expected to first reach the coast in the hurricane warning area Friday. These conditions are likely to persist into Saturday in portions of the hurricane and tropical storm warning area.

SURF: Swells generated by Harvey are likely to affect the Texas, Louisiana, and northeast Mexico coasts by Friday.   These swells are likely to cause life-threatening surf and rip current conditions.

Please consult products from your local weather
office.
TORNADOES: Isolated tornadoes are possible
across portions of the
middle and upper Texas coast on Friday.

NEXT ADVISORY

Next intermediate advisory at 100 AM CDT.
Next complete advisory at 400 AM CDT.

<<<<<<<   >>>>>>>

Taking a gaming break, I look in the refrigerator for something to snack on. There's half a bear claw from the coffee shop. Grabbing it, I close the door. A picture falls out from beneath a magnet. Reaching down, I retrieve it, putting it back on the refrigerator door where it belongs. It's one of my favorites; Mom, Dad and me in front of the Runaway Mine Train at Six Flags over Texas. When I was a kid, I thought it was the best roller coaster in the whole world. Now that I'm older I realize how small it is, but it's still a lot of fun, if only for all the nostalgic happiness it brings me each time I ride it. There's also pictures somewhere of us at the log ride and going to the top of the oil derrick. Looking back, I realize that the main reason we drove all the way up from San Antonio (where our house used to be) was for me. My happiness was important to them and I'm only just now beginning to appreciate how much. They could have stuck me with a relative and flown to someplace like Vegas, but they didn't. We also went down to Port Aransas during summer vacations; spending time playing on the beach, enjoying the ocean. It's where I learned the basics of surfing and how to throw a frisbee, snorkeling too. Dad even took me deep sea fishing a couple of times, but I could just never get past being seasick. There's a picture there of me and him on the boat as well.

Thinking back to the last few months before they died, it wasn't a bad relationship, just strained. They were in San Antonio and I was here in Aransas Pass having fun on the "3rd coast," as we Texans call it. They gave me the space I asked for, hoping I'd go to college, find a direction for my life. But that's eluded me for some reason. Working, spending time on the beach, having a girlfriend (until recently) was enough. So why am I thinking about them all of a sudden? It's simple. I'm angry at them less for being gone, now just missing them more. Missing the family I once had.

My phone beeps at me to let me know I have a text—it's from work. A general message for all employees letting us know that based on the 10pm announcement from the national weather service this thing is getting serious, and that the store is closed until further notice. Basically, to stay away, get out-of-town if you haven't already done so. Seconds later an email pops up on my laptop saying the same thing.

A couple of my online gaming friends call me during the next hour, concerned because they know I live on the Texas coastline--but I promise them I'll be fine. Yet, the more I think about it, the less sure I become.

Chapter 6

BULLETIN
Hurricane Harvey Advisory Number 20
NWS National Hurricane Center Miami FL
AL092017
400 AM CDT Fri Aug 25, 2017

...HURRICANE HARVEY DANGEROUSLY
APPROACHING THE TEXAS COAST...

SUMMARY OF 400 AM CDT...0900
UTC...INFORMATION

LOCATION...25.9N 95.4W
ABOUT 180 MI...290 KM SE OF CORPUS
CHRISTI TEXAS
ABOUT 185 MI...295 KM SSE OF PORT
OCONNOR TEXAS
MAXIMUM SUSTAINED WINDS...105
MPH...165 KM/H
PRESENT MOVEMENT...NW OR 320 DEGREES
AT 9 MPH...15 KM/H
MINIMUM CENTRAL PRESSURE...967
MB...28.56 INCHES

WATCHES AND WARNINGS

CHANGES WITH THIS ADVISORY:None.

DISCUSSION AND 48-HOUR OUTLOOK

At 400 AM CDT (0900 UTC), the eye of
Hurricane Harvey was located
near latitude 25.9 North, longitude 95.4 West.
Harvey is moving
toward the northwest near 9 mph (15 km/h), and
this general motion
is expected to continue during the next couple of
days. On the
forecast track, Harvey will make landfall on the
middle Texas coast
tonight, or early Saturday.   Harvey is then
likely to meander near or
just inland of the middle Texas coast through the
weekend.
Maximum sustained winds are near 105 mph
(165 km/h) with higher
gusts. Some strengthening is possible, and
Harvey is expected to
become a major hurricane before it reaches the
middle Texas coast.

Hurricane-force winds extend outward up to 25
miles (35 km) from the center and tropical-storm-force
winds extend outward up to 140 miles
(220 km).
The minimum central pressure reported by
NOAA and Air Force planes was 967 mb (28.56 inches).
HAZARDS AFFECTING LAND

RAINFALL: Harvey is expected to produce
total rain accumulations
of 15 to 25 inches and isolated maximum

amounts of 35 inches over
the middle and upper Texas coast through next
Wednesday.   During
the same time period Harvey is expected to
produce total rain
accumulations of 7 to 15 inches in far south
Texas and the Texas
Hill Country eastward through central and
southwest Louisiana, with
accumulations of up to 7 inches extending into
other parts of Texas
and the lower Mississippi Valley. Rainfall from
Harvey will cause
devastating and life-threatening flooding.
STORM SURGE: The combination of a
dangerous storm surge and the tide will cause normally
dry areas near the coast to be flooded by
rising waters moving inland from the shoreline.
The water is
expected to reach the following heights above
ground if the peak
surge occurs at the time of high tide...
N Entrance Padre Island Natl Seashore to
Sargent...6 to 12 ft
Sargent to Jamaica Beach...5 to 8 ft
Port Mansfield to N Entrance Padre Island Natl
Seashore...5 to 7 ft
Jamaica Beach to High Island...2 to 4 ft
Mouth of the Rio Grande to Port Mansfield...2 to
4 ft
High Island to Morgan City...1 to 3 ft

WIND: Hurricane conditions are likely within

the hurricane warning area late Friday and Friday night, with tropical storm conditions expected to first reach the coast in the hurricane warning area later this morning.   These conditions are likely to persist into Saturday in portions of the hurricane and tropical storm warning area.

SURF: Swells generated by Harvey will begin to affect the Texas, Louisiana, and northeast Mexico coasts later this morning. These swells are likely to cause life-threatening surf and rip current conditions. Please consult products from your local weather office.

TORNADOES: Isolated tornadoes are possible across portions of the middle and upper Texas coast on Friday.

NEXT ADVISORY

Next intermediate advisory at 700 AM CDT.
Next complete advisory at 1000 AM CDT.

<<<<<<<   >>>>>>>

Friday-- August 25th, 2017

I awaken to rain striking my bedroom window. Stretching and yawning as I look through the glass, it appears that the wind has picked up because the rain's coming in at an angle. Not good.

It's a little after 9am and although I haven't had much sleep, it begins to sink in just how serious my circumstances have become. Checking the weather app on my cell it informs me the temperature is slowly dropping from our norm; it's 76 degrees now (that's good—it's usually mid 80s by this time) but the wind is now averaging about thirty mph and climbing (not so good).

Turning on the TV, something I rarely do, I look to see what the local stations have to say about Harvey. It's the usual. Some out-of-state broadcaster standing on the local beach, camera facing the waves, as they tell you how bad it's getting, while people *play in the surf* directly behind them. Ha! I knew it wasn't all that bad! While that's blaring in the background I put on a pot of coffee and check my iPhone for text messages. Several of my friends are asking me if I've bugged out yet, as the meteorologists on TV are "yelling" at me to do the same thing. Harvey is now hurricane status and intensifying quickly. The emergency lane on Highway 37 that leads from Corpus Christi to San Antonio has been opened to accept the extra traffic flowing out, and for an emergency type situation, it's proceeding smoothly. Here's the part that's beginning to worry me though; the best guess for Harvey's direction is that it's coming right for the coastal bend and expected to make landfall sometime tonight. Holy crap, maybe this is something to take more seriously.

Going online I double check my bank account to see if I can go to San Antonio anyway (assuming there will be any hotel rooms left when I arrive). I conclude that ninety-seven dollars won't go very far, no matter where I end up, unless I want to sleep in the jeep. Facing the hurricane head on is not quite as romantic as it was just 24 hours ago and now seems rather foolish. What would mom and dad say if they were here? As much as I pretend I'm grown up, there are times I miss them and could really use their seasoned advice. And even though two of my online friends have offered to put me up, it's a no-go because they're at least two states away. What to do, what to do.

A thought begins to nag at me, and I keep pushing it back. But as I watch the sheets of rain pelt my windows even harder, the solution becomes obvious. Especially since I have no plywood to board over those windows (I'm on the second floor and can't reach some of them anyway). This should be the apartment manager's job, but I see his car is gone already. Giving in to this growing uneasy feeling I pull out Matt's business card. There beneath his work number is his personal cell number. It'll just be for a day, right? Beggars can't be choosers, right?

I punch in his number and he answers on the second ring— "Matt Murchison."

"Hi Matt, this is Paul from the coffee shop, and I'm embarrassed to ask you this, but when your wife suggested I stay with you through the storm, well, is the offer still open?"

Matt takes my groveling politely and says, "No worries. My only rules Paul are no drinking and no drugs. If you're OK with that come on over. Jen convinced me you're worth taking a chance on; she's got a sense about people and I trust it. But you'd better hurry though, the wind's picking up fast."

"Thanks Matt, I'll be there as soon as possible."

"From where you are drive down to FM 1069 and turn right. Armstrong Rd. is about three miles down, then turn right again. You've got the house number on the back of the card. Just be sure and close the gate behind you when you get here."

Pulling a suitcase out from under my bed I throw in enough clothes to last a few days. The "just in case" stuff gets zippered in too. Let's just hope the electricity isn't out for long. Most storms around here it's out a couple of hours, but then, this *is* a hurricane. The Xbox gets bagged and put into a duffel along with my laptop, a pillow and a couple of blankets too, since I'm not sure where I'll be sleeping.

Opening the door, the wind grabs it out of my hand slamming it against the wall. Just how fast *is* the wind blowing? I realize I'm not going to be able to carry everything downstairs all in one trip, so I break it up into two. Wind gusts threaten to carry away the suitcase, the duffel bag as well. A little rain soaked I pull out of the parking lot and head for Matt's, a bad feeling welling up inside of me; wondering if I should have loaded up more of my belongings. But living on the second floor, I don't have to worry about flooding, right? I turn right on Wheeler and drive towards Armstrong Rd.

Several minutes later, I arrive at the gate and see Matt's house vaguely through the rain, one hundred yards away at the back of the property. It's obvious he and Jen have a few acres, with lots of scrub oaks clustered about. The horses appear to be huddled near the opening of a small barn-like structure to the right of the home. Climbing out of the jeep, trying to shield my face from the rain, I don't notice the hand that reaches out until it touches my shoulder.

Jumping two feet off the ground I turn and scream, "Who the hell are you?"

Covered up in a green Army poncho is Eliot, water dripping from his face and beard, and despite how long the poncho is, I'm convinced he's soaked from head to toe.

He shouts back over the sound of the wind, "Matt told me down at the coffee shop I could come here if things got bad--- it's bad."

With my pulse racing I gather my wits for a second and reply, "Tell you what, you get the gate and I'll drive us up to the house."

Without saying a word Eliot removes his soaked backpack and sets it on the floor of the passenger side of the jeep. I jump in as he opens the gate, then drive through as he closes it behind me. Eliot climbs aboard. Even in this driving rain and layers of protective clothing Eliot has a very pungent scent about him; a shower, no, maybe two showers would do him good. In front of the house are two large oaks where it appears someone frequently parks beneath, so I do as well. Maybe the trees will provide some protection from the wind, more importantly the stuff being driven by this torrent. We exit the vehicle, carrying what the gusts will allow and stumble for the door. Matt must have seen my headlights through the tiny half-moon window in the top of the front door (all the other windows I can see from here are boarded up) and he quickly ushers us into the foyer.

"Welcome Paul, you too Eliot, I *thought* you might both decide to join me out here. I wish you would have called me Eliot; I would have come out and picked you up." He hands both of us a large towel to dry off with.

"Dropped my phone in a puddle this morning." And that was all he said, a man who's direct and to the point I decide.

Drying my hands and face I go back out. Grabbing the rest of my gear I let myself back in and promptly begin to dry off, more thoroughly this time. Spotting a shoe rack next to the front door I remove mine and set them there as well.

"Thank you so much for allowing me to stay here tonight Matt, I realize you don't know me, or owe me anything for that matter… and uh… thanks."

Eliot looks at Matt and simply says, "Yeah, me too."

"So, Eliot, if you walked all the way here I know you've got to be soaked. Why don't you put your boots next to the fan on the floor there and let's get you some dry clothes. Down the hallway to the right is a bathroom, and if you'd like to take a shower, I'll leave some things outside the door to put on."

"Sounds good," Eliot replies, "everything in my pack is wet."

"Don't worry too much about the storm guys," Matt encourages, "this house was built in the 50s and it's been through a couple of hurricanes already. She's a survivor. I inherited this home from my grandmother when she passed on a couple of years ago."

Eliot heads down the hall, peeking in doorways

until he finds the bathroom.

"Make yourself at home Paul," Matt says as he leaves to go find some clothes for Eliot.

Glancing around the living room I notice the radio on low, a news station giving weather updates between the talk show host and his callers pontificating about the approaching storm. To the left is the kitchen past a half wall; immaculate and organized, painted antique white with light green cabinets. Pictures of flowers and Christian hangings adorn the walls. Going in I sit at the table, retrieving my phone to check for messages and updates. While replying to friends texting me their concerns, I notice Matt back in the living room.

"Would you like a quick tour of the house Paul?"

"Sure," I reply as I join Matt in the living room.

"You've seen the kitchen, and the living room— this is a basic 'L' shape home. Down the hall to the right is a bedroom, a bathroom (where's Eliot's showering) and then another bedroom. Opposite the bedrooms is an open den as you can see. At the end of the hall is the master bedroom with its own bath. There's a separate two car garage next to the house outside and just past that is a small barn for the horses. My only concern, and the reason I stayed behind, is to care for the horses through this, although I'm not sure the barn can stand up to any serious wind."

"First of all, Matt, thanks again for taking me in. If there's anything I can do to earn my keep just tell me what to do. I know it's only one night, but I appreciate it all the same."

"You're welcome."

"And I'm glad you suggested Eliot take a shower to warm up and get clean, he really needed it," I add trying to hide the grin on my face.

"That was sneaky I know, but I've known Eliot a while, and I try to be careful about how I say things to him. He's a nice guy when you get to know him, just messed up in a way because of some things he was asked to do during the war in the middle east. He doesn't like to talk about it, but what he's shared with me was bad. Killing people who later turned out to be innocent bystanders really set him back a-ways, and he punishes himself for it now. If you guys talk, don't bring up the military unless he does first, Paul, it's a very touchy subject."

"Ok," is all I can come up with, I'm not sure I understand the whole middle east war thing anyway. Matt leads me throughout the house—pointing out the linen closets, through the den opposite the bedrooms with sliding glass doors to the backyard, (boarded up of course) and then back down the hall. He ends up at the bedroom closest to the master bedroom explaining this will be mine tonight. It contains a twin bed opposite a stack of boxes on the wall that were never unpacked from their move-in two years ago. As we're walking through the home, I continue to hear the wind and rain as it continually throws sheets of water against the boards protecting the windows.

We walk past the bathroom and where there was once a stack of clean clothes; Eliot's dirty clothes are now piled up. Matt picks them up holding them out at arm's length and leads me to the washing machine. "No time like the present," he says trying not to breathe in.

Chapter 8

BULLETIN

Hurricane Harvey Advisory Number 23
NWS National Hurricane Center Miami FL
AL092017
1000 PM CDT Fri Aug 25, 2017

...EYE OF CATEGORY 4 HARVEY MAKES
LANDFALL BETWEEN PORT ARANSAS AND PORT
O'CONNOR TEXAS...CATASTROPHIC FLOODING
EXPECTED DUE TO HEAVY RAINFALL AND
STORM SURGE...

SUMMARY OF 1000 PM CDT...0300
UTC...INFORMATION

LOCATION...28.0N 97.0W
ABOUT 30 MI...45 KM ENE OF CORPUS
CHRISTI TEXAS
ABOUT 45 MI...75 KM SW OF PORT
OCONNOR TEXAS
MAXIMUM SUSTAINED WINDS...130
MPH...215 KM/H
PRESENT MOVEMENT...NW OR 325 DEGREES
AT 7 MPH...11 KM/H MINIMUM CENTRAL
PRESSURE...938 MB...27.70 INCHES

WATCHES AND WARNINGS

CHANGES WITH THIS ADVISORY:

None.

SUMMARY OF WATCHES AND WARNINGS
IN EFFECT:

A Storm Surge Warning is in effect for...
* Port Mansfield to High Island Texas

A Hurricane Warning is in effect for...
* Port Mansfield to Sargent Texas

A Tropical Storm Warning is in effect for...
* North of Sargent to High Island Texas

DISCUSSION AND 48-HOUR OUTLOOK

At 1000 PM CDT (0300 UTC), the center of
Hurricane Harvey was
located near latitude 28.0 North, longitude 97.0
West.   Harvey has
just made landfall on the Texas coast over the
northern end of San
Jose Island about 4 miles (6 km) east of Rockport.
Harvey is
moving toward the northwest near 7 mph (11
km/h).   The hurricane is expected to slow its forward
motion and move slowly over
southeastern Texas during the next couple of
days.

Maximum sustained winds are near 130 mph

(215 km/h) with higher
gusts.   Harvey is a category 4 hurricane on the
Saffir-Simpson
Hurricane Wind Scale.   Weakening is forecast
during the next 48
hours while the center of Harvey is over
southeastern Texas.

Hurricane-force winds extend outward up to 40
miles (65 km) from the center and tropical-storm-force
winds extend outward up to 140 miles
(220 km).   A Texas Coastal Ocean Observing
Network station at
Aransas Pass recently reported sustained winds
of 111 mph (178 km/h) and a wind gust of 131 mph (211
km/h).

The minimum central pressure just reported by
an Air Force Reserve
Hurricane Hunter aircraft is 938 mb (27.70
inches).

HAZARDS AFFECTING LAND

RAINFALL: Harvey is expected to produce
total rain accumulations of 15 to 30 inches and isolated
maximum amounts of 40 inches over the
middle and upper Texas coast through next
Wednesday. During the same time period Harvey is
expected to produce total rain accumulations
of 5 to 15 inches in far south Texas and the Texas
Hill Country over
through southwest and central Louisiana.

Rainfall of this magnitude
will cause catastrophic and life-threatening
flooding.

STORM SURGE: The combination of a
dangerous storm surge and the tide will cause normally
dry areas near the coast to be flooded by
rising waters moving inland from the shoreline.
The water is
expected to reach the following heights above
ground if the peak
surge occurs at the time of high tide...

Port Aransas to Port O'Connor...9 to 13 ft
Port O'Connor to Sargent...6 to 9 ft
N Entrance Padre Island Natl Seashore to Port
Aransas...5 to 8 ft
Sargent to Jamaica Beach...4 to 6 ft
Port Mansfield to N Entrance Padre Island Natl
Seashore...3 to 5 ft
Jamaica Beach to High Island...2 to 4 ft
Mouth of the Rio Grande to Port Mansfield...1 to
3 ft
High Island to Morgan City...1 to 3 ft
WIND: Hurricane conditions are occuring
along the coast in the Port
Aransas to Port O'Connor area and should
spread over other portions
of the hurricane warning area during the next
several hours.
Tropical storm conditions are occurring in other
portions of the
hurricane and tropical storm warning areas.

Tropical storm
conditions are likely to persist along portions of
the coast through
at least Sunday.

SURF: Swells generated by Harvey are
affecting the Texas,
Louisiana, and northeast Mexico coasts.   These
swells are likely to
cause life-threatening surf and rip current
conditions. Please
consult products from your local weather office.

TORNADOES: Tornadoes are possible through
Saturday near the middle and upper Texas coast into
far southwest Louisiana.

NEXT ADVISORY

Next intermediate advisory at 100 AM CDT.
Next complete advisory at 400 AM CDT.

<<<<<<<   >>>>>>>

Looking through the small window in the front door, I shine my flashlight out into the darkness. The rain is horizontal, and the sound is distressing, I can't imagine what a tornado would be like. Rain seems to hit the ground and then, amazingly, bounces up and is swept back into the air. I've never seen anything like it.

I consider opening the door for a better look, but instantly think better of it. Shaken, I walk back down the hall to see how the guys are doing.

Arriving at Matt's bedroom, I find a chair and sit near Eli (who has his eyes closed—resting) I think to myself: It's close to midnight and I don't know what's going on exactly. Has the eye of the hurricane hit yet? It seemed to have eased up a little but now it's howling again. All I know is that I've never been more scared than I am right now; feeling lost, not a clue as to what to do next but wait this thing out. There's no outside communication whatsoever. Never been so disconnected in all my life. How did people do this in years past? I know that sounds like a stupid question but if having all this technology is all you know… well, I just don't know how people did it before. So much for being the captain of my own ship.

Matt fell asleep a couple of hours ago despite the "jet stream" rushing past the house outside. I look over at Eli and tell him, "Eli, I'm going to my room and try to rest, I just don't know what else to do."

"Ok kid. I'll come get cha' if I need ya."

With that I grab my flashlight and head to the next room down the hall. I throw my blanket and pillow on top of the mattress. Turning the light off I lay down fully clothed, figuring if something happens to the house I've got to be ready to run.

Flashing back, the last time I felt anything like this was on February the 12th earlier this year. It was 9 o'clock in the evening and I'd just gotten home from work. My cell phone rang, almost not answering it because I didn't recognize the number.

"Is this Paul Stevenson?" a man's deep voice

asks.

"Yes," I respond, a sense of unease coursing through me.

"Are your parents William and June Stevenson?"

I've never heard anyone call my dad by his full name---it was always 'Will', now I'm scared. With a slight tremble in my voice I answer again—"Yes."

"Mr. Stevenson, this is Officer Garcia with the Texas Highway Patrol. I'm sorry to have to inform you that your mother and father were involved in a car accident on Highway 37 less than an hour ago. They were air lifted to Christus Spohn Memorial Hospital on Shoreline in Corpus Christi. They should be there by now."

My mind goes blank, I'm stunned. "How are they?" was all I could think to ask.

"Mr. Stevenson, I don't have any details to share with you, I would suggest you get to the hospital as soon as possible. From what I saw of the car they were in, it's not good. I'm sorry."

I mumble thanks and hang up. Moving through a fog of emotion I pick up my keys and head for my car downstairs. Jumping in I fly down Wheeler and then onto highway 181. I'm giving my little Toyota a run for its money, pedal to the metal not caring if there's a cop along the way. In no time I'm at the Harbor bridge, then crossing over I come quickly to my exit. There's almost no traffic this time of night; a good thing because I'm not doing my best. Driving down Shoreline I see the hospital and go straight for the emergency entrance.

Trying to be strong I locate the front desk and

seek out my parents' whereabouts.

The nurse looks at the computer screen and then back at me. "Are you related to the Stevenson's?" her voice flat and serious.

"Yes, I'm their son," emotion coloring my reply.

"Mr. Stevenson," she says as she stands up and walks around the counter, "Please follow me."

Walking thirty feet down the hall she opens the door to a room with a desk and some chairs in it—looks like a doctor's private office. Holding the door she ushers me in and invites me to sit down.

"What's wrong? Why are you putting me in here, I want to go see them!" I practically shout.

"I'll have a doctor come as soon as possible to explain their condition. Please be patient."

She leaves me there with the door cracked open. It wasn't more than two minutes when there's a light knock, then a middle-aged woman in a doctor's coat walks in, hand extended. I shake it.

"I'm doctor Winthrop, one of the ER doctors who worked on your parents."

"What do you mean *'worked'* on your parents, I thought they just barely got here?!?"

Doctor Winthrop sits down across from me, folds her hands in front of her on the desk. "Mr. Stevenson, there's no easy way to tell you this. I'm sorry to tell you that both of your parents have passed away."

I look at her, disbelieving, sputtering, "What?"

"They were brought in forty-five minutes ago by Halo Flight, from a horrible wreck up near Three Rivers. All we were told is that they were hit head on by someone driving the wrong way on the freeway.

The first responders were able to free your parents, but your father died of his injuries in flight. We began emergency surgery on your mother as soon as she arrived, but it was too late, the trauma was too extensive. She passed on a few minutes ago. I'm sorry for your loss."

Numb, all I feel is numb. This can't be happening. This is something you see on the news; it happens to people you don't know. I stare at the wall trying to think of something to say.

Sensing my thoughts, she says, "Is there anyone I can call? A relative? A friend perhaps?"

I have an aunt and uncle who live in Arizona—no help right now. "No," I reply. "What happens next?" I ask through the tears running down my face.

"We'll have someone contact you tomorrow morning to make arrangements for your parents. There are some wonderful people here who can help you through this if you like. Is there anyone close by who can assist you?" She's looking at me with genuine care in her eyes.

"No, I'm their only child, the closest family member is out of state." Sitting there for a moment I finally ask—"Can I see them?"

Looking at me she slowly replies, "Mr. Stevenson, I wouldn't want you to see them the way they are. Please believe me when I tell you it would be best to simply remember them as they were."

Just like that moment six months ago, I feel like my life has been dropped into a blender. The longer I lay there the heavier my eyes get, I'm mentally exhausted. I should be terrified but knowing that Matt and Eli are here in the house, I feel a sense of peace come over me. It shouldn't, but it does. Before you know it, the noise of the wind and the debris peppering the house begins to fade, and despite all my concerns I fall sleep.

Chapter 7

BULLETIN
Hurricane Harvey Advisory Number 22
NWS National Hurricane Center Miami FL
AL092017
400 PM CDT Fri Aug 25, 2017

...MAJOR HURRICANE HARVEY BEARING
DOWN ON THE TEXAS COAST...CATASTROPHIC
FLOODING EXPECTED DUE TO HEAVY RAINFALL
AND STORM SURGE...

SUMMARY OF 400 PM CDT...2100
UTC...INFORMATION

LOCATION...27.5N 96.5W
ABOUT 60 MI...95 KM ESE OF CORPUS
CHRISTI TEXAS
ABOUT 60 MI...100 KM S OF PORT OCONNOR
TEXAS
MAXIMUM SUSTAINED WINDS...125
MPH...205 KM/H
PRESENT MOVEMENT...NW OR 325 DEGREES
AT 10 MPH...17 KM/H
MINIMUM CENTRAL PRESSURE...941
MB...27.79 INCHES

WATCHES AND WARNINGS

CHANGES WITH THIS ADVISORY:

The Tropical Storm Warning has been discontinued south of Port Mansfield, Texas.
The Storm Surge Watch has been discontinued south of Port Mansfield, Texas.
The government of Mexico has discontinued the Tropical Storm Watch north of Boca de Catan.

SUMMARY OF WATCHES AND WARNINGS IN EFFECT:

A Storm Surge Warning is in effect for...
* Port Mansfield to High Island Texas
A Hurricane Warning is in effect for...
* Port Mansfield to Sargent Texas
A Tropical Storm Warning is in effect for...
* North of Sargent to High Island Texas

DISCUSSION AND 48-HOUR OUTLOOK

At 400 PM CDT (2100 UTC), the eye of Hurricane Harvey was located by aircraft reconnaissance aircraft and NOAA Doppler radar near latitude 27.5 North, longitude 96.5 West. Harvey is moving toward the northwest near 10 mph (17 km/h), but its forward speed is expected to decrease significantly during the next couple of days. On the forecast track, Harvey will make landfall

<u>on the middle Texas
coast tonight or early Saturday.</u> Harvey is then
likely to meander
near or just inland of the middle Texas coast
through the weekend.

<u>Data from an Air Force Reserve Hurricane
Hunter aircraft indicate
that maximum sustained winds have increased
to near 125 mph
(205 km/h) with higher gusts.   Harvey is a
category 3 hurricane on
the Saffir-Simpson Hurricane Wind Scale.</u>
Some additional
strengthening is possible before Harvey makes
landfall overnight.
Weakening is then expected over the weekend
while the center moves
inland over Texas.

Hurricane-force winds extend outward up to 35
miles (55 km) from the
center, and tropical-storm-force winds extend
outward up to 140
miles (220 km).   A station at Aransas Pass,
Texas, recently
reported a sustained wind 56 mph and a gust to
71 mph.

The minimum central pressure based on aircraft
reconnaissance data
is 941 mb (27.79 inches).

HAZARDS AFFECTING LAND

RAINFALL: Harvey is expected to produce
total rain accumulations of 15 to 30 inches and isolated
maximum amounts of 40 inches over the
middle and upper Texas coast through next
Wednesday. During the same time period Harvey is
expected to produce total rain accumulations
of 5 to 15 inches in far south Texas and the Texas
Hill Country over
through southwest and central Louisiana.
Rainfall of this magnitude
will cause catastrophic and life-threatening
flooding.

STORM SURGE: The combination of a
dangerous storm surge and the tide will cause normally
dry areas near the coast to be flooded by
rising waters moving inland from the shoreline.
The water is
expected to reach the following heights above
ground if the peak
surge occurs at the time of high tide...

N Entrance Padre Island Natl Seashore to
Sargent...6 to 12 ft
Sargent to Jamaica Beach...5 to 8 ft
Port Mansfield to N Entrance Padre Island Natl
Seashore...3 to 5 ft
Jamaica Beach to High Island...2 to 4 ft
Mouth of the Rio Grande to Port Mansfield...1 to
3 ft
High Island to Morgan City...1 to 3 ft

TORNADOES: A few tornadoes are possible through Saturday near the middle and upper Texas coast into far southwestern Louisiana.

NEXT ADVISORY

Next intermediate advisory at 700 PM CDT.
Next complete advisory at 1000 PM CDT.

It's almost four pm. Eliot's sitting at the kitchen table with me as Matt finishes up an early dinner on the stove. Bacon and eggs with fried potatoes are on the menu; things that we need to eat up if the power goes out, he explains. The wind is really howling, and I'm worried about how much worse it might get. We listen to the news on the radio (Matt just has an outdoor antenna for television and with this weather, we can't pick anything up but snow) and hear that Harvey is gaining steam, coming directly for us. I'm wondering once again if I shouldn't have headed west; money or no money. I'm putting my faith in Matt and his house, wait, did I just say faith? I'm trusting in Matt. My cell phone reception is becoming spotty and I fear it's not going to work here shortly. If the power goes out, it will too I'm sure. Matt brings the food over to the table and serves everyone before sitting down.

"Let's give thanks," Matt proclaims as he closes his eyes, head bowed. I look over at Eliot--he has his head down too. He thanks God for the food and asks him for a safe night, seeking his guidance and for strength of will to see us through the storm. As he says amen, I quickly bow my head pretending to be praying too.

"Man, that was a loud one," Matt declares as something heavy strikes the roof above us.

"Probably just some branches off the trees outside," Eliot declares in between bites.

At that, I become concerned about my jeep. Should I move it? Do something with it? But then it occurs to me, no place is really safe in a hurricane. As we eat the radio news interrupts with the latest: "---The winds are gusting now at 60 to 70 mph and the National Weather Service is telling us that Hurricane Harvey is going to make landfall just north of Corpus Christi (that's us) by midnight tonight with winds somewhere between 100 and 140 mph. Total rainfall is expected in the 15 to 25 inches range, and just to recap the Mayor Pro Tem in Rockport (we're sitting 10 miles south of Rockport) has advised anyone deciding not to evacuate should write their social security number on their arm with a sharpie, for easier identification once the hurricane passes." Okay . . . Is he just trying to scare us I wonder, or does he really believe we might die?

Just then the power goes off, the lights flash back on a time or two and then goes out completely. Matt's battery powered radio continues, "The news from AEP is to expect power to be down anywhere from three days to three weeks depending on where you live in Nueces or San Patricio County (that us again)."

Sitting in the dimly lit room I try to absorb what I've just heard. The radio announcer drones on for another minute or so but I'm oblivious to what's being said. Matt gets up and takes a couple of candles out of the cupboard above the sink, lights them, and sets them on the table. All I can think about now is my stuff left back at the apartment, and more importantly, what about my job? How bad is the flooding going to be, are we really safe here tonight? It's quickly becoming overwhelming.

Matt looks at the two of us, saying, "Time to make a plan gentleman. You all finish eating while I talk. First of all, you're both welcome to ride this out with me for a few days. It looks like things are quickly going from bad to worse. If there is a bright spot, Jen and I have made some preparations here at the house just in case something like this came along, and now it has, so here's what we have available. Candles, matches, flashlights and spare batteries are in the cupboard over the sink. We'll eat up the food in the refrigerator and freezer for as long as it lasts and then start in on the dry goods if things aren't better by then. The bad news about the water is that we're on a well out here, so no power means no water. The good news is we have fifty-five-gallon rain barrels in the back yard located beneath three rain gutter down spouts. And you'll find a five-gallon water bucket in the bathroom to refill the toilet tank after you flush; we'll be refilling those as we go. One bucket should be good for two or three flushes. We're on a septic system out here so we're better off than those in town if the sewage system stops working, they won't have our luxury. (Flushing a toilet, a luxury? Wow, this is getting crazy.)

"What about drinking water?" Eliot chimes in.

"There's two cases of bottled water plus what Paul brought with him, as well as several gallons in the pantry. Once that's gone, we'll use a special filter I have and then boil it to kill any bacteria. I've got a Coleman stove in the spare bedroom to cook with and even a camp style percolator for making coffee."

I silently cheer that last statement since coffee's not a luxury to me! As I ponder his words, the candlelight flickering in the room magnifies the serious of our condition. I pull my cell out of my pocket and notice that it has 54% left on the battery and no connection to a tower. Immediately I put it on super battery saver mode.

Looking over at Eliot then back at Matt I ask, "What do you want us to do?"

"Let's watch our resources and conserve whatever we can. I'm hoping the power comes back on quickly, but the last hurricane to hit us head on was Celia where the power was out for three weeks. But that was a long time ago--I'm sure things are built better now. I think we should plan on the electricity being out for a week or two. Of course, you can leave anytime you like, just saying things may be 'Little House on the Prairie' around here for a while."

"I've seen worse," Eliot states. "Living on the streets ain't much different from this. By the way, if we're going to be cooped up in here a day or two, call me Eli."

"Fine Eli. I just realized the fuel for the Coleman stove is in the garage, I'll check on the horses and grab the fuel. Be back in shortly."

"Ok Matt, do you need help?"

"No thanks Paul," replying as he walks to the door.

Eli looks at me, saying, "So, kid, I've seen you at the coffee shop a few times, Emily seems to like you," with a deep cowboy drawl, a little drill sergeant mixed in. He runs his hand down and over his mustache and beard.

I'm not quite sure what to say, Eli strikes me as someone who once carried some power and authority, 'gravitas' I think they call it, a bit of it still present here in this room. But life has taken its toll on him it's obvious; I hear the pain in his voice. "Yeah, I like her a lot myself. She's always nice, super cheerful, and I don't think it's all an act just to sell coffee. She's mentioned you a time or two as well, all good I might add."

I gather my courage and decide to ask, "So, what's it like to be homeless?"

Through the whistling of the high wind outside I hear the sound of breaking branches; loud cracking and popping coming from the front yard where my jeep is parked. Eli jumps up and heads for the door, glances through the tiny window and calls me over, "Kid, grab your jacket, it looks like Matt's hurt."

Finding my shoes, I throw on my coat and follow Eli outside. The wind is gale-force, with rain stinging my face, but that's nothing compared to the feeling I get when I see a large limb laying across the roof of my jeep. I start to mutter, "Son of a...", then my eyes follow to where Eli has run to and see Matt laying on his side beneath the branches extending from the heavy branch laying across my jeep. By the time I get there Eli is on his knees calling out Matt's name but there's no response.

"Kid lift up on this branch over there," pointing to a limb as Eli shouts to be heard over the wind. "While you lift, I'll try to pull him out."

I grab the branch and lift with all my strength, but it barely moves. I try again with no luck.

"Swap with me," Eli shouts.

I trade places and grab Matt's feet. Eli gathers his strength and lifts the main branch a few inches, enough so that I can drag him straight back and away. Eli jumps back over and quickly finds a pulse, but Matt's out cold.

"Help me carry him in."

I oblige and do my best, fortunately Eli is stronger than I thought (stronger than me and I work out!). Together we get him into the house, then lay Matt down on the carpet in the living room. I run back outside for the gallon of fuel laying in the water, come back and strip off my coat. Eli is soaked again yet his focus is totally on Matt. He runs his hands gently over his body looking for trouble as if he's done this before. When he touches his lower left side along the rib cage Matt groans. Eli continues his examination and instructs me to find some bandages for cuts he has on his face. Coming back with a first aid kit I find in the hall closet; I find that Eli has Matt's shirt pulled up with heavy bruising visible along his left side.

"I don't think the ribs are broken, but he's going to be hurting for a while. He's got a bump on the side of his head too. We'll have to watch him. I'd say go to the hospital to be sure, but who knows if it's even open."

"He's lucky to have you here Eli, the only first aid I know is CPR from work."

Standing back, I realize Eli's a lot smarter than I've given him credit for, someone I could learn from. As I begin to see him in a different light, it dawns on me that 'homeless' doesn't automatically mean uneducated or not so bright. I feel ashamed.

"Ok kid let's get him into his bed, but gently. Grab a blanket off his bed and bring it in here."

Coming back into the living room with me Eli beckons me to the same side he's on. Together we roll him towards us and as Eli holds him I spread the blanket beneath Matt as much as possible. Eli rolls him onto it taking special care with his head and neck and we pull it under him so that he's now completely on top. Dragging him down the hall into the bedroom, being careful not to jostle him too much, we then lift him into his bed.

"I'll grab a candle from the kitchen. Do we need anything else?" I ask.

"Yeah, a bottle of water," Eli responds as he's removing Matt's shoes and socks.

I get back and find Eli has removed his pants and shirt as well and is covering him up with a sheet. Grabbing a washcloth from the bathroom, he takes the water from me and starts to work on the cuts on the side of his face. It doesn't look bad; more like long scratches, plus that bump on his left temple. Eli then bandages the worst of it as I hold a large jar style candle close to where he's working. Glancing towards the windows I see fading light peeking around the outside edges of the board. Sunset's still a ways off, but the hurricane is moving in fast. Out of habit I check my cell phone for messages, but there's no coverage. I may as well turn it off to save what juice it still has left. The howling of the wind is getting louder.

"I'll be back, gotta' check on my jeep."

"Waste of time kid, nothin' you can do right now, anyway."

I ignore Eli and head for the front door. Looking out through the little window I see he's right. It's getting worse outside, and seriously, what could I really do at this point? The branch is across the roof on the front half, preventing me from moving it even if I wanted to. A chain saw is the next thing I'll need. Resigned, I spend the next couple of hours walking back and forth, listening to the radio and checking in on Eli and Matt. Eli has taken a seat next to Matt's bed and assumed the role of nurse. Putting my suitcase and duffel bag in my room I prepare for the long night ahead. The weather guy now says Harvey will make landfall between 10 pm and midnight, winds around a hundred and twenty mph—maybe more. How I wish there was a beer in the refrigerator, heck, a whole case! This is way more than I can handle and here I am holed up with two strangers.

Eli walks into the kitchen and sits down at the table. "You hungry kid?"

"Not really, wish I had a beer though."

"Yeah, me too."

"How's Matt doing?" I ask, trying to get my mind off the storm.

"Seems ok for now, we'll just have to take it one step at a time, but I think he's gonna' be alright. I saw a lot worse in the war, and those guys healed up just fine. Besides, Matt's tough."

I pull my cell out and turn it on again hoping against all odds there'll be a signal. There's not.

Habit causes me to look at the weather app, but then of course there's no update with no cell tower connection. Checking the time, I realize sundown is minutes away. It's growing dark outside, and the house is being bombarded constantly, the wind loaded with rain, debris blasting us, water pooling in the yard.

It hits me hard as I realize how screwed up things are, and mentally I begin to lose it. My jeeps under a tree, my laptop and cell phone are useless, all my stuff at the apartment may be destroyed at this point, the power may not be back on for days or weeks, and who knows when the grocery store will open again—my job! I have $97 dollars left in the bank, to which I now have no access to. What the hell!?

"This just totally sucks Eli, what the hell are we doing here? This is just bull sh…" I shout----

"Hold on Kid, attitude is gonna' make us or break us tonight, you just need to quit yer' bitchin' and get a hold of yourself. It could be worse."

"Worse?" I scream, *"how could it be worse*?!?" glaring at Eli.

"You could be back in your apartment, and I could be in my tent," Eli simply states staring back at me.

His calm demeanor washes over me, calms me down. He's been to war. If he thinks we'll be ok, then maybe we will be. But what about all my possessions? The internet, iPhone, Xbox, even if it's for a few days, what'll I do? I'm lost without my transportation, my job, my apartment, not to mention my gaming world friends. God, I wish my parents were here. My whole world has dissolved around me, and it only took twelve short hours for it to happen.

Realizing he might be correct I take a deep breath, "I guess you're right, it's not like I had anywhere else to go. My jeep wasn't safe, and I don't think my apartment is safe right now either."

"Nope," Eli replies. "Grab me a bottled water, would you kid?"

I grab one for both of us out of the pantry and sit down, my mind still reeling.

The winds outside now sound like the roar of a

jet engine, or even a freight train, the sheets of rain now horizontal. Looking over at Eli, I see his eyes are closed, his head tilted down. I can't tell if he's resting or praying. No harm in that I guess, they say there are no atheists in foxholes.

Hearing moaning from Matt's room down the hall, Eli gets up to check on him. I follow. Arriving we see Matt rotating his head back and forth, wincing with his eyes shut, obviously in pain.

Eli moves a chair closer to the bed and says, "Matt, can you hear me?" Pausing, "Can you hear me Matt?"

A second later Matt answers, his eyes still closed. "Yeah...what happened," he mumbles.

"It looks like you got hit by a branch coming down and it knocked you out. The kid and I brought you in. How you feelin'?"

"My head's killing me and my side hurts."

Eli responds, "Best I can tell—you've got some bruised ribs and a good size bump on your head."

Matt's eyes flutter open and he glances around, "What's that noise? Is that the wind?"

"Yeah. The hurricanes almost on top of us. Last I heard, before the radio cut out, the wind was at 90 with gusts up to 120 mph."

He tries to sit up, but the pain stops him instantly, so he lays back down. "I've got to check on the horses, make sure they're ok," he croaks.

Eliot firmly replies, "Sorry bro, no one's going out in that, you couldn't even stand up in it. Just pray for them and we'll check on them once this settles down some. Besides, I think horses are smarter than we are sometimes," a grim smile popping up on his face.

"So," I ask in disbelief, "You think if you pray, that God will protect the horses in a hurricane?"

They both look and me as Matt answers, "God doesn't promise there won't be bad things that happen in your life, he just promises to walk by your side when you go through them Paul. And yes, I believe God can protect them if he decides to, but I have to pray about it first."

"Why?" I respond, "What good will that do?"

"Jesus tells us that, 'We do not have, because we do not ask.' So we ask first and wait for His response. Sometimes it's yes, sometimes it's no. But even when it's no it usually becomes obvious over time why—many times because God has something better for us down the road. That's called having faith."

"I don't know Matt, I'm trying to be respectful and all, but that just seems like so much bull s..., ah, hocus pocus to me. Trusting in something I can't see, feel or touch seems foolish."

Matt winces in pain again and asks for water. Eli hands him a bottle, and he carefully takes a drink.

"Look kid, let's argue about this tomorrow, find something for Matt's pain will ya?" Turning to Matt, Eli asks, "What cha' got around here to help with them ribs?"

"Look in the bathroom cabinet, I've got some ibuprofen—just bring the whole bottle please."

As I'm in the bathroom something heavy (and loud) slams against the plywood over the window to my right and scares the bejeebers out of me. This is getting serious.

Walking back into the bedroom I hand the pills to Matt, "I can't wait for this to end, I know you said the house has survived this before, but it feels like the winds' going to rip the roof right off. I'd do anything not to be here right now."

"That makes three of us Paul, that makes three of us."

Chapter 9

Saturday August 26th

Awakened by the crashing sound in the kitchen, I don't know what time it is, but it seems early because there's faint light peeking around the boards covering the windows. I grab my phone off the nightstand and turn it on. It's almost 7am (still no signal) and I can't believe I slept through this. More importantly, I'm ALIVE! Turning my phone back off I walk into the kitchen to see Matt sitting at the kitchen table, his head in his hands, obviously in pain. His ribs are wrapped, his head too.

"Matt, are you ok? Do you need help getting back to bed?"

"Nah, I'm just dying for a cup of coffee. But I'm too dizzy to stand for very long."

Looking over at the kitchen counter I see where he's pulled down some pots and pans, now scattered about, hence the noise that woke me up.

"Look, I'll fix the coffee while you sit there, you just tell me what to do."

"It's a deal, Paul."

Matt guides me through setting up the Coleman stove, and has me crack a window next to where it's sitting on the kitchen counter. With the wind still blowing outside it's siphoning the air right out. He points out the percolator and has me fill it with water from a jug in the pantry. I pump up the Coleman fuel tank (it's one of the old fashion kind) and light a burner. Using the coffee I brought, I put it in the top of the coffee pot, set the cover over the bowl and add the lid with the little glass 'knob.'

"Should I check on the horses for you?"

"Thanks Paul but that was the first thing I did this morning. From the porch I could see them huddled in the open garage, out of the rain. It's still very windy but nothing like last night. The worst of it seems to be a missing roof off the barn and broken tree limbs and palm branches down everywhere; some trees uprooted. Fortunately, the front porch is up high enough to avoid being flooded. Sorry about your jeep by the way."

That comment snaps me back to reality. My jeep sits beneath a huge limb and my life feels like it's been crushed right along with it. There's no telling what shape my apartment is in.

"Eli's asleep on the floor in the back-spare bedroom, I think he sat up with me most of the night. He could have slept in the bed, but I guess it's just not his way." Matt looks towards me and says, "Thanks for bringing me in and fixing me up."

"Eli's the one to thank, I think he's got some type of 'medic' training because he seemed to know exactly what to do last night."

Sitting there quietly for a while, I listen to the wind outside, occasionally hearing the bubbling of the coffee on the burner.

"Nothin' better than the smell of a Coleman stove and coffee percolatin' in the mornin'," Eli says with a smile as he ambles into the kitchen. "How're the ribs Matt?"

"Hurting but I'll manage. Paul if you don't mind, if the coffee's done, pour me a cup please."

"Happy to," I reply, "Creme or sugar?"

"Sugar, thanks."

"I'll take a cup too kid, black."

"On the way," I respond as I prep three cups of Colombia's best. Sitting down I take a sip and begin to wonder if all coffee fixed in a percolator tastes this good, or does it taste better this morning because I've just survived a hurricane? No matter, I savor the flavor and let the caffeine do its thing. I watch the flame dancing on the candle sitting in the middle of the kitchen table as I try to wrap my mind around what's happened in the last 24 hours.

After a couple of moments Eli speaks up, "Matt I think I'll get the kid here to help take some of the boards down over the windows and see how bad things look. Then we'll fix you a little breakfast and try to get something on the radio."

"Sounds like a plan, thanks Eli."

I should be irritated by the way he keeps calling me 'Kid', but in a strange way, I kind of like it. Eli's the kind of guy you would like to back you up in a fight. Forget that, he's the guy you would want to fight it for you! He's scary and calming all at the same time. And yet he seems to be like Matt somehow, I just can't put my finger on it.

"The boards are held in place by simple clips along the edges by the brick," Matt explains, "a flat blade screwdriver should do the trick. You'll find one in the drawer next to the refrigerator. Speaking of the refrigerator, we need to cook and eat everything we can since the powers going to be out a while, expect a big breakfast this morning."

"No complaints here, I'm hungry," I chime in.

"Excuse me."

Getting up I head back to the bathroom as the coffee's already working its way through me. Taking care of business, I flush and realize although the bowl is now cycled and full again, I don't hear anything refilling the tank. "Oh yeah" I mumble out loud. The water pump is out. Time to refill the tank with the five-gallon bucket. This is going to be a bit of a hassle, but it's better than going out in the trees, and in the rain for that matter.

Walking back into the kitchen with my jacket and hat on, I announce, "I'm ready if you are Eli."

"Matt, do you have any waders or rain boots?" Eli asks.

"Yeah," taking a second to think, "you'll find both wedged between the cab and bed of my truck in the garage."

"Let's go kid," Eli says as he grabs his poncho and heads out the front door.

We walk out into a gray, rainy, very windy overcast day. It feels more like November than August. If it weren't for all the destruction, I would be enjoying the cooler temps. Walking the short distance to the garage I'm thankful there's only an inch or two of water here; parts of the acreage between the house and the road are much deeper.

The horses take up most of the garage next to the truck. Eli heads straight towards the back where a 55-gallon metal drum sits. As he opens it, the horses take instant notice.

"What are you doing?" I ask.

"Matt asked me to feed the horses while you were in the powder room." He scoops out a couple of quarts of pellets (smells like alfalfa), pours them into a metal bucket and hands it to me. "Hang on to this for a second." Eli fills another bucket, hands it to me as well and then fills a third. It's all I can do to keep the horses from sticking their great big noses into the food. "Follow me," Eli says.

Heading out to the side of the garage facing away from the wind, we set the buckets down several feet apart on a dry piece of ground and they eagerly chow down. Going back inside I ask, "How do you seem to know so much about things?"

Eli replies with a phrase I used to hear my Dad say, "I'm a jack of all trades, but the master of none." He glances my way and follows up with, "Some from the military, some from different jobs. I read a lot."

He hands me a pair of rain boots that come up almost to my knees. They're too big but that's better than too small. Eli puts on the waders and we head' back to the windows on the house. He pries the clips out and hands them to me. The boards come down quickly and we lean them up against the house under the front porch. Soon we have them all off and survey the house from a short distance. Besides missing a few shingles, she appears fine, but then there's my jeep. Walking up to it I take a good look at it. I don't know whether to get angry or throw my hands up in frustration and walk away.

"Doesn't look so bad to me," Eli states in a matter-of-fact sort of way.

I look at him likes he's grown a third eye, "Seriously!?"

Taking it all in, "Get a saw, cut that limb into pieces and I'll help you remove the branches that are sticking down inside. There's a chance it might be drivable, but we won't know how bad it really is until that's done."

Standing there with a light rain coming down I think he's crazy, but you know what? I'm just too frustrated to care right now.

"What next," I ask Eli.

"Let's walk the fence line, make sure the horses don't have any way of getting out."

It takes 45 minutes to walk it (slosh through it is more accurate), Eli thinks it surrounds about four acres. We find two sections of the chain link fence laying over, but we prop them back up for now with limbs we find floating around us. More than once the water is high enough to spill over the tops of my boots (a good 12 to 14 inches), but I just push through because this must get done. It's the least I can do for Matt as it's clear I'll be here now for more than just a day or two.

We walk back to the house removing our boots, shoes and socks. Once inside, it's nice to see light coming through the windows, it looks like a whole different home. I head back to my room and change out of my jeans, soaked from the thighs down. Walking into the kitchen barefoot I smell the wonderful aroma of bacon. Matt's already cooked it while we were working, and has it set aside in a covered bowl, something he could do and not have to stand over it the whole time.

He comes trudging down the hall from the bathroom, his arm across his ribcage, saying, "If one of you gent's will scramble the eggs in the carton next to the skillet, we can eat."

I volunteer. Eli is already sitting at the kitchen

table and fills Matt in on what we found, and that the horses have now been fed. Matt responds by telling us he's tried the radio and his cell phone but there's nothing working so far.

I fill three plates with bacon and eggs and set them on the table. Grabbing three bottled waters I sit down; Matt then gives the blessing and we eat. I close my eyes this time. (I don't want to be rude, right?)

"So," Matt begins," it looks like we've still got light rain coming down and wind, but I'm glad it's still only in the 70's out there. Which makes it comfortable in here for the time being. I fear the heat will be back once this all blows out of here and it won't be much fun without air conditioning."

"Worse than that," Eli adds, "the mosquitos are going to be horrible in a few days with all this water standing around, and there's already little mounds of fire-ants floating around out there hoping to drift by something to latch on to."

I'd seen that before, it's pretty amazing what they'll do to survive. I had to direct some of my friends to YouTube videos before they would believe me.

Matt replies, "You know, I usually tell people to take it one day at a time when they find themselves in a bad way, I think it's going to be more like one hour at a time for us."

One hour at a time is about all I can handle right now. We eat in silence for a bit and then I realize I should try to go and check out my apartment.

"Matt, what are the chances I could get you to take me to see what shape my apartments is in?"

He thinks for a moment. "Well, I'm not in the best of shape, and although my head feels a lot better--

my ribs are still sore." Pausing for a second, "You drive and I'll ride shotgun, I really want to see what the town looks like myself."

Chapter 10

BULLETIN
Hurricane Harvey Advisory Number 25
NWS National Hurricane Center Miami FL
AL092017
1000 AM CDT Sat Aug 26, 2017

...HARVEY DRENCHING TEXAS...
...TORRENTIAL RAINS WILL CONTINUE FOR
A FEW MORE DAYS...

SUMMARY OF 1000 AM CDT...1500
UTC...INFORMATION

LOCATION...28.9N 97.3W
ABOUT 25 MI...35 KM W OF VICTORIA TEXAS
ABOUT 80 MI...130 KM ESE OF SAN ANTONIO
TEXAS
MAXIMUM SUSTAINED WINDS...75
MPH...120 KM/H
PRESENT MOVEMENT...N OR 350 DEGREES
AT 2 MPH...4 KM/H
MINIMUM CENTRAL PRESSURE...984
MB...29.06 INCHES

WATCHES AND WARNINGS

CHANGES WITH THIS ADVISORY:

The Storm Surge Warning for the Texas coast
south of Port Aransas

has been discontinued.

The Hurricane Warning for the Texas coast has been replaced with a
Tropical Storm Warning.

DISCUSSION AND 48-HOUR OUTLOOK

At 1000 AM CDT (1500 UTC), the center of Hurricane Harvey was
located near latitude 28.9 North, longitude 97.3 West. Harvey is
moving slowly toward the north near 2 mph (4 km/h), and little
motion is anticipated during the next several days.

Maximum sustained winds have decreased to near 75 mph (120 km/h)
with higher gusts. These winds are confined to a small area near the
center. Weakening is forecast during the next 48 hours, and Harvey
is expected to become a tropical storm this afternoon.

Hurricane-force winds extend outward up to 25 miles (35 km) from the center and tropical-storm-force winds extend outward up to 140 miles (220 km).

The estimated minimum central pressure is 984 mb (29.06 inches).

HAZARDS AFFECTING LAND

RAINFALL: Harvey is expected to produce total rain accumulations of 15 to 30 inches and isolated maximum amounts of 40 inches over the middle and upper Texas coast through Thursday. During the same time period Harvey is expected to produce total rain accumulations of 5 to 15 inches in far south Texas, the Texas Hill Country and southwest and central Louisiana. Rainfall of this magnitude will cause catastrophic and life-threatening flooding.   A list of rainfall observations compiled by the NOAA Weather Prediction Center can be found at: www.wpc.ncep.noaa.gov/discussions/nfdscc1.html

STORM SURGE: The combination of a dangerous storm surge and the tide will cause normally dry areas near the coast to be flooded by rising waters moving inland from the shoreline. The water is expected to reach the following heights above ground if the peak surge occurs at the time of high tide...

Port Aransas to Sargent...4 to 7 ft
Sargent to High Island including Galveston Bay...2 to 4 ft
High Island to Morgan City...1 to 3 ft

An hour later we're throwing on our rain gear and boots. Mine are still wet but I don't care, at least it's warm water and not cold. Walking out the front door we head for the backyard, Matt picking up two empty white five-gallon buckets on the way. There are stickers on both saying, "Food Grade, Heavy Duty, BPA Free." We slosh back to the first rain barrel beneath the gutter. It's sitting up on a pedestal so that we can put the first bucket under the spigot at the bottom making it easy to fill. I notice that between the gutter and the top of the barrel, Matt's placed a filter preventing leaves and small debris from running in with the water. Smart.

"Very cool," I tell Matt. "What a great idea!" as I turn on the spigot.

Glancing around the backyard he says, "It's great for times like this, but we also use it to water Jen's plants and garden. Our well water has lots of minerals, but the worst part is the high sodium content being this close to the Gulf of Mexico. We had to bring in good topsoil for the garden and use raised beds because all we have here is beach sand. With our climate we can get two, sometimes three crops a year depending on what we've planted."

Seeing the vegetables destroyed by the storm, I want to ask him what they grow, but I realize now's not the time. Having filled both buckets we head back to the porch and set them next to the front door. Matt sticks his head inside and yells, "Eli, we're taking off, please use this water out here to wash dishes with."

"No problem Pardner," he calls back—there goes that whole cowboy thing again.

The horses have found comfort huddled under one of the larger oak trees up on a small rise out of the standing water, so getting the truck out of the garage is easy. We drive up to the gate through water measuring from several inches deep up to a foot or more. Matt gets the gate and then we head down the road, slowly, taking our time.

After turning left on FM 1069 we soon reach the intersection with highway 35, the water standing beneath the overpass is too high for most cars. Matt's truck has high clearance, so we slowly plow through as others are turning around and heading a different way. I then turn left at the dark stop light onto Wheeler. As we continue down the road, I notice that the hospital on the right appears to be closed, not a car in sight. Debris is everywhere whether on the street or in the business lots—remains of roofs, signs, fences, you name it.

"Would you look at that--" Matt says, pointing out a Sonic on the left where the 'roof' above the car stalls is now a mass of twisted metal in the parking lot. The roof of the main building may be partially gone too, it's hard to tell. Some structures look so-so, others are broken up badly; walls missing, rooftops gone, it's like a movie scene.

Turning left onto my street we encounter an alligator in front of us in the middle of the road. He looks our way, we stare back. He doesn't seem eager to move. It must be at least six feet long.

"I knew we had alligators in the area, but this is the first time I've seen one in town," I comment.

"Me too," Matt replies.

Giving him a wide berth, I pull into the apartment's parking lot a hundred yards down the road and it doesn't look good. The wall along the north side is ripped away exposing the interior of my neighbors' apartment. Mine next door looks sketchy from here; the front window is gone, and from this angle you can see sky through it. *Definitely* not good.

Matt hands me a couple of black heavy-duty trash bags he'd brought along and says, "Sorry Paul, with my ribs this way I don't feel up to hauling stuff downstairs, I'll wait in the truck for you if you don't mind. Just grab what's important for now."

How could I complain? I'm just thankful he's allowing me to stay at his place for a while. It's unspoken between us, but it's obvious I can't stay here at the apartment tonight, and I've no place else to go. I'm humbled by the thought that I yelled at him for his comments about "God loves you," and now he's putting up with me at his home. Actually, humbled doesn't begin to cover it. I'm feeling pretty scummy right now.

Climbing the stairs, I unlock the door. It's a disaster plain and simple. The windows are blown in (or out, depending on which ones you're looking at) and water is everywhere. And it stinks, like seawater stinks. Rummaging through what's there, I find the things I value most; pictures of family, clothes in drawers not soaked by the rain, important papers in a plastic file box. I remember a small lock box in a bottom drawer which holds my parents' mementos. Nothing fancy; some jewelry like earrings from mom and a silver ring with a green stone my dad liked to wear.

The cross my mom wore around her neck is in there too; two silver nails formed into a crucifix on a long silver chain. Holding back the emotions I 'gut it up' and head back down to the truck where Matt's waiting. I never knew just how much these things would come to mean to me until now.

After loading what I could salvage into the bed of the truck, I climb in and ask Matt for a favor, "Do you mind if I drive by my grocery store just to see how it's looking?"

"Sure Paul." Five minutes later we arrive.

The scene blows me away. Not by the fact that the store looks good for having survived a hurricane, it's the water tower across the street. What's left is laying in pieces on the ground across from us, like the sections of an orange; split apart, amidst the legs that once held it at least sixty feet in the air. That's the only water tower for Aransas Pass that I know of, what will they do for water now?

Parking in a corner of the lot, we just sit there for a while with the engine idling. It's gray, rainy, and a steady wind continues to pummel us. What's there to say? This is the aftermath of a hurricane, and what's done is done. We can complain about it or think about how we'll react to it and rebuild our lives. My mind is on overload, too much to take in; I just zone out.

Pulling back out onto the street—it appears to be a ghost town. There's no electricity, water fills the streets, a car or truck occasionally passes by, probably as overwhelmed as we are. "Let's go home," Matt says, and all I could think of to say is, "Sounds good."

PART TWO

Aftermath

Chapter 11

Arriving back at the house I'm surprised to see a new car there parked in the water close to my jeep. It's a green four-door Subaru of some kind. Matt announces, "Looks like Sarah's here." And that's all the explanation I get.

Pulling into the garage I get out and grab my bags from the truck bed and head to the front door. We walk inside, strip off our rain gear and find a girl sitting in the kitchen at the table.

"Hey Matt, I came by to see how you and the horses made out, didn't know you had company!" she states, glancing at Eli across the kitchen table. Looking my way, she adds, "Who's this?"

"Sarah Connors, I'd like you to meet Paul...", Matt realizes he doesn't know my last name.

"Stevenson," I complete, "Paul Stevenson."

"Hey," I say grinning, "Is that 'Sarah Connors' like in the Terminator Movies?"

"Yeah, only I'm a brunette and she's a blond. Besides, I don't believe in time-traveling robots."

"But she's just as scrappy," Eli says with a wink.

"So, you two know each other?" I query Sarah and Eli.

Matt chimes in, "Eli joins our bible study group at the coffee shop from time to time. Anyone and everyone's welcome," he concludes glancing my way. I think it's his way of inviting me.

Recognizing me from the other day, Sarah looks at me in an accusing sort of way and says, "You're that guy that yelled at Matt at the coffee shop, aren't you?"

"Guilty as charged, but I have apologized," I sheepishly respond.

Matt glances between the three of us and sits down. "So, Sarah, catch us up on what's going on with you. Where were you last night during the storm and why back in the area so quick today?"

"The short answer is I stayed in Kenedy last night with friends. According to a radio station out of San Antonio, the weather's worse there than it is in Corpus, where my apartment is. The hurricane turned northeast last night after making landfall and headed more towards Victoria. Still, it was raining buckets when I left this morning, but it's not as bad here. Along with wanting to be sure everything's ok at my place I thought I'd stop by yours and check in on you."

Eli stands up from the table saying, "Hey, while you all chat, I'm going to catch up on some sleep from watching 'sleeping beauty' last night," and walks off down the hall.

Matt and I chuckle while Sarah gives him a curious look, "What's he talking about?"

"Well, as you can see I've got a bump on my head, plus, some really sore ribs. I went out last night during the storm to check on the horses and grab some things out of the garage, and as I was making my way past Pauls' jeep, a limb came down on me. I don't think I'd be talking to you right now if his jeep hadn't taken the brunt of the fall. Paul and Eli came out and pulled me out from under the branch and brought me inside. So, Eli sat up with me last night playing nurse."

"Are you ok? Do we need to get you to a doctor?" Sarah says.

"I think I'll be alright; Eli's had some medical training; he thinks the ribs are just bruised and I'm feeling better this afternoon. I believe I'm in better shape than Pauls' Rubicon."

"That reminds me, do you have a chainsaw Matt?" I interject.

"I do. When the rain quits, we'll see if we can't do something with that branch and find out just how much damage was done."

"Thanks, I just hope it's still drivable," I say.

"So, how'd it go here last night?" Sarah asks Matt.

"Paul would be the one to answer that, I was out for most of it."

I give Sarah the rundown of the evening. She in turn tells us that hurricane Harvey made landfall between Port A and Rockport, putting us almost dead center. The winds were estimated at 120 to 150 mph, estimated because the equipment in the area quit working after 75 mph, even at the Corpus Christi International Airport. It was classified as a category 4 hurricane just before landfall by the NOAA.

"I believe we're lucky to be alive," Matt sighs.

"More like blessed Matt," Sarah corrects.

"You're right, we should give thanks--"

Matt and Sarah bow their heads as he offers thanks to God for seeing us through. Again, I just don't get it. We've been hit by a hurricane, with no power; no water; no phone or internet. It's gonna' get hot and muggy soon with no AC and they're giving thanks. Never mind mosquitos the size of Mini-Coopers. I find it hard to be thankful with my jeep under a tree, not knowing if I still have a job or not. I shake my head and sigh.

"Seeing as you're here Sarah, would you like to stay for lunch?"

"I wouldn't want to impose," she replies.

"You'd actually be helping out. We've got food in the fridge that needs to be eaten up before it spoils."

Sarah thinks for a second, then says, "Ok, but one condition—I cook."

"No arguments here," Matt replies smiling.

Sarah gets up to see what's available for our meal.

"Paul, I've got a favor to ask: not knowing how long the power's going to be out, hence no well water, would you fill up several 5-gallon buckets from the rain barrels and put them on the front porch?"

"Sure Matt. Where are the extra buckets?"

"In the garage in the back right-hand corner. Please use the lids with the spout, they're so much easier to pour with."

"Consider it done."

Once again, I put my rain boots and jacket back on, then go outside. The rain is more a light drizzle or mist now, and the temp is still moderate—I'm glad. If it was in the nineties as usual this time of year it would feel more like a tropical rain forest. Grabbing a stack of white buckets, I head towards the rain barrels in the backyard. Making another trip to the garage I retrieve enough lids to cover them all. As I'm walking back, I notice what appear to be turtles (I can see what looks like their heads) swimming over in a deeper part of the standing water, in a depression about 100 feet away. It looks like maybe four turtles (two pair) watching my approach. As I get closer one set of turtles disappears beneath the surface, then the second set of turtles does the same. A chill runs down my spine. Either those are two pair of turtles, perfectly synchronized, or those are two alligators in the yard.

Chapter 12

Walking quickly back to the house I poke my head inside the door and shout towards the kitchen, "Matt, we may have a serious problem out here."

"What's up Paul?" he calls back.

No matter what, he always seems cool, calm and collected. I envy that. "I think there's a chance we've got two alligators in the yard. Do alligators attack horses?"

"They can, but that's unusual. The problem is, how did they get inside the fence, and how are we going to get them out? And are there more than two?"

"Eli and I found part of the fence down this morning," I reply, "maybe they got in that way. But it's back up now."

Matt walks outside with me after gearing up, and we make our way towards the area where I first spotted them. Sure enough, there's two sets of eyes looking at us. Sarah joins us a minute later and says, "Definitely looks like alligators. If the Parks and Wildlife office was open for business today, they'd come remove them for you. But I doubt you can reach them since all the phones are down."

"Are you sure they're alligators?"

"She's working on her degree in Marine Biology Paul," Matt answers," if anyone can be sure, it's Sarah."

"Okay!" I reply, "So, what's the plan?"

"Well, unless someone or livestock is in immediate danger, it's illegal to kill them. We need to be sure the horses are protected first, then try to figure out a way to get them off the property."

"Easier said than done." Matt comments. "They must have followed the drainage ditches along Armstrong road, especially since they're deep and overflowing right now, then into the yard in search of food."

"Believe it or not, there's also a lot of fish out there, must have come in with the flood waters," I add.

"Yeah, I can see some from here Paul." Sarah points out.

Matt thinks for a second, "For now, let's get the horses into the paddock next to the barn. The barn roof's gone but the chain link fencing is still up and will keep them protected for the time being."

I have no clue how to handle horses, but Matt and Sarah direct me as we coax them back towards the enclosure. I begin to think to myself; just how much more surreal can this whole thing get? I wish there was an app for this, chuckling to myself.

Completing that job, Matt makes sure the horses get fed as Sarah returns to the cooking and I finish filling water buckets.

Having lined up ten five-gallon containers on the porch, I return inside to the wonderful aroma of food cooking on the stove. Matt's set up a battery powered fan in the window next to the Coleman to suck all the gas fumes out. Checking my cell phone once again I find there's still no signal. The battery power is way down, so I dig through my stuff and plug in my portable battery charger. The problem is, what'll I do when *that's* gone? Oh, how I wish I could log on to the internet, catch up with friends, find out what's happening at work. I may be the captain of my own ship but right now it feels like it's a tiny rowboat in the middle of an empty sea. Looking at the positive, I guess I should be grateful for my new friends; Matt, Eli and Sarah. Eli's right, it could be much worse.

Lunch turns out to be chicken breasts cut into strips, frozen vegetables and O'Brien potatoes all from the thawing freezer. We begin a conversation about what the Hurricane may have done to the beach along the coastline, how bad it might be at this point. It then progresses into a discussion about the damage that must have been done to the homes and businesses in Port Aransas. There's also Aransas Pass and Rockport to consider. From what little we saw when we drove to my apartment, it's got to be horrendous. Listening to radio reports on the way over, Sarah says the storm surge in the streets of Port Aransas was somewhere around four to six feet, maybe worse. I couldn't help but think about the restaurants, the shops, the folks who live there year-round. My heart going out to them, many of those people I consider friends. Although it's a tourist destination to most, for me, it's my second home.

Looking towards Matt, I ask, "So where do you work?"

"At the lumber store there on Wheeler. When we passed it earlier it looked damaged, but it was hard to tell just how bad. I'll have to keep checking in until I find out when we might re-open."

Staring down at the table, feeling a little depressed, I remark, "Me too, I need to get back to work. But with no electricity, or water, it doesn't look good."

"Guys, I'm still not feeling to well, I'm going to

lay down for a while," Matt groans.

"Go get some rest," Sarah responds, "we got this."

As Matt makes his way back to his bedroom, Sarah takes over rather quickly. "Paul, please bring in a bucket of water and let's get these dishes knocked out."

Bringing one in I fill both sinks with cool water. Adding soap to the left side, Sarah begins to wash. I rinse and then dry with a towel I find hanging on the oven handle.

Making conversation Sarah says, "It sounds like you can't go back to your apartment, and the grocery store is closed for the time being. What will you do now Paul?"

Good question, I think to myself. "I really don't know. I'm guessing I might be able to get some hours at one of our other stores in Corpus Christi, assuming they're open. But I don't even know if my Jeep is drivable yet. Once the rain quits, that's my first project. It looks like this is my home for a while as long as Matt will allow. I'm lucky to have somewhere to stay right now."

Sarah pauses for a moment, then stops and looks at me. "Paul, you may not want to hear this, but you might consider that Matt being at the right place at the right time is more providence, than luck."

"What do you mean?" Looking at her suspiciously, thinking a sermon is coming my way.

"Just that. If you and Matt had not crossed paths at Coastal Bend Coffee, you wouldn't be here right now. A safe place to sleep, food to eat. And come to think of it, you happened to be here just when Matt needed someone to pull him out from under that tree."

"Coincidence," I reply, "nothing more."

Before we can get into a knock-down-drag-out I hear something outside. Walking to the living room window, a spy a woman getting out of a Ford crew cab truck similar to Matt's, only newer, nicer. It's his wife Jen with two labs in tow; one chocolate, the other yellow.

Walking in she removes her boots as she orders the dogs to sit on the front door mat. Spotting us, she says, "Hi Sarah, hi Paul, where's Matt?"

Taking a towel from Sarah, she wipes off the dog's paws as Sarah informs her that Matt's in the back bedroom taking a nap.

"Any coffee available?" She asks.

"No but I'll get some started for you." Getting up, I retrieve the percolator from the cabinet.

As I fill the pot with water from a gallon jug, I catch Jen up on what's happened in the last 24 hours. As soon as I get to the part about Matt's injuries she races to the master bedroom.

"He's gonna' be ok!" I shout after her, but it's too late. She's concerned for her man.

Sarah grabs a mug and pours herself some coffee. She sits back down at the kitchen table and looks my way again. "I'm sorry about your parents Paul."

Her comment catches me off guard. I was expecting a fight, not sympathy. Glancing outside through the kitchen window I see the sun beginning to peak through the clouds, a welcome sight. "Thanks," was all I could muster. I'd forgotten she was at the coffee shop when I yelled at Matt a few days ago.

Without being prodded, Sarah continues, "My sister and I were adopted when I was two; I don't remember my biological parents. My adoptive mom and dad couldn't have kids, so I think that's why they treated us like princesses. But I've often wondered what my real parents were like."

"I guess I should consider myself lucky I knew mine, they were really good to me," I reply. "I had an older sister, but she died when I was very young, so they spoiled me as an only child. I sometimes wonder about what it would have been like if she were alive today."

Why did I just tell her about Hannah? I never tell people about her. Maybe it's because she's being so open with me. I feel vulnerable all of a sudden.

Jen comes to my rescue by joining us back in the kitchen, obviously relieved her husband's doing alright. Grabbing a mug from the cabinet and pouring some freshly brewed coffee, she says "Matt's looking pretty good—I guess I overreacted a little. And the dogs are happy to be home. They're taking a nap with him now," a smile crossing her face. "So, tell me the rest of the story."

I continue with my part; the visit to my apartment and what the town looks like now, ending with the discovery of alligators on the property. She raises her eyebrows but doesn't seem to be too ruffled by the news. Sarah finishes up with up with her story and what the roads to and from San Antonio were like.

Jen responds with, "Well, here's where we're at with Hurricane Harvey. It's moving slowly to the east and drenching the hill country. The winds are still around sixty to seventy miles an hour. The fear is that it will head back into the Gulf of Mexico and strengthen all over again. Then, God forbid, make landfall once more."

"Damn," is my response, "Oh my Lord," is Sarah's.

"Port Aransas, San Patricio county (where we live) and Aransas county took the brunt of it. Before I lost the radio signal they were saying that Harvey became a level four hurricane just before landfall. Word is, Port Aransas is seventy to eighty percent damaged or destroyed."

Chapter 13

Sarah left to go see her apartment and the afternoon goes by slowly. With no TV, radio, internet, etc... Jen and I spend the time talking about what we know, and what we need to do if things don't get better soon. It's going to be at least a week or two for electricity to come back on, which means no water flowing out of the tap either (being on a well). I can't afford to stay in a hotel in Corpus, so my options are few, actually--none. I'm at the mercy of a couple who less than a week ago I looked down on as naïve Christians. Eating crow is something I seem to be doing more and more of lately.

The labs come running down the hall followed by Matt. Eli is right behind him.

"Well, looks who's up, Butch Cassidy and the Sundance Kid!" Jen says with a grin.

Matt and Eli glance at each other with a "Who's she talking about?" look on their faces. Obviously, an old joke between the three of them.

"How are you feeling Matt?" I ask.

Sitting down at the table he replies "Better. Not great, but better. The ribs are not as sore, and I can breathe again," he says with a slight grin.

"Good to see you Jen, how are ya?" Eli pipes up.

"I'm well Eli, and you?"

"I'm alright. Moving things along she adds, "Well, gents, it's almost supper time. Any thoughts?"

Matt answers, "Why don't we fire up the grill and cook the steaks in the freezer, they're probably thawed by now. We can bake the potatoes in foil at the same time."

"Sounds like a plan." Jen responds. She gets up and heads to the freezer.

Looking my direction, Eli says, "Hey kid, while they're getting supper going, let's go feed the horses."

"Happy too," I answer as I get up to follow him out the door.

It's still slightly windy, cloudy, and the water has receded some, but there's still plenty to slosh through. Approaching the garage, we hear the horses acting up, neighing rather loudly. Looking over in that direction Eli spots something. Reacting quickly, he shouts, "Run back to the house and see if Matt's got a big rifle—I need one *now*."

Trying to run through six inches of water is difficult, but I arrive seconds later and stick my head in the door. "Matt —Eli needs a big rifle, quick!"

Taking my word for it, Matt heads to his bedroom and returns with some type of hunting rifle with a scope. He gives it to me and then proceeds to put his own boots on.

Running (more like splashing) back to the paddock I see what the trouble is; one of the alligators has gotten under the fencing. Handing the rifle off to Eli, he takes a quick look at it and checks the breach. Satisfied there's a bullet in there he walks closer to the fence line and takes careful aim. The gator has the horses backed up along one side. He pulls the trigger with a loud report; the animal is hit and starts thrashing about. Eli reloads, then walks closer to where he is and shoots again, this time striking the head. The thrashing stops and he begins to float half submerged in the shallow muck, his feet contracting in a slow movement. Opening the gate Eli walks in, stands directly over the gator, then points the gun at the top of the skull. A shot rings out and Eli looks towards me, shouting, "Just making sure."

By this time Matt's with us and Jen is heading our way too. "Are the horses alright?" She asks.

Matt walks into the fenced area and slowly approaches them. Hands held out in a soothing manner, he reaches towards the closest one and quietly speaks, assuring them it's all over. After assessing them all he turns to Jen, "They seem fine, although I don't know why they didn't bolt when they had the chance. Especially with all the shooting."

Eli hands the rifle to Matt and attempts to drag the alligator by the tail out of the enclosure, leaving a trail of blood in his wake. Nothing seems to frighten this guy.

"Let me help you," I offer, walking his way. Caught up in the moment, I set aside my fear of grabbing on to the slimy, leathery tail and help pull this big guy out. He looks to be at least six feet long, the head bigger than mine. Giant teeth (at least to me) poking out from the mouth remind me of how dangerous they are if they can get a hold of you. I did a report in high school once (I was fascinated by them) and their bite force is 3700 pounds per square inch. Yours and mine is around 150. Nothing can get an alligator to release its prey, except for maybe a really big branch, or a bullet.

Letting go of him beneath some trees on dry ground Eli walks his length. "Almost seven feet," he proclaims. "There's some good eating there."

"Seriously? And who's going to skin him?" I ask,

knowing the answer before the question leaves my mouth. My heart slows its pounding as the adrenaline wears off. Jen and Matt console the horses while I just stand there and try to take it all in. The last twenty-four hours have just been unbelievable. I find myself wishing Sarah was still here, there's just something about her. She's pretty and easy to talk to. A little voice inside my head reminds me she's a Christian, and that I don't like Christians. Ignoring the little voice, I decide I like her anyway, and look forward to seeing her again soon.

"I'll skin him," Eli replies. No surprise there.

Just then a neighbor next door walks up to the property line thirty yards away, "Hey Matt, Jen, I heard the shots, is everything ok?"

"Hi Brian, yeah, we're alright. Had to take out this gator; he was in the pen with the horses," Matt says.

At first glance Brian reminds me of a burly, bearded teddy bear, the kind that wears a leather vest covered in patches. Another Eli only with a "Ride to live and live to ride," frame of mind.

Walking out of the pen and towards Brian he continues, "Did you stay during the storm too?"

"No, I just got back; had to see how the homestead held up. So, you stayed here last night? Really? What was that like?"

"I wouldn't want to do it again, although I slept through most of it." Matt then proceeds to fill Brian in on the last 24 hours as I decide to wander around the property. About a third of the trees are down, some uprooted. The few palm trees they have are in better shape, still, some of the fronds are missing. Little islands of grass pop up in places as the rainwater is slowly either running off or being absorbed into the soil. The temps' still moderate, but the sun threatens to break through the cloud cover from time to time. After circling back to my jeep and taking a good long look, I feel slightly encouraged. Once I get this big limb off it, it may not be so bad. The floorboard is full of water, but this vehicle is made to take in dirt, water, mud; you name it. Limbs poke down inside but the seats don't seem to be torn up. And the steering wheel and dashboard look ok, the back half not bad at all. Unless I'm missing something, the major trauma is to the soft top which can be replaced. Tomorrow I'll get Eli to help me work on this.

Walking back towards the paddock, Matt and Jen are checking the fence where the alligator appears to have worked its way under.

"Could you give me a hand Paul?" Matt calls out.

"Sure." I walk over, and we spend the next hour working on the paddock fence to ensure the safety of the horses. The second alligator is nowhere to be seen, but I'm confidant he's not far away.

By the time we get back to the house Jen has supper just about ready. She's brought out a portable card table to the porch and set it up; plates, silverware, and condiments for the potatoes. Matt and I wash up using some barrel water on the front porch. Removing our gear, we sit down in the white plastic chairs near the grill where the steaks are just coming off. Glancing over towards Brian's spread I see him and Eli working on the alligator, happy it's not me.

Just as Jen is setting the plates of food on the

table a familiar looking Subaru pulls up. It's Sarah, a smile creases my face.

"You couldn't have shown up at a better time," Jen calls out, as Sarah walks towards the porch. "Come, help us eat up some of this Sarah."

"Thanks Jen, I'd like that."

Matt and I bring our chairs over and we all sit down at the table. Jen joins us, and Matt gives thanks for our meal.

"So, what happened in Corpus?" Matt directs a question at Sarah.

"Driving through Portland and Corpus Christi wasn't too bad. They didn't get hit quite like Aransas Pass did. Where my apartment is (near the university campus) being near the bay, well, there's a lot of cleaning up to do. The power is out for the moment, although after talking to some people there, it may be back on in the next 24 to 48 hours. I had to take the stairs up to the fourth floor where I live, and fortunately everything's ok. I'm grateful for that. But, if you don't mind, could I stay here with you and Jen until the powers back on down there?"

Matt and Jen look at each other, nodding approval. "Sure Sarah." Looking my way, Matt says, "Paul, would you mind taking the couch while Sarah's here for a day or two?"

"No problem, I just feel privileged to get to stay here. Whatever you need me to do," I reply.

We chat while we eat, again, grateful that it's still not up into the 90's temperature wise, as is normal for August. Sarah talks about what the hurricane may have done to the coastline, not to mention how it might have affected the birds, turtles and sea life. I'd never thought about that before. People are always focused on how it affects them, but little is said about how it might also affect the wildlife.

I sit thoughtfully for a moment and then ask Sarah, "When I take the ferry to Port A, I frequently see dolphins. I especially like to watch the ones that leap out of the wake in front of the tankers that come through the channel on their way to the gulf. This may sound like a stupid question, but I've always wondered; *how do they sleep,* when they have to come up to the surface to breathe air every few minutes? It seems like they would just fall asleep and drown."

Looking my way as she finishes a bite of baked potato, "That's actually a good question Paul," smiling. "It's been discovered that dolphins are able to sleep with only half of their brain at a time, the other half awake. It allows them to continue to swim, and breath of course, and then when one half is rested, the other side sleeps. Whales do the same thing. I'd Google it for you and show you the details, but no such luck today."

"That's amazing," I respond.

"It's a God thing." Matt simply states.

"What about evolution Matt?" I shoot back.

Pausing for a moment, "Let's think about this Paul, the more you observe in nature, the more you see a pattern in things. The perfect symmetry in seashells, flowers, snowflakes, or the amazing complexity of the human body; you name it. The DNA for everything is contained in a single strand; and it doesn't matter if that's for a grain of wheat, or a Blue Whale. Only our best super-computers can now begin to unravel it." Looking directly into my eyes he says, "So, convince me that all this happens by chance." Pausing, I'm not sure what to say, so he adds, "Ok, I've got a question for you Paul. Have you ever heard of Dark Matter or Dark Energy?"

"Yeah, I think scientists have recently discovered it, it fills most of the universe I guess."

"Something like that." Matt comes back, "I was just looking it up on Wikipedia last week and at this time, most scientists believe it to be real. The theory goes that the world you and I can see, touch, and feel only makes up 5% of the universe. That 27% of it is made up of Dark Matter, and the last 68% is Dark Energy. Yet none of this can be measured, seen or felt. So, you tell me, who's crazier; the scientists who tell me to believe in something that fills 95% of the universe that I can't verify, or, the Bible that tells us a spiritual world surrounds us, filled with things at least some of us has seen; things like angels and demons."

Feeling backed into a corner with no clear answer I go with the safe one, "I guess at this point it's a matter of who you believe the most."

"Almost comes down to a matter of faith, wouldn't you say?" Matt replies, a calm assurance to his voice. Sensing my rising anger Matt adds, "I'm not trying to make you mad Paul, but it's easier to believe, at least to me that this was all created on purpose, rather than it all just started with a big bang, and a swirl of chemicals in a pond somewhere."

"Alright, I'll give it some thought," I reply, deciding that's all I care to hear. I guess the sermon comes with the free lodging. But somewhere in the back of my mind, I can't say he's completely wrong either.

As we're clearing the table, stunned, I spot Eli

walking over; covered head to toe in mud—and I don't want to know what else.

Addressing us all, "Brian's going to put the gator meat in plastic bags and save it for us. We're splitting it 50, 50. He's got a chest freezer over there running off a generator and we can come get some any time we want. I like Brian . . . he's a Vet too," ending with a smile.

Looking Eli over Matt tells him, "Okie Dokie. Well, it looks like you need a shower big man! Jen, would you go in the house and grab that portable camp shower in the spare bedroom, you know, the one we used last summer on the trip to Big Bend?"

"On the way," Jen replies getting up.

"Paul, you grab a couple of those buckets of water next to you and come with me." Glancing back at Eli, "We're gonna set you up a shower."

As we head for the trees Matt asks Eli, "So, what did you all do with the carcass?"

Eli responds, "Brian and I drug it over to a pond on his property." Smiling he adds, "He says the turtles who live there will have a chance to get a little revenge."

"What do you mean?" Matt asks.

Chuckling, Eli replies, "Alligators eat turtles; now the turtles are gettin' even."

I never would have thought of that. Kind of interesting and gross all at the same time.

Hooking up the shower bladder in a tree, everyone including me, is happy about getting it going. Hanging the curtain was the hard part, getting it just right. We *all* ended up taking a shower using the rainwater from the buckets. It felt good even though my last shower was only two days ago. And by this time the large rain barrels in the back yard had filled up again, so I refilled all the five-gallon buckets and replaced them back on the porch.

Upon reflection, I found myself thankful for people who had the sense to prepare for unexpected challenges. It occurred to me that having stuff like they have; rain barrels, buckets, Coleman stoves, portable showers, etc. is like insurance. It can cost a lot of money, and you hope you never have to use any of it. But you're glad you have it when you do. My education was just beginning.

Later that evening as Matt starts a pot of coffee, Jen surprises us all by bringing out a large flat box—it's Monopoly! I haven't played that game in years. Probably the last time was with my parents and Arizona relatives. Warm memories come flooding back.

"I'm the shoe," I toss out early. Everyone picks out their favorite too.

"Who wants to be the banker?" Matt asks.

"I'll do it," Jen replies.

"I'm in, but we play by the written rules. Not all this crazy made up stuff, and no wheeling and dealing!" Sarah announces.

"Wait, wait, wait," I retort. "Not even putting all the fines in the middle and getting to collect it all when you land on Free Parking?"

We debate for the next couple of minutes about what the "rules" will be as Jen counts out everyone's starting cash. And I'd like to know why you get six twenties and not five? Just one of those little mysteries of life I guess. After a few compromises we begin with Sarah going first. Three hours later Jen stands victorious (you can tell she hates to lose) with hotels on the orange and red corner. It didn't seem to help much that I had all the railroads, Boardwalk and Park place. But it was fun. I'd forgotten just how *much* fun it could be. And with real people sitting at a table playing a simple board game. Not some online game with people I've never met. It felt kinda' like a family. Breaking up after the game we go to our own spaces within the house, for a little quiet time before bed.

It's been dark outside for a while now and interestingly enough; I find that I'm not checking my phone every minute. I kind of like not being so dependent on it, I just know it's late and time to get some sleep. It's about getting up with the sun now and taking advantage of the daylight more than anything else. Grabbing my belongings, I make a little camp in one corner of the living room, laying my blankets on the couch. Sarah comes out of her room for a bottled water and sits down in the chair facing me. A soothing candle on the coffee table has replaced the electric lantern we used earlier during the game. It's only one, but it fills the whole room with a soft yellow glow.

"What's up?" I ask Sarah.

"I just need to think for a while, and I didn't want to be alone. Do you mind if I sit out here a while Paul?"

"Not at all, I'm a night owl anyway, or at least I was."

Looking around Sarah asks, "Where are the dogs?"

"They went to bed with Matt and Jen."

Listening carefully towards the front door, "Sounds like the wind has finally stopped," she says.

"I'm so glad too," I reply. "I used to love the wind, especially coming off the gulf. Now, after this storm, I'm not so sure."

"Don't let it bother you too much. It is what it is." She replies. "Things like Hurricanes are a part of life. You never expect it to happen to you, but it does. You just have to have faith it will all work out."

Afraid of being drawn into another religious discussion I change the subject. "So, tell me about your parents, you said you were adopted?"

"My parents are Mitchell and Samantha Connors, although they go by Mitch and Sam. My dad is a retired American Airlines pilot, my mom still teaches Junior High. They live in Irving just west of Dallas, but these days it all feels like one big city to me. We used to come to Port Aransas on summer vacations, which is why I know so much about this area. We always saw it as the perfect 'undiscovered' seashore; not overly crowded like Florida or the California coastline. And I love the fact you can drive golf carts on the streets in Port A and park them on the sand while you spend time enjoying the waves. It's where I first fell in love with the ocean, and all that's in it. To me the beach and the Gulf of Mexico are so much more than just having a place to party."

"Like you, I love the coast," I reply smiling. "It's why I moved down here two years ago. There's just something about the ocean that make me feel free. Even though the waves aren't that big, I still enjoy surfing."

"I like kayaking, especially through the Lighthouse Trails this side of the ferry," Sarah adds. "I was thinking about going over to Port A tomorrow, would you like to go with me?"

How could I turn down those beautiful brown eyes? "I'd love too," I reply.

Chapter 14

Sunday August 27th

Waking up the next morning, I hear the sound of a radio in the kitchen. Jen has a pot of coffee going and it smells great, the aroma from the blend I bought from CBC a few days ago. Seems like a lot longer than that. Wait, I just said radio. The radio's working? What about my cell phone? Eagerly I sit up and root through my stuff. Finding my iPhone, I turn it on. Yes! Yes! I actually have a signal! It's only one bar, but I'll take it. Alerts start to pop up because of all the missed calls, emails and text messages. Getting up, I walk down the hall and into the kitchen.

"Good morning Paul, how'd you sleep?" Jen asks from the kitchen table.

"Not bad, not bad at all."

Looking over several texts, I find one from Alex. He wants to know if I'd like to help with a mobile kitchen being brought down Monday, that will be set up in the store's parking lot. "Yes", I reply, "just let me know when you need me."

It makes me happy to know I still have a job! He must be up early too because a minute later I receive his reply: "Be at the store Tuesday, eight am." I fire back a 'thumbs up' emoticon.

Walking over as she offers me a mug of coffee, Jen asks, "I'm going to go out on a limb here, but would you care to go with us to church this morning after breakfast?"

Thinking for a second, I realize Sarah will probably go, making my answer easy. "Sure. Given all the hospitality you and Matt have shown me, how can I refuse?" Besides, I've been to church lots of times with my parents, I can handle this.

"That was quick!" Jen replies, "Couldn't have anything to do with Sarah going, now could it?" A sly grin crosses her face.

Wow, she's sharp! There won't be getting much past her. I just smile as I take my first sip of Columbia's best.

Matt walks in with the labs, "Where's Eli? He's not in his room."

Jen responds "He's outside, looking at Pauls' jeep. Figuring out the best way to get that limb off of it."

The labs come over and start licking my arm where I sit. Looking in Matt's direction I begin to scratch one of them behind the ears, "So what are their names?"

"The golden lab's a girl, she's Molly. The chocolate is Max, a boy."

"Hi Molly, hi Max," I scratch them both behind their ears.

"What's on the news?" I ask Jen as Sarah appears in the hallway entrance.

"Good morning everybody," she says.

"You're just in time for coffee Sarah, come on over and sit down. To answer your question Paul, what's left of Harvey is past Victoria now heading slowly towards Houston. Winds are still around 40 mph, and its leaving serious flooding behind everywhere it goes. The mayor of Houston is not going to ask for mandatory evacuations; he seems to think the city's just too big for that to be practical. Locally, most of Corpus Christi has power now, but here, Ingleside and Rockport will be out for seven to fourteen more days depending on how rural you are. There's a mandatory curfew after dark, and signs have popped up in front of some homes saying: 'looters will be shot.'" Looking at everybody she adds, "By the way, it looks like cell phones may be working, Paul got a signal just now. "

Everyone searches for their cellphone, excitement in their eyes. We all take some time, responding to friends and family. I let my Aunt and Uncle know I'm well, which is good, because they were ready to pack a bag and come find me.

I find myself torn between the joy of reconnecting with 'the world' and feeling the anguish of knowing hundreds of thousands of people are only just now being pummeled by the remnants of Harvey. Their homes and lives being destroyed. You can watch it on TV, but it's totally different living it.

After breakfast we change clothes, then all pile into Jen's four door crew cab truck (it's huge). Even Eli comes with us. Driving to church we witness the devastation firsthand; from shingles missing on most homes to entire roofs being gone. Cars crushed beneath trees (mine doesn't look so bad at this point) and fences in pieces, some completely missing. No businesses open whatsoever. It's a depressing sight.

Pulling in, the church parking lot has a few cars in it. Walking in the double doors a barrel-chested man with salt and pepper hair greats us. Matt offers an introduction, "Pastor Weaver, this is Paul Stevenson,

Paul, Pastor Weaver."

"Nice to meet you," I offer as I shake his hand. "Glad you could come," he replies with a warm smile. Next, he gives Jen and Matt a hug, shaking Sarah's hand afterwards. "Eli, I haven't seen you in a quite a while! Welcome, welcome! "He shakes his hand too, Eli simply responding, "Preacher."

We find a seat in the brightly sunlit sanctuary. Long padded burgundy pews fill the room, an elevated carpeted platform before us. Large potted plants hide the speakers at the corners of the stage, musical instruments stand next to them. A back-lit wooden cross hangs from the center of the back wall, a clear plexiglass podium stands front and center. *Looks a lot like my parents' old church.* Glancing around I see maybe thirty people in a room designed to hold a hundred and fifty. Pastor Weaver walks up to the pulpit and addresses us.

"Thank you for coming everyone," he announces, glancing my way. We even have a visitor today." Turning to his notes, "This morning, we will not have a regular service, instead I feel the Lord is leading me to guide this body towards how we might be able to help our community in the aftermath of the hurricane." Bowing his head, he says, "Matt, would you lead us in a word of prayer?"

Without hesitation Matt gives thanks for our good health, and the chance to help others through their trials. He asks for guidance, strength and the forgiveness of our sins. It's at this point I realize he's well respected in this congregation, a man of stature. I feel even more lucky to have been taken in under his wing. Some would even say blessed.

Pastor Weaver then outlines a plan; a beginning for the days ahead. We'll divide into groups, each according to what best suits our individual talents. As most of the flock is still away, he assigns temporary leaders and we talk openly about the needs people have now, or will, once they get back. Things like meals, help with homes wrecked by flooding, ways to get people to jobs if their cars no longer run. Looking around, I can almost sense my mom and dad here, a warm feeling comes over me. Thirty minutes later Pastor Weaver closes in prayer, asking us to come together again Wednesday afternoon at five while the sun is still up, assuming the power isn't back on by then.

I must admit, it wasn't so bad being in church today, but then there was no sermon either. It felt good to be surrounded by people who despite their own circumstances, were eager to get out and help their fellow human being. We hang around afterwards while Matt, Jen and Sarah chat with several people. Finding Eli, he and I head outside. Checking my phone's weather app, the temperature will hit 82 degrees today, still cloudy and breezy, but not too bad.

Walking towards the truck Eli points to a pond a hundred feet away, just past the pavements edge, "Look," he says.

Once again, I spot a pair of eyes at the surface watching our every move. "They're everywhere!" I comment.

"Yep," Eli responds. "All the flooding has brought them out of the streams and drainage ditches. The turtles around here are going to be mighty unhappy."

I almost forgot about that. Turtle equals lunch for an alligator.

"Too bad we can't drop by Dairy Queen for some ice-cream," Matt says, as he, Jen and Sarah approach the truck.

"Ohhhh- don't say that," Jen rebukes, "That sounds really good right now!" bringing a smile to Matt's face.

"Let's drive through town; see what's going on," Matt says as we load up and head east on FM 1069. Despite the improving weather, I feel gloomy seeing all the destruction. There are a few people out, removing waterlogged furniture from homes, cutting up fallen trees with chain saws--you get the idea. But for the most part it's still a ghost town, businesses boarded up, stop lights out. Everyone comments sadly as we pass their favorite stores and restaurants. Trees are down everywhere, yet I notice there are still flocks of birds in the sky as I try to be optimistic in our journey from Ingleside into Aransas Pass.

"I'm glad you gassed up before arriving home yesterday Jen, I don't think there's going to be any open stations close by for a while. Of course, we could always drive into Corpus Christi, for that and groceries, but it's nice we don't have to just yet."

Matt makes a right at the corner where my Grocery store is, and my heart smiles as I spot gulls once again in the parking lot— 'One legged Willie' amongst them. I imagine they're eating minnows in the standing water. The place is still closed, boards over the glass doors, nobody in sight. Heading down the road that leads to the Port A ferries we don't get even a quarter of a mile before we're stopped by a roadblock.

The familiar black and white sedan driven by Texas State DPS officers sits in our way. Easing up to a trooper Matt rolls his window down.

"Good morning, is it possible for us to get to Port Aransas, officer?" Matt says respectfully.

"Only if you are a current resident of Port Aransas with proper identification," the trooper responds. "And, you couldn't go this way anyway, the ferries are not operational right now."

"Any idea when things might change?" Matt asks.

"Nope. You need to turn around and head back the way you came." His tone indicating he's heard this way too many times already.

"Thanks," Matt replies, then makes a U-turn and drives back towards my store. This time I'm staring out the window at the twisted wreckage of the water tower opposite of where I work, amazed and overcome by how much power it had to take to bring down the steel structure.

Staring into my stores parking lot Sarah remarks, "Look over there, a laughing gull with one leg. How cute!" A woman after my own heart.

Chapter 15

Back at the house Sarah and I discuss a change in destinations.   Finding Matt, she tells him, "Since we can't go to Port Aransas, Paul and I are planning to go to Corpus Christi and pick up a few things. I know we need more bottled water, so if you'll make me a list, we'll pick it up."

"And I'll pay for it," I add.

"Sounds fair to me," Matt agrees. He jots down a list on a piece of paper and hands it to us.

"When you get back, we'll get that log off your jeep kid." Eli tells me.

"I can't wait," I reply. Actually, if Sarah weren't so cute, I'd let her go to Corpus by herself, and I'd be working on the jeep already.

"See you in a couple of hours," Sarah announces. We walk outside to the Subaru and climb in.

"So why a Subaru?" I ask as we head for the front gate.

"They're just good cars, besides it's a four-wheel drive, great for either the beach or the snow. I can't tell you how many people I've helped who were stuck in sand."

Laughing, I reply, "Yeah, I'd be rich if I charged every person I winched out of the sand with my jeep. There's a lot of people who have no clue how to drive on the beach."

Pulling up to the gate, I hop out and open it up for Sarah, she pulls through and I reverse the process.

Turning right onto 1069 we've only gone a mile when Sarah spots something in the road and stops right beside it on the shoulder.

"What are you doing?" I ask, climbing out on my side.

Glancing both ways to be sure there's no traffic, she walks over to what turns out to be a dinner-plate size turtle, picks it up and carries it over to the other side where it was heading.

"Turtle Patrol," She calls out. "Whenever I can, I try to help turtles, so they don't get run over. My friends and I came up with the name: "Turtle Patrol."

She really does love animals. I'm impressed.

Jumping back in the car, it's not long before we're driving down highway 181, passing through Portland. Sure enough, going over the bridge crossing Nueces Bay, a brown pelican is in flight paralleling us, catching the wind-shear rising from the elevated roadway. He flies along hardly flapping a wing, gliding it seems at 50 mph.

"Beautiful, aren't they?" I ruminate.

"Glancing over, Sarah notices the pelican and responds, "You're the first guy I ever met that thought so. Are you interested in birds?"

"My ex-girlfriend is a birder. I never noticed them until recently, but I have to admit, some of them are pretty cool."

Eyeing a sports car on the road in front of us, Sarah asks, "Do you like fast cars?"

"Yeah, why?"

"Then you'll appreciate this, the highest measured speed of a Peregrine Falcon is over 220 mph."

"Seriously!? That's incredible."

"The fastest thing on the planet," Sarah

responds. "And the fastest fish is the Sail Fish; they've been clocked at 70 mph, which is amazing for underwater. We have those here in the Gulf of Mexico by the way."

"Yeah, that *is* amazing," I respond, "I guess most people don't care about stuff like that Sarah, but I enjoy learning about nature, and especially the ocean. For example—everyone is afraid of sharks, but I know that they usually want to avoid you, just like you want to avoid them. That's why it doesn't bother me when I go surfing, or diving for that matter."

"You dive?" Sarah says smiling.

"I've been a few times, out to the abandoned rigs they turned into artificial reefs. It's really fun, and peaceful. There's not much I enjoy more besides maybe video games."

"You're talking about the rigs 40 miles off the coast here, right?"

"Those are the ones," I reply.

The day couldn't be much better. Talking with Sarah on the way into Corpus seems to make the rest of the world disappear, problems and all. I find myself feeling happy for the first time, in, well in six months.

Locating an open grocery store, we load up on canned vegetables, dry foods like pasta and rice, even some spam, foods that don't need refrigeration. In a separate cart we add several cases of canned drinks and bottled water. Gallons too. Candles, matches, batteries and mosquito repellent are on the list as well. I buy an ice chest with two bags of ice the limit), and we head to the register. The total is over a hundred dollars, but my card goes through anyway (I was worried because I was down to my last ninety-seven). My latest paycheck must have been deposited yesterday on time. 'Thank you, Lord!' I think to myself. Wait, did I just say that? Matt must be rubbing off on me.

Driving back to Aransas Pass I gather my courage. Looking at Sarah, "Can I ask you a strange question?"

Without hesitation she responds, "Shoot."

"You're a Christian. I'm not. As a matter of fact, I yelled at Matt the other day and said some cutting things in front of you."

"So, what's the question?" She asks.

"Why are you so nice to me? I mean, I thought that would make me part of the 'untouchable, don't talk to that guy,' group?"

Sarah pauses for a second, then responds, "I respect you."

"Come again?" not sure I was hearing her right.

"Paul, you can say you're mad at God, now, today, out-loud. It took me years to admit that to myself, much less tell other people that."

"I'm not sure I understand."

"You're one of the few truly honest people I've met in quite a while. And your past reminds me of mine. It makes me feel close to you—in a way. Your openness is refreshing."

"I never thought about it like that before," looking down.

Sarah continues, "When people find out you're adopted, they frequently feel sorry for you, or change the subject, because they don't know what to say. They're in unfamiliar territory. Not you. You recently lost your parents while I feel like I 'lost' mine when they gave me up. That used to make me feel angry and hurt. A lot. Sarah looks directly at me, "Paul, that day you walked into the coffee shop and yelled at Matt, I knew exactly how you felt."

Stunned, I sit silently for a while as we near home.

"So, you're not mad at God anymore?"

"No, He showed me how much he loves me through this group I'm in, and the church you saw today. The day I gave my life to him, He took that pain away. I can't tell you how, I just know He did."

Arriving back at Matt's house I'm excited to find the limb is off my jeep. Hopping out of Sarah's car I walk over to see the damage, minus branch. There are log sections stacked up neatly next to the fence, and a pile a brush nearby.

Sarah joins me, "They must have done it while we were gone."

"This helps a lot!" I reply. "There's still a lot of cleaning up to do, but the heavy work is done."

Together we unload the groceries and water and go inside.

I spot Matt and Eli walking into the kitchen, "Thanks guys for getting the limb off my jeep, but I wished you would have let me help. I feel guilty now."

"It's all good kid," Eli responds. "I'm sure you'll return the favor one day."

"I'll get this put away Paul," Sarah says, "Why don't you see how it's running? I know you're dying to get back out there."

"Thanks, Sarah!" I run to my gear in the living room and grab my keys. In two seconds I'm out the door and back to the jeep.

Walking around to the driver side, it doesn't appear as bad as it did before. The soft top is torn up where the branch went through, but besides the interior filled with leaves, dirt and two inches of water on the floorboard, it could be worse. Opening the door, I reach over into the glove box for a towel I use for polishing. Wiping the seat clean, and letting the water run out, I climb inside pushing the tattered shreds of the roof back. Inserting the key, I slowly turn it as I cross my fingers. Cranking it over, it quickly catches. Yes! It runs!

Sarah appears standing next to me, holding a broom, dustpan and trash bag. "Thought you might need these," She offers, a grin on her face. "It runs! That's great Paul!"

"You have no idea how happy this makes me! Yeah, it's in need of repair, but I can get to places on my own now. I go back to work in two days, and it would have been a long walk."

She leaves the cleaning supplies with me and heads back inside. I spend the next hour and a half removing what's left of the soft top, sweeping out debris and removing the muck. Now's the time I regret not buying full insurance. Having paid cash for this I only purchased liability. This little repair's gonna' be all on me. Pushing that thought aside, I'm happy anyway because I'm driving again. Yes, Yes, Yes!

Already grimy from cleaning, I decide to drive down to the apartment and see what else I can salvage. Poking my head inside the front door, I let the gang know my plans, then walk back to the jeep. Getting in I plug in my cell phone charger.

Driving towards the gate I look for the alligator

trapped inside the fence line, but he's nowhere to be seen. I let myself through the gate and head towards FM 1069. The water is no longer covering the roadway, but the drainage ditches alongside are overflowing. Turning left, heading into town there are people in front of their homes dragging furniture out along with pieces of sheetrock; anything ruined by flood waters that entered the house. Arriving at the Wheeler intersection, the streetlights are still out. No surprise there, but if there is one, it's how many police and state patrol cars are out and about. In minutes I arrive at the apartment complex, then walk upstairs to find my door ajar.

The place is trashed, and it's obvious it's not all from the storm. Looking around, I realize my belongings have been rummaged through as anger begins to rise in me. I guess the cops missed my thieves.

An hour later I've bagged up salvageable clothing and personal items. I'm sad and still very angry about the way I feel 'violated', yet thankful I'd removed the important things already. The worst part is that my surfboard is gone. As banged up and scared as it was, I loved it. By now the place smells bad; like mold and sea water mixed together. The furniture, bedding and carpet will all have to be hauled off.

Carrying bags back to my jeep there's an officer waiting for me. He checks my driver's license to confirm I *actually* live here (used to live here) and then checks to see what I've bagged up. Complaining about belongings that were stolen he suggests I fill out a police report with a detailed description in case it's recovered. I mumble some thanks, realizing they're doing the best they can, and climb back into the jeep.

Checking my dashboard, I've got half a tank of gas; I'll be ok for a while. The breeze blowing through my open windows is not bad, as the weather is still somewhat cool and cloudy, but that'll change quickly. The forecast in the next day or two is back to normal; hot and humid.

Arriving back at the house I throw a tarp over the jeep and use rubber tie downs to keep it in place. Carting my stuff inside, I discover our next-door neighbor Brian along with Jen, huddled over the kitchen table, talking quietly. Moving closer I see a reddish colored wiener dog laying on a towel. Max and Molly are on the other side, trying to see what's going on, noses along the table's edge sniffing back and forth.

"What's up?" I inquire.

Turning around Jen responds, "Oh, hi Paul. Brian found this little girl hobbling down the road and brought her to me. I work in an animal hospital, so I have some experience with this." Explaining as she works, "It looks like little 'Mindy' may have a broken front leg."

"Mindy?" I ask.

"She has a dog tag with her name and a San Antonio phone number on it. We've called but no one answers."

"What are you going to do?" I inquire.

"For now, I'll do my best to set it, but without an x-ray that's not wise. Since my clinics closed for the next few days I'm going to take a chance. Better to try that than allow it to heal the way it is."

Mindy has her eye's closed, being good for Jen. I think they call her color 'cinnamon'. She's different somehow, it's the long hair I realize. It makes her floppy ears look even longer.

"Most dachshunds are short hair, right?"

"Yes they are." Glancing back down she adds, "And she's really cute, I'm sure someone's looking for her."

Glancing around, I ask, "Where's Matt, Eli and Sarah?"

Brian responds, "Matt and Eli are two houses down inspecting the barn roof. It's laying in pieces in the Merrill's front yard."

"Sarah headed back to her apartment." Jen adds. "Hey Paul, if you don't mind, would you refill any of the empty buckets out front, and fill the portable shower outside too?"

"I'll get on it after I put my stuff away, I'm ready for a shower myself."

"How did it go at your apartment?" She says, without looking up.

"It was ransacked, but I got a few things out of it, mostly clothes."

Brian and Jen both look up, startled. "I am so sorry to hear that! What about your furniture?" Jen asks.

"It's soaked in smelly, moldy water. I don't think it's salvageable. Maybe the kitchen table and chairs can be saved, but the bed, a chest of drawers, anything else with a cloth type covering is gone. I was lucky to get what I could."

"Well, I'm glad you're safe here with us. With your apartment unlivable, I've talked to Matt, and you're welcome to stay with us until you can find something else."

Taking a moment to gather my thoughts, I look at Jen, "Thank you for all you've done for me, I don't know where I'd be right now otherwise. I'll pay you rent as soon as I start working again, I promise."

"We'll work something out Paul. By the way, dinner's at 5:30."

Later on, after dinner and dish washing, I spend the evening on my phone; catching up with old friends, checking Facebook and Snapchat posts, and discovering the storm's still powerful. The Houston area is now inundated with some of the worst flooding it's ever seen. Sadly, Aransas Pass is not even in the news anymore, we're 'old hat' as they say. In local news our Aransas Pass Mayor has placed us under a curfew from 7 pm to 7 am. Grateful for a dry place to lay down, I blow out my candle and go to sleep. Sarah fills my dreams.

Chapter 16

Monday, August 28th

Waking up to thunder, I curse to myself thinking this was all supposed to be behind us. A storm is pouring more rain down upon an already soaked landscape. Sadly, I used to love a good thunderstorm, but after the Hurricane, it's just not the same anymore. 'What's today?' I wonder. Checking the phone, I discover it's Monday. It's only been five days since I was drinking CBC coffee and driving to work; it now feels like weeks ago.

Getting up I stop at the bathroom where I no longer try to turn on the light switch every time I walk in, finally accepting the power's off. Looking in the mirror I notice a beard growing, and it doesn't look half bad! Grinning, I exit out into the hallway.

Eli spots me coming into the kitchen, "Mornin' kid. Coffee's ready if you want some."

"Don't mind if I do, thanks."

Pouring a cup, I ask, "Are Jen and Matt up yet?"

"Nope, they were up late tending to the pup," Pausing, "Jen told me about your apartment, sorry to hear it."

Sitting down at the table opposite of Eli, "I don't know whether to be madder at the Hurricane, or the thieves."

"It don't make much difference either way." Eli states flatly.

Absorbing his last comment, I conclude he's right. "By the way, thanks again for helping with the jeep. I appreciate what you and Matt did."

Ignoring my compliment, "So, kid, what's the plan for today?"

Walking into the kitchen, with little Mindy held close to his chest Matt answers for Eli, "He's working with me, today. We're going to be helping some people in need." Then glancing my way, "We could use your help too if you're still willing."

"I am." Rising from my chair, I offer it to him; "Sit down Matt, I'll get you some coffee."

"Thanks Paul, my ribs still don't feel so good, and this little thing kept me up half the night." Looking down at her he adds, "But she seems to be doing better now." Mindy looks up and licks Matt on the chin, a bandage and 'coat-hanger cast' wrapped in white cloth tape on her right front paw.

Looking out the kitchen window as I pour Matt's cup, "Can you believe it's raining again?" A nearby bolt of lightning fills the kitchen with a flash of light. The thunderclap that follows causes Mindy to bury her nose beneath Matt's arm. Pulling her up close he replies, "There won't be any work done until this stops though. I checked the weather and we should have some sun by this afternoon. I think I'll use this time to prepare for my next bible study."

"Well, I need to wash a few clothes, but unless I drive into Corpus and find a laundromat, I'm not sure how to go about it. Any ideas guys?"

"Two," Eli responds. "You can pour a bucket of water and some soap in the bathtub, scrub the clothes by hand with a brush or nylon scrub pad, then rinse and hang them over the shower rod. Or you can take that same bucket, pour in a little soap and water, add clothes then close it up and roll it back and forth to get them clean. Be sure you find a bucket with a Gamma Seal Lid; it has a screw on top. Then rinse and hang."

"Sounds like experience talking there Eli," Matt adds with a grin. "And with this rain coming down, there's no shortage of water for all this cleaning."

"Well, if it's going to be awhile for breakfast, I think I'll tackle this right now."

Forty-five minutes later, with a sore back and very clean hands I find Jen in the kitchen alone at the table. Eli's cooking at the stove.

"Smells good Eli, what's for breakfast?"

"It's gonna be fried spam, with potatoes, toast and jelly."

I think silently to myself, "Eli cooks?"

Sensing my thoughts, Jen says smiling, "Eli has experience from cooking in the Navy; some of the best I've ever tasted. Isn't that right Eli?"

Staring into the skillet he replies, "I'll take your word for it pretty lady."

Hearing the radio on in the background prompts me to ask, "So what's in the news this morning?"

Jen answers, "Well, it looks like the President is coming to Corpus Christi tomorrow to survey the damage from Hurricane Harvey, and may come out to Aransas Pass or Rockport, but they're not sure yet. Power and water will be off for a few more days, the hospital nearby is still closed, and telephone poles are down everywhere."

"That's bad, but it would be fun to see the president, if he makes it by."

Thinking for a moment, I ask, "How are we able to use our cell phones then?"

"The major carriers brought in portable towers with their own power source," Jen replies.

Matt walks into the kitchen just as Eli is serving breakfast.

"Perfect timing Matt, It's ready." Eli states.

Everyone sits down at the table after getting something to drink. "Let's pray," Jen says as she bows her head in thanks.

Chapter 17

Later that afternoon a county work truck shows up. Turns out Jen knows the people who can haul this now lonely alligator away (good riddance). The rain has stopped, but it's still windy, overcast and very humid. We all head out to the field following two men with long poles and ropes. Sloshing through a few inches of water, keeping a sharp eye out, it's Eli that spots him first.

Pointing north he says, "Right there near the fence, close to that palm tree."

Sure enough, sixty yards away a pair of eyes watch our movement, just above the surface of the water. I can also see spine knobs running down his back as we slowly move in.

"If he goes deep, we're going to have to come back another day. We're only going to try this if we can clearly see him," Greg states (one of the two county guys).

"Shouldn't be an issue," Matt replies. "I don't think it's deep enough anywhere on the property now where he can completely submerge."

Walking around to opposite sides of the big boy, using the long poles with a loop of rope at the end, they get a noose around both his nose and tail. Working their way in, the alligator thrashes about, trying to get free. Greg falls into the water losing his pole, but quickly recovers and grabs the stick just as the alligator tries to whip his head around towards him.

Slapping at my face I realize I'm surrounded by

mosquitos. There seems to be hundreds of them. "Paul, run back and find a can of mosquito repellent, please," Matt says, slapping at his own arms.

Without a word I slosh back to the house and locate it. Returning I see everyone swatting the air while trying to finish their work on the animal. As they take turns spraying themselves down, I take the pole from Greg near the gator's head, so he can spray himself as well.

Instead, he walks to the truck and grabs a brown blanket from the cab. Ignoring the mosquitos, he walks up behind the animal from Mark's side, and slowly works his way along the torso. Carefully sitting down on the gator, it begins to thrash again. Not waiting for him to stop he lays the blanket over the head, covering the eyes. This seems to calm him somewhat. Asking Eli for a roll of black duct tape he must have handed to him earlier, Eli hands it back, and then kneels close to help hold the jaws shut. (Like I said, nothing seems to scare this man.) Greg works the tape several times around his long snout, restraining his powerful jaws.

"Ok Mark, bring the truck around," Greg directs his coworker.

Mark pulls the truck up next to us, then lowers the tailgate and clears the eight-foot bed. He, Mark, Eli and I together lift the heavy reptile into the back end.

After closing the gate Mark comments, "Looks to be about six feet, maybe a hundred and fifty pounds."

"What'll be done with him?" I ask, brushing mud off my shirt and jeans.

"We've got a place about twenty miles away where we let these guys go. He'll be safe there."

I laugh softly to myself, it's not *his* safety I'm

worried about. Greg takes the can of spray from Jen and covers himself from head to toe.

"The mosquitos are going to be really bad for a while with all this standing water, it's gonna' suck." Eli proclaims.

No argument here.

"Thanks fellas for coming out on short notice," Jen says, "and helping get this guy out of here."

"It's the least we can do," Greg replies, "For all the times we've needed your help with a sick or injured animal, you were always there for us."

"Well, I can't take all the credit, I work for a wonderful group of veterinarians. Can we get you two anything to eat or drink back at the house?" Jen asks.

Glancing at Mark for confirmation, "No thanks, we'll take our 'guest' and drop him at his new home. There's a lot to do today as you might imagine. We're going to be busy for weeks."

"I'll get the front gate for you then," Matt declares as he heads in that direction.

"Thanks so much, we really appreciate your help." Jen adds once more.

"You're welcome," Greg and Mark reply together.

As we all slosh back to the house, Jen remarks, "Thank God no one was hurt."

Before I realize what I'm saying, I reply, "Amen."

"You did pretty good there kid, most people your age are afraid to get their hands dirty."

"Thanks Eli, I'll take that as a compliment."

Matt catches up to us as we near the house, "We'll gentlemen, we have two options. Get cleaned up and then head to a home nearby where an elderly couple needs a fallen tree cut up, or head straight over and get cleaned up afterwards."

I look at Eli, he looks back, "Let's just get it over with," Eli replies as I nod in agreement.

Jen addresses us as we split off towards the garage, "I'll feed the horses and get dinner ready. Try to be home by five."

"Yes ma'am," Matt answers for the three of us.

We load up two chain saws, some heavy rope and a come-a-long into the bed of Matt's truck. Fortunately, he has three sets of gloves, all different kinds. It doesn't matter to me though; any set of gloves is better than none.

It turns out the house we're visiting is on the next street over; a quick ride.

Getting out of the truck, a grey-haired woman and her husband (using a walker) greet us in the front yard. I recognize her; it's Mrs. Henry, my favorite customer from the grocery store.

Matt walks up to her, and introduces Eli, but when he gets to me, she says, "Yes, I know Paul," with a big smile on her face. "He's the kind young man at the store where I get all my groceries."

"Good to see you Mrs. Henry. How are you doing?"

"I'm fine Paul, just fine. This is my husband, Joshua."

I lean in and shake his hand, "Nice to meet you sir."

Joshua simply nods.

Looking at me she says, "I didn't know you go to our church? I don't remember seeing you there before. Are you part of Matt's group?"

Sensing my embarrassment at the thought of being a Christian, Matt quickly replies, "No ma'am, he and Eli are staying with Jen and me until they can get back on their feet from the storm."

Looking at Matt, "How nice of you to do that. There are times we all need to be the good Samaritan," responding with a gentle smile.

Ready to get busy, Matt asks where the tree is that needs to be removed. She leads us around to the back yard while Mr. Henry returns indoors. Fortunately, her place is on higher ground and the soil is only wet, not muddy. We find a huge oak, laying on its side, roots pulled up. The top of the tree on the back patio, blocking the sliding glass door leading outside.

"You're lucky the tree missed the house!" I comment.

"Yes," Mrs. Henry responds. "We are very fortunate this hurricane did so little damage, not everyone can say that."

As Matt surveys the situation, Eli and I head back for the truck, and grab the equipment. After Eli shows me how to properly lube and gas up the chain saws, we return and get a quick run-down of the plan.

Matt and Eli begin cutting limbs away as I drag them away from the trunk. For thirty minutes they cut the side branches off leaving some on top, and others beneath the fifty-foot behemoth. As we take a short break to refuel the equipment, Mrs. Henry brings out three bottled waters for us.

"Thanks so much," Matt says, "perfect timing."

While we sit on the cleared portion of the tree,

Matt outlines the next step.

"I don't have much experience doing this, but I think we need to cut the side and lower branches, so the tree will roll, and then we can take out the top branches. Your thoughts Eli?"

"I can't think of a better way, let's get 'er done."

Grabbing the chain-saw, Matt looks at us, saying, "We'll take it one limb at a time. As the branches are cut away, the tree will start to roll, so we need to be ready to jump, in case it comes over faster that we think." They work on some of the smaller branches clearing a path to the larger limbs. Then Matt asks Eli for some room to work on one of the biggest ones.

Eli stands clear, giving a wide berth. I walk to the opposite side of where he's cutting, thinking it will roll towards him. Sure enough, the limb he's working on cracks, and the tree rolls slightly right in Matt's direction. Then, without warning, loud cracks are heard from underneath, and the tree suddenly rolls left. I turn to run, but a heavy branch catches me, slamming me to the ground. I see feet running my direction through the leaves just as the clouds on the horizon turn to black.

Chapter 18

I find myself walking down one of the many paths between attractions at Six Flags over Texas; an amazing amusement park. I'm in the Boomtown section. It takes a moment to realize I'm alone; not a soul in sight. It's daytime and the weather is perfect; not the hot, humid remembrances of being there during past summers. I must be dreaming because Six Flags is always crowded, and it's never this cool out, unless you come during the fall. There's a tranquility I feel here like being with good friends, not a care in the world. And now that I look around, I see that all the colors are vibrant, the trees and shrubs; perfect shades of green, the sky a deep blue. There's no sun in the sky, yet there's light everywhere. It's like I've stepped into a perfect, brand new version of the park. I'm very happy at this moment.

Walking for several minutes, pleasant memories begin to assail me from my past. Sensing that I'm near my favorite ride; The Runaway Mine Train, I walk around a corner, finding it. There, in front of me are three people at the entrance to the roller coaster. Speechless, I stop to catch my breath. On the other side of some kind of golden railing (that was never there before). It's my mother and father with someone I've never met, and my parents look different; younger I think. They're smiling as if they've been expecting me and begin waving as I walk closer. My eyes are drawn to the young woman standing with them; an odd feeling comes over me. She looks a lot like my mom. Same brown hair, same eyes. A little taller maybe, like

Dad. Stunned, I think that's what Hannah would probably look like if she were alive today. No . . . no way. This is crazy. As if reading my mind, she stops waving, and then nods her head as if to say "yes, I am she." How could this be possible? Wiping away the tears rolling down my cheeks, I begin to walk quicker, trying to figure out how to get around this railing, to talk to them. Then, as I near the fence line, the vision dims, and I find myself waking up.

"He seems to be coming to," I hear a strange voice say.

Finding myself on an orange couch I open my eyes to the blurry image of a Hispanic man with a handlebar mustache, looking down at me. "Hello, Paul. If you can hear me, please tell me how you're feeling?"

Taking a second, I look around, hoping to see my family, but they're gone. Matt, Eli and Mrs. Henry are here in the living room with me.

"It hurts, my right shoulder hurts. And my head."

"I'm Doctor Bautista. You don't seem to have any serious external injuries that I can see, but with your permission, I'd like to continue my examination."

"Sure, whatever," groggily I reply, my eyes closed.

My emotions are churning from the dream. Why did I see my parents? And was that really Hannah? And why Six Flags? Was it all nothing more than a deep desire played out in a dream?

"I'm going to lift your right arm, Paul."

"Ok," I respond. He gently lifts it off the couch and then bends it inward towards my body. Sensing I'm not feeling pain, he reverses the movement, lifts it back out towards him, away from the couch, then lifts it up towards my head. Pain causes me to howl, and he gently sets it back down by my side. He touches my right shoulder, pressing in different spots until the pain reveals itself in my face.

He stops, then looks towards everyone and states; "Without an x-ray I'd say his right shoulder was separated, but it's back in now. The bruise on his forehead is from a blow but doesn't appear to be serious." Looking down at me, he continues. "Paul, it's tender now, but to be honest, the real pain will come tomorrow. I'd like you to take some ibuprofen to keep the inflammation down, it'll help with the pain as well. But the important thing is to wear a sling when you're up and moving around, until it's healed up enough for the shoulder to support the arm properly. This is important, because if you don't, it will take a lot longer to get better." He hands me a couple of pills he shakes from a bottle, and some water. I gratefully swallow them down. Laying my head back down, I feel sleepy again and the room grows dark.

<<<<<<<   >>>>>>>

I must have dozed off, because I wake up to the smell of cooking in the kitchen, the familiar hum of the exhaust fan in the window. I'm back at Matt's house but I'm not sure how I got here. As I try to move there's two things stopping me. First, my right arm which is now in a sling, and it hurts. The other is finding Mindy asleep, wedged between me and the couch, head on top of her little cast.

Sarah spots me moving around and walks over.

"Need help getting up?" She says.

"Please," I respond. "How did Mindy end up with me?" I inquire.

Helping me to a sitting position, she replies, "I watched her hobble over to the couch a little while ago. She managed to crawl up the throw pillows piled up on the floor down by your feet, and she made herself at home next to you."

Sitting up, Mindy realizes I've moved, then crawls up next to my leg and lays down again. She's back asleep in seconds.

Grinning, Sarah adds, "I think she's taken to you."

Looking at my arm, "I guess it's because we've both been 'winged.' My right arm, her right front paw." I realize just how cute she really is, a warm little bundle pressed up against me.

Looking at my clothes I realize I'm not covered in mud anymore. "How'd I get cleaned up?" I ask Jen.

"Matt and Eli helped you change when you got here, you helped a little, but they did most of the work."

"Well, that's embarrassing," I reply. I don't remember any of it, but I'm glad for it all the same.

Looking at Sarah, "Can I talk to the doctor?"

"I've got his number if you want to talk to him. By the way, he's Mrs. Henry's neighbor, it's a miracle he was there. He had only been around for an hour to check on his house when she walked over and asked him to come look at you. Up until now he's been in San Antonio because of the hurricane. She said his bill is on her since you were working on her behalf."

Moving my arm around (supported by the sling)

didn't feel too bad. I consider taking it off, but then remember the doctors' admonition.

Looking towards the kitchen I realize Jen and Matt have been following the conversation. Jens cooking, and Matt's got his bible open and working on a study.

"How are you feeling Paul?" Jen asks.

"Much better, thanks."

Matt looks up at me, happy to see me moving around. I direct a question towards him, "What happened? I thought for sure the tree would roll the other way?"

Closing the cover, he answers, "Me too. I'm sorry about that. I've cut up a few trees and that's the first one that ever did that. All I can think of is that when I cut the one big branch on my side, it removed enough support to allow the smaller ones on your side to crack in half and cause the whole thing to roll back towards you. The doc thinks you dislocated your shoulder when you put your hands out to break you fall. It only took a minute for me and Eli to get you out from under it, but by that time you were knocked out. How's your head?"

Touching a lump on my forehead, "Feels like the time I had a surfboard smack me good, coming off a big wave. Fortunately, I didn't pass out that time, but friends had to help me to shore."

Subconsciously I've been petting Mindy. She's soft and cuddly. Looking down at her, "I know how you feel little girl," I think to myself.

"How am I going to be able to work tomorrow?" The question directed at no one. "I can't afford to miss any hours right now."

"I'm sure they'll have something you can help with. With the situation we have right now, I think they'll even take a one-armed-surfer like you." Matt replies as everyone laughs.

"I hope you're right," I reply.

Jen jumps in, "We're just glad it wasn't worse, the doctor said you should be fine. And don't get mad, but we've been praying for you."

"Thanks Jen. I guess it couldn't hurt."

Adjusting my arm in the sling I look back at Sarah sitting in the chair in front of me, "So, what brings you here? I mean I'm happy to see you, don't get me wrong, but I thought you were in Corpus?"

"Jen called me when she heard you'd been injured. I was working at the church just a couple of miles away, so I thought I'd come by and see how you were feeling," a blush crossing her face.

"Does this mean you care about me?" I ask, doing a little 'fishing' as it were.

"Yes, I do." Thinking for a second she adds, "You're different Paul. You talk to me like a real person, not like someone's next conquest." Hesitating, "It makes me feel valued-- good about myself."

"I like you too Sarah. You're more mature than most of the girls I know, someone who knows what she wants in life." Taking a chance, I say, "Besides, I think you're very pretty."

She closes her eyes. Then says, "Prove it."

"I don't understand." I reply.

"What color are my eyes." She says, with her eyes clearly shut.

Without hesitation I respond, "They're brown, like a Hershey's kiss; your auburn hair really brings them out. I think they're beautiful." This is the first time I haven't tripped over my words with a girl. This self-confidence is something new, it feels good.

Sarah's eyes slowly open, surprised, hesitant to respond. "You're the first guy I've ever met that could tell me what color they are. Saying I'm pretty is usually just a pickup line." Her smile speaks volumes.

"Supper's ready you two," Jen announces.

I pick up little Mindy and lay her on a doggie bed next to the couch. Max and Molly come over and lay on the floor next to her, as if she needed to be guarded, their heads next to hers. Talk about your 'calendar picture,' it would be perfect.

Sitting at the table, Jen serves up spaghetti with meat sauce. Canned corn and a small bowl of fruit cocktail rounds out the meal.

"A strange combination I know, I hope you all like it." Jen throws out there.

"It looks great to me!" I reply.

"Me too," Matt adds. "Sarah, would you give thanks please?"

We all bow our heads as Sarah says grace over the food. The last sentence is unexpected, but nice to hear. "And Father, thank you for bringing Paul into our lives, please help him heal quickly."

A round of amens is followed by the sound of forks digging in. I can't help but think, that besides all that's happened to me over the last few years, I really like these people. Maybe Christians aren't so bad after all.

Chapter 19

Tuesday, August 29th, 2017

My phone alarm is going off, it's 6:30am, and I have to be at work in an hour and a half. Rolling over on my right arm, I stifle a scream. The pain from that shoulder is like a knife going down to the bone. No sh--, the pain would be worse the next day, I think. Rolling back the other way, I grab that shoulder with my left hand to stabilize it and attempt to sit up. Swinging my legs off the edge of the bed I almost step on Mindy, who is lying next to me on the floor, eyes looking up at mine.

Ignoring the shoulder pain, I reach down to scratch her head. "Good morning, girl. How'd you get in here?" Wondering out loud.

Glancing over I see my door ajar, unsure whether she did it on her own, or if she had some help from Jen. (I'm only now beginning to realize just how sneaky Jen can be.)

Mindy follows me out to the kitchen, walking a little better than yesterday. I check her water bowl and then find a treat for her from a drawer where I've seen Jen hide them.

Breaking the large treat into smaller pieces I place them in her food bowl, whispering to her, "Don't tell anyone Mindy, this will be our secret."

I hear the toilet flush in the hallway bathroom, and then Eli joins me in the kitchen.

"Hey Eli, could you refill the tank in there, I

couldn't get it this morning with my arm and all."

"Already done kid. I had a feeling you were gonna' be incapacitated for a while."

"Thanks," I reply.

Turning on the fan in the window, and grabbing the percolator Eli comments, "I'll get the coffee going, you just sit there." He lights the Coleman stove. "Are you really going to work today kid?"

"No choice," I respond. "If they're going to want my help while everything else is shut down, I'll count myself lucky to be employed. I'm not sure how they're going to make it work down there with no water or power, but I'm going in anyway."

"Good man," Is Eli's quick reply.

In my mind I take that as a compliment, especially coming from him. It's funny, Eli has gone from being some homeless guy I saw occasionally, to practically a hero in the last week. I've never met anyone tougher. Yet, polite in a way, almost gentle.

"Eli, can I ask you a question?"

He pours water into the coffee maker, adds the basket, then scoops the coffee in. "Shoot," he replies.

"You seem so tough sometimes, I know I'd never want to cross you, yet you're so nice all at the same time."

"It's a common misperception," he replies with that cowboy-like drawl.

"What do you mean?"

He turns around, looks me dead in the eye and says, *"Never mistake kindness for weakness Paul."* I feel like I'm looking into the eyes of a grey wolf.

Wait, did he just call me Paul?

"The willingness to be nice to others, even

nasty people, doesn't come from feebleness, it comes from inner strength." Turning back around he continues, "You show me respect, I'll do the same for you. Cross me or my friends in a way that looks like trouble, and I'll make you regret it."

Continuing, "The real men, and women in this world don't have to show off, you just know it when you look at them. Some Navy Seals I know are the nicest guys you'll ever meet, but I wouldn't want to piss em' off either," Eli says—just as Matt enters the kitchen.

"Good morning gentlemen, I smelled the coffee and couldn't help myself," Matt says with a grin. "How's the shoulder Paul?"

"Hurts like hell. Oh—sorry Matt."

Chuckling Matt replies, "I cuss too, just not very often. Thanks for trying to watch your language around the house, it's appreciated."

Eli fixes a simple breakfast, and Jen joins us right before we eat. Turning on the radio we find out that Texas Governor Greg Abbott has deployed the National Guard already, 12,000 in all. Schools in the immediate area are still closed and will be for some time. Some parents are opting to move their children to other school districts as a result. FEMA and other disaster response teams will be setting up soon in our area, some have already done so, and electric company repair trucks are beginning to show up. Not just from other Texas cities, but from all over the nation. Churches and community centers have opened their doors, to help feed and provide shelter to those in need.

It makes your heart swell with pride the way we can all pull together after something like this.

Refreshing we can forget which side of the political isle we fall on. We're just people helping people.

After breakfast, back in my bedroom, getting dressed is difficult but not impossible. Walking through the living room afterwards Jen hands me a bottled water as I head to work, Mindy tracking my movements from her little blanket on the floor as I go. Pulling the tarp off the jeep takes a few minutes, one handed, but I succeed and head out. I must admit, I miss working, and seeing my coworkers every day. I didn't realize just how much until now.

Driving down the road with the wind in my hair, I see once again how much destruction is out there. Piles of junk, sheetrock, and destroyed belongings have appeared in front of homes and businesses. Some heaps are four to five feet high. It's sad. Fortunately, the sun is shining for the first time in days and it feels good, although I can tell it's going to get hot, the forecast is for ninety plus. And the mosquitos are leaving me alone (but only because of the spray I put on before I left).

Getting close to work, in the parking lot of a 'Dollar type store', I see men and women in national guard uniforms handing out cases of bottled water and food packages to folks. The cars are lined up in the parking lot patiently waiting their turn. Pride in our military fills me, I've always appreciated those willing to serve our country. They, in my mind, are our unsung heroes; the average soldier. I imagine many of them (and their families) are suffering right along with us, and yet, here they are, helping others. As Matt, might say, "God bless em."

Pulling into the store's parking lot I notice a line

of port-a-potties along the back edge where I would usually park. There's a mobile kitchen set up and people already lined up for breakfast. I park and start to walk towards the store in search of Alex. The glass entrance doors are locked in the open position, and as I enter the smell hits me. There's going to be a lot of cleaning up to do; between the spoiled food and the seawater that managed to find its way in.

Laughing causes me to turn around, and I find Alex pointing at me, standing next to two other associates.

"What?" I ask in mock anger.

"I've just never seen you with a beard before," he replies, "and with your brown hair, I didn't think it would be red!"

"I know." Replying, "My grandfather was from Scotland."

Once the laughter dies down Alex gives me an idea of what the next few days will be like. The goal is to get the place cleaned up, with the resources at hand. We're limited by daylight, and by the availability of water, (it's not running). The generators are helping some, but are mainly used for fans and lighting the walk-in cooler and freezer while we work. The mayor has expressed his optimism that both will be back by Thursday or Friday, (two or three days from now). The scale of the job seems overwhelming. Yet, I find myself grateful for a job, and the fact he doesn't seem to mind that I'm crippled, so to speak. My day is spent being the "gopher." Assisting anywhere and everywhere; cleaning, using pallet jacks to move things, helping people load free bags of ice (limit two), I get through the day in reasonable fashion. I'm hot, very sweaty, and tired. But It feels good to be useful.

"Thanks, Paul for what you've done today. Same time tomorrow?" Alex asks.

"I'll be here," replying with a tired smile.

As I climb into the jeep, I notice that the gulls are back, looking for crumbs left by the people who took advantage of the mobile kitchen today. I spot "one legged Willie," and think to myself, "I know how you feel my friend, I know how you feel."

Heading towards home I take a different route, driving by the war memorial where an army helicopter was mounted on a tall pedestal. Sadly, it's now fifty feet away laying on the ground, kids climbing on it, a group of people standing nearby chatting. Across the street at the Civic Center, there must be a hundred vehicles present. I'm guessing it's now the staging ground for some of the recovery efforts. Driving further down Wheeler my heart sinks as I spot the remains of a roadside shop where seashells of all sizes were sold. It's been there forever--now it's a pile of rubble. The good part is, occasionally there'll be tables on the side of the road, with offerings of free food or drink. People helping people. I must thank Jennifer again for suggesting I stay with them.

Chapter 20

Arriving back at the house it's only five—still a couple of hours till sundown, but I'm tired and my arm's hurting too. I wish Sarah was still here, but I know she went home last night. She's growing on me, her Christianity and all.

Climbing out of the jeep I opt to leave the tarp off, no rain forecast for the next few days, at least I hope not. It's good to see most of the water covering the property is gone leaving damp beach-like soil behind. Everything is really green now; I just wish there weren't so many mosquitos. And it's smelly too, dead minnows cover the ground along with remnants of sea water, even a few small fish.

Walking inside I greet Jen, then ask, "Where's Matt?"

"He got a call from work and is down assessing the situation at the lumber store. Looks like I'll be back at work next week too, the clinic should be up and running by then."

"Great!" I respond, "And Eli?"

"Back in his room asleep." She replies, then adds in a more serious tone, "Paul, I need a favor from you."

"Anything," I reply.

"Eli's the kind who can't sit still for long. He's talking about going back to sleeping on the beach, living out of his tent, being homeless again. I know he doesn't like being cooped up in a house, but try to encourage him to stay, would you?" Her eyes pleading with me.

"You got it, Jen."

A moment later she adds, "By the way, we're having a bible study tonight, you're welcome to join us if you like. With the coffee shop closed, we're having it here at the house for a while." Then adding with a sly smile, "Sarah's coming."

Like I said before, you can't put anything over on her. "Why not," I reply, trying to hide my grin.

Grabbing some clean clothes, I head out to the portable shower hanging from a tree near the garage. Fortunately, the last person to use it has refilled the bladder up top. Closing the curtain around me I remove the sling and strip down. After a quick rinse I turn it off and soap down. Then, rinse again. There's only five gallons up there if you're lucky. I towel off and get dressed as best I can. Tonight, I'm wearing cargo shorts and a t-shirt, it's hot out and I dread what sleeping is going to be like this evening. This will be the first night it's been above seventy-five degrees. With no air conditioning and temps in the mid-eighties, plus seventy to eighty percent humidity, it's going to be ugly. Swatting at the mosquitos as I grab my dirty clothes, towel, and soap. Barefoot I run for the house.

It turns out Jen is preparing food for the study group as well as us—a nice thing to do. Not everyone has a pantry full of food to see them through, or the means to buy more in Corpus Christi. There's a lot of people who are unemployed because of the hurricane, some who may never go back to the same job again.

Stowing my gear and clothes in what was Sarah's room, I come back to the kitchen and ask Jen if she would like some help. Setting the table and putting out bottled waters only takes a minute. I hear whimpering and glance towards the living room.

There, looking my direction is Mindy. Walking over I pick her up with my good hand and carry her to the couch. Just as we're sitting down Matt enters the front door, Eli in tow.

"Hi, everyone," he says, glancing around, "How was work today Paul?"

"Not bad, considering. It felt good to be busy again, knowing I was helping others, not just bringing home a check."

"I know what you mean." Going straight into the kitchen and giving Jen a hug, he asks, "What's for supper beautiful?"

"We're keeping it simple tonight. I'm expecting four from the group and with us, that makes eight. Ham sandwiches and potato chips, with those fried pies you like so much for dessert."

"I can't wait," Matt replies.

They go clean up while I remain on the couch staring out the window. It's still a while until sunset but the trees in the way make it appear as if it's already twilight. Mindy crawls from my lap and into the sling, lays along the top of my arm with her head buried. "How can you breathe like that?" I say out loud.

"Oh, that's nothing." Jen answers, "Wait to you catch her sleeping under the bed covers. Then you'll really be amazed."

Looking back outside, I can't help being thankful the cloud cover is gone. For some reason I think of the dream I had. Wondering if they really were who I thought they were, and if so, why did I see them. After a moment I write it off as a desire that became a dream, and check my cell phone for messages, also to see what's going on in the world. Thankful I can charge it with my jeep. Too bad I can't use it to play any of my favorite video games.

Thirty minutes later three people show up, and Jen introduces them as Debbie and Steve Reyes, and Cindy Smith. Debbie looks at me funny, then says, "Aren't you that guy from the coffee shop the other day…"

And before she can complete the sentence I say "Yeah, yeah, that's me."

Jen laughing from the kitchen, adds, "It's a long story, I'll fill you all in later."

As they sit down in the living room Sarah appears in the door, bringing in an extra-large gift bag. It looks heavy.

"Hi Sarah, you look really nice tonight," Matt proclaims coming back into the front room.

"Electricity is back on at the apartment. I can't tell you how wonderful it is. Oops, I forgot you're still in the dark here."

"No worries," Matt replies. "We're getting by, it shouldn't be too much longer."

That sounds a little too optimistic to me. Then, looking at Sarah, I ask, "What's in the bag?"

"Just a few things for you all. You'll find out later." She sets the bag down next to her chair.

Dinner is served cafeteria style and we all end up in the living room. Conversation covers the latest from the flooding in Houston to the devastation in Port Aransas and Rockport. Fortunately, Corpus Christi came through well in comparison. Sarah is kind enough to help me with my plate, making me feel two years old again. Despite my complaining, I secretly enjoy her attention.

Jen takes Mindy to a large kennel, with her own dinner waiting inside, a little water bowl too.

"Those of you who have your bible handy, please get them out. We'll be starting in the book of Acts tonight." Matt begins from a kitchen chair placed at the entrance of the living room. Waiting for everyone to find the right page, he asks Steve to open with a word of prayer.

Afterwards, Matt announces, "The title of tonight's teaching is, 'Would you die for a lie.'"

As the next hour progresses I'm taken with how it's more of an open discussion; everyone able to speak their mind without fear of being shot down. It was refreshing. Going back to the four gospels Matt points out that all of Jesus' followers ran off and hid when he was arrested and then crucified. Matt tells us how over the coming months and years, starting with Steven, all the apostles suffer things like being stoned, imprisoned, shipwrecked, beaten. It's not the happy-go-lucky, 'let's go out and share the gospel' with a flowery happy ending (the kind I was expecting). In the end they all sacrificed their lives for their beliefs.

It was his closing that really caught my attention. "So, if Jesus never did rise from the dead, and was not seen by hundreds of people afterwards, then why would the apostles be willing to give up their lives, many in horrible ways?" An open question to us all. Sensing that no one wanted to answer —Matt follows up, "They wouldn't. Twelve people would never come out of hiding to face the possibility of a painful death to preach the 'Good News', unless they truly believed in what they were sharing. This to me, is one of the greatest reasons to believe what's in this book," Matt says as he holds up his bible. "The confidence that your sins would be forgiven, and that heaven awaits you."

Looking around, I decide to speak up. "Not to be a mood killer, but if they all knew hard times awaited them, well, then why did they continue? If I think the same is in store for me, that is, if I become a Christian, then why would I want to?"

"Excellent question. When you know the answer to that Paul, you'll know why we're all here tonight. The short answer is the peace that comes with having your sins forgiven. That nothing and no one can remove you from God's hand. The joy of knowing God's got your back, even when faced with difficult circumstances."

A reference to my parents dying I think. Matt has given me a lot to think about tonight.

After some more debate, we close in prayer. Once the young couple and Cindy have left, the rest of us move to the kitchen table. By this time the sun is down, and we light a couple of candles. Pouring some water over glasses of ice, I consider what a luxury it is now. Ice water as a treat. I know. Sounds crazy.

Lifting the gift bag up on the table, Sarah pulls several packages of D cell batteries out, separating them into three piles.

"What are these for?" I ask.

Reaching back in she removes three boxes, all the same; battery powered fans.

"One for you," handing one to Jen and Matt, "And one for you," she hands the other to me. "The last one is for Eli."

I never thought something so simple could make

me so happy.

"Thank you very much," Matt exclaims.

"Yes, thanks Sarah! The one we use in the kitchen as an exhaust fan is almost dead. This is a God-send," Jen adds.

"Sarah, I don't know what to say. I'll be able to sleep tonight now. I owe you one." I say sincerely. "I don't know when I'll be able to pay you back."

"You don't have to, but dinner one of these days would be nice." She smiles, and then a wink only I can see makes me grin.

She gets up and says her goodbyes—I hate to see her go.

Splitting up for bedtime, I realize I haven't seen Eli all evening. I guess he never came out of his room, not even to eat. I hope he's alright. Setting his fan and batteries outside his door, I proceed to my room, set up my own new fan, and crawl into bed. Checking my cell phone one last time, I return some text messages and down some ibuprofen. Making sure not to lay on my right side, I turn the fan on low, and nod off with a light breeze blowing across me—it's wonderful. Somewhere in the middle of the night, a little dog crawls in bed, and nuzzles up close. I need to have a little talk with Jen tomorrow.

Chapter 21

Wednesday, August 30th, 2017

This time, when the alarm goes off, I roll *away* from my bad shoulder, making sure not to roll over Mindy in the process. Turning the fan off, then putting my jeans on, I head to the kitchen with the pup in tow. She paws at the front door, and I let her out to do her business. Come to think of it, I have a little business of my own to take care of.

Afterward, I go back into the living room to find Mindy is back in. Jen, who's in the kitchen, must have let her back inside.

"Coffee?" Jen says, holding a cup out towards me.

"Thanks," I respond. "Is Eli ok?"

"What do you mean?"

"He didn't even come out to eat supper last night."

Lowering her voice slightly as we sit at the table, "Matt and I think there's some medical problem, but Eli won't admit to anything. He doesn't eat sometimes, and he's really thin. He seems to have stomach pain occasionally. That's one more reason we want to try to help him, get him to stay here. Maybe he'll open up."

Not sure how to respond, I change the subject. "I want to thank you again for suggesting I come to stay with you and Matt, riding out the hurricane and all."

Taking a sip of coffee, she replies, "You're welcome."

"Matt told me you have a 'sense' about people, that you all should take a chance on me. Is that true?"

"Are you sure you want to hear my response?" She says with a sense of caution.

Guardedly I reply, "Yes, I do."

"The Holy Spirit led me to invite you to stay with us."

Pausing, not sure how I should respond, Jen continues. "When you accept Jesus as your Lord and Savior, and ask him to forgive your sins, He sends the Holy Spirit to live inside you. If you stay grounded in Him, and seek His guidance, trusting He'll take care of you, the Holy Spirit will lead you in the direction you should go. It doesn't always make sense to you, but it always turns out to be the right thing to do. You may not know for weeks or months, maybe years, but God has your best interest at heart."

"You make it sound so appealing. So, does God *talk* to you?"

"Not in words. Think of your conscience telling you, you should or shouldn't do something. Two things guide me from there. One, it must line up with scripture, and two, a sense of peace comes with the decision."

"She's right Paul," Matt says as he walks into the kitchen. "That's how I got over the death of my mom. God led me to ask forgiveness for how much hatred I had for my father, and for how much anger I had towards Him for letting my mom die. He replaced those crushing feelings with a peace I had never known. That's why I didn't take it personally when you yelled at me at the coffee shop."

"That just seems so hard to accept," I reply.

"That's why the Word calls it, 'The peace that passes all understanding.' You can't explain it, you just have to experience it."

"Well, thanks you all. I've got to finish getting ready and head to work. Thanks again for letting me stay here."

"We're glad you're here Paul," Jen replies.

Climbing into the jeep I grab the mosquito spray and not only douse myself with it, I spray it all around me. The mosquitos seem to like shade and dark places to hide, my jeep being one of them. As I plug my cell phone in to the charger, I can't help but notice it's already eighty-five degrees, and it's not even 8am yet.

Driving to work, there's a young couple with a backpack and a baby in a stroller walking down FM 1069. Pulling over I ask, "Where you are headed?"

A young man with sandy brown hair replies, "We heard they're handing out MRE's and water on South Commercial street somewhere, we thought we'd check it out."

"I'm heading that direction, hop in." I reply.

"This is Lisa and my names Kyle," he says as he takes off his backpack and places it in the floor. Lisa disconnects the carrier from the stroller and straps it into the seat next to her. As Lisa climbs in the back seat with the baby, Kyle loads the rest into the back of the jeep, then joins me up front.

"I'm Paul," I respond.

"Thanks for picking us up." Pausing, "Do you know where the foods being given away in town?" Kyle asks.

"Yep," I reply, raising my voice a little to compensate for the wind in the open jeep. "The

National Guard was at a Dollar Store yesterday, I'm sure they'll be in the same place again."

We all chat on the way into town, and notice as we pass the coffee shop, there appears to be people inside working. "Yes!" I think to myself. I hope it won't be too long until they reopen.

Nearing the line of cars waiting for the National Guard help, I pull into the parking lot close by.

"That would have been a long walk guys, you sure took a chance on catching a ride from someone."

"Not really," Lisa explains, "We said a little prayer, and then you showed up. Thanks so much for the ride, God bless you, Paul."

"You're welcome. Take care," I respond, a bit surprised. I guess God can use anyone, not just Christians.

They shut the doors and head for the tables where everything is stacked. They seem happy, despite the lack of basics like electricity and running water. Maybe there is more to this faith thing than just pasting a silly smile on their faces. Their joy seems genuine.

Pulling up in the parking lot at work, there are more people here than yesterday. Both employees, and those looking for a meal and/or ice. Parking near the gulls I pull out a small bag of crushed crackers I prepared just for this moment. I think they recognize me because they all come flying over as soon as I'm out the door. Tossing the crumbs around, I make sure 'one legged Willie' gets some.

The sweat is already running down my back as I walk inside the building, and unfortunately, it's not much cooler in here. I see large fans running all over the place, long extension cords running to the door, there must be several generators out there. Finding Alex, he hands me a can of mosquito spray, which I politely refuse.

"Thanks, anyway, already took care of that on the way here."

"Good news Paul, it looks like we may be able to reopen tomorrow afternoon or Friday, most likely Friday. They're telling us the power should be on soon. So, we'll put you to work today, and then have you take tomorrow off. If you don't mind, we're hoping you can work Friday, Saturday and Sunday. I'm not sure how busy we'll be, but we need our best people this weekend just in case."

"Sure, I'm happy to do that." I beam with pride, being thought of as "one of the best."

Today turns out to be a repeat of yesterday, only there are lot more employees here helping. The store looks better, smells better too. With my arm in a sling, I help out where possible, feeling good just being able to contribute.

Having skipped breakfast this morning was not my best idea; I was more than ready for lunch at noontime. I was impressed to see the company had catered BBQ for the employees, with all the fixings from a restaurant in Corpus Christi. I had a reason to give thanks for my meal today. And silently I did. I don't know if He heard me, but I thanked Him all the same.

At five I clock out, grab a couple of bags of ice and go home. Once I get there, I noticed Matts' truck is gone. Walking inside with one of the bags I spot Eli in the kitchen.

"Where is everyone?" I ask.

"There was a meeting at the church, they'll be home in an hour or so."

Eli replies. "Here, give me that." He says, reaching for the ice. "Is there anymore?"

"Yeah, one more in the jeep."

Setting the bag on the kitchen counter he states, "I got it," as he heads for the door.

Walking down the hall to my room I grab some dry clothes and then outside for the shower. Getting cleaned up, then coming back in, I see Eli's got a large thirty-two-ounce tumbler of iced tea waiting for me.

"You have no idea how good that looks, thanks Eli." I drink it half-way down, careful not to spill a drop.

"You're welcome, kid. You want to help me fix dinner for the folks?"

"Sure. Just help me put my stuff away." And we precede to make a meal.

Fifteen minutes later Jen, Matt and Sarah walk through the door, and the labs come bounding out of the bedroom to see them. Little Mindy comes hobbling out too.

"It's not fancy, but the kid and I have dinner ready. Grilled cheese, pickle spears, potato chips, and once again there's fruit cocktail for dessert." Eli announces.

"Looks yummy," Jen says. "And I'm glad to see you moved the Coleman stove out on the porch. No more cooking inside as long as the weather cooperates. We were taking a chance with using the fan in the window to clear the fumes, anyway."

"My thinking exactly," replies Eli.

"What brings you by Sarah?" I ask, as Eli and I

set the table, Jen and Matt heading back to their bedroom.

"I was at the church meeting this afternoon, and there's a request for clean-up crews in Port Aransas. Several churches are combining forces and heading over there tomorrow. I realized I didn't have your phone number, so I thought I'd drop by and see if you'd like to join us."

"I don't know how much help I'd be," raising my arm and sling up in the air, "but I'm off and I've been wanting to see how things are looking over there, anyway. Count me in."

Matt and Jen return as we all sit down. After Jen says grace, we chat about the day; Eli tells us about some of his adventures in the Navy, and Matt let us know he's going back to work tomorrow. Jen will be going back to work as well— it seems everyone will be cleaning up, repairing, etc. after Hurricane Harvey. Matt asks us all to pray for those whose jobs are now gone, for the businesses that will not reopen, and for families left homeless by this devastation.

Eli and I are clearing the dishes from the table while Matt, Jen and Sarah chat. Sarah's phone rings and after checking to see who it is, she answers. Getting up from the table she walks slowly into the living room, speaking quietly. Watching her stare out the window, I can tell by her body language something bad has happened. She puts her phone down on the coffee table and begins to cry.

"What's wrong?" Jen asks.

At first Sarah doesn't respond, so I walk over to her, hoping somehow to help. She looks up at me, then presses her head against my chest, tears still flowing.

Unsure how to react, I wrap my arms around her, holding her close. After a moment she indicates she wants to sit down, so we head back to the kitchen table. Everyone else sits down as well, waiting to hear the bad news.

Matt hands her a napkin, and she blows her nose. Looking around at all the concerned faces she says, "I just found out from a friend at the Marine Science Institute in Port Aransas that the place was wrecked by hurricane Harvey. It won't be open again for months. The good news is, all the animals and birds were evacuated beforehand, and are fine."

"Yes, but we kind of expected that, didn't we?" Matt hesitantly replies.

"We did." She responds. "But the worst part is that it's been confirmed that Tony Amos has cancer and isn't expected to live much longer." The tears begin to roll once more. "He's my inspiration for becoming a Marine Biologist. Tony is my friend."

Chapter 22

Thursday, August 31ᵗʰ, 2017

Getting up a little early, I prepare to meet Sarah in Corpus Christi near her apartment, it's on the way to Port Aransas going 'the long way' (the ferry is the 'short way'). There's a Whataburger nearby, and we thought we'd have breakfast there before going into town.

After dressing, I walk into the kitchen. Sitting at the table, Eli looks up as I enter, and says, "Hey kid."

"Good morning Eli, how are you?" I ask in greeting.

"Never better," sounding sarcastic as I see his left hand grabbing onto his stomach. He picks up a mug with the other and takes a sip of coffee.

Seeing the coffeepot on the stove, I grab a cup myself and proceed to pour some in.

"How long will the coffee stay hot, if you brew it outside on the Coleman, and then bring it in here?" I ask.

"Long enough." He replies, gruffly.

Deciding he's not to be messed with this morning, I change tactics. "I'm going into Corpus today, is there anything I can get you?"

"Nah, Thanks kid."

After drinking a few sips, I walk back to the bedroom and load up a backpack with a spare change of clothes, a multipurpose knife, some bottled water I have squirreled away, and give little Mindy a scratch on the head. She's found her way under the covers on my bed and seems quite content.

"Have a good day Eli," I call out as I go out the door.

Climbing into the jeep, I begin to spray myself down with repellant, the mosquitos already active. The sun is hot; eighty-five degrees, and there's 80% humidity. With my gear stowed safely behind me, I begin to take off when I see Matt walking towards me.

Holding out some cash Matt says, "Can you do me a favor Paul? Pick up some more water; bottled and gallon, and if you find a cheap cell phone for Eli, get it for me."

"Sure thing," I reply, "See you all this evening."

"Thanks Paul."

Pulling up to the gate, I see the horses are roaming the acreage and feeding off the grass. It's a pleasant sight. Like things are back to normal if only in small ways.

Driving down FM 1069 I turn right onto the highway heading into Corpus. Passing through Portland, things don't look near as bad as Aransas Pass, and I'm hoping to spot some of my feathered friends on the bridge before me. Nearing the Harbor Bridge, I see Roseate Spoonbills on a tiny island to the right that's usually covered with all types of sea birds. The spoonbills' beautiful pink shade makes most people think they're flamingos, but they're not. It reminds me of something my old girlfriend once told me that Corpus Christi is considered one of the best places in America for bird watching. I can see why.

Crossing over the bridge I merge with I-35 and then hang a left onto SPID (South Padre Island Drive).

Passing the mall on the left I see lots of cars already. It's amazing how something this close to Aransas Pass seems to be doing fairly well, compared to the devastation just thirty minutes away. Several miles down the road I find my exit and pull into the restaurant parking lot. Sarah's already here, the Subaru parked near the front.

Walking in I spot her at a table, reading something on a tablet. Taking a moment just to look at her, I realize she's one of those women who looks naturally pretty — without makeup. And she's wearing a Columbia button down shirt in a bright pink color, the kind most people think of as a 'fishing' shirt. Mine's Columbia too, only it's a light blue. We're both wearing cargo shorts I notice; great minds think alike. A smile creases my face.

"May I buy you breakfast?" I ask, approaching her table.

Glancing up she replies, "Sure Paul, give me a second to decide what I want."

Considering her options, she tells me, and I head for the counter. Along with our meals I ask for two large cups for ice water. It's going to be a long, hot day.

Sitting down across from her I inquire, "Doing a little better today I hope?"

Closing her tablet cover she responds, "Yeah, I guess I am. Sorry about all the blubbering last night."

"No worries, Sarah. The way you speak about this Amos guy, he means a lot to you."

"Tony Amos is a local hero to many of us. If it wasn't for him, I wouldn't be working on my degree in Marine Biology. But you don't want to hear about all this."

"Sure I do, please tell me. I've heard of the ARK (Animal Rehabilitation Keep) before, and how he rescues sea turtles, but that's about it."

"Are you sure? I don't want to bore you."

"If there's something I know we share Sarah, it's a love for the ocean."

One of the things I enjoy about Whataburger, is that even though it's fast food, they bring your meal out to you when it's ready. Sure enough, it quickly arrives, and Sarah says grace, quietly so as not to disturb others near us.

"Well, it all started about three years ago when I was driving from Aransas Pass to the ferry landing (crossing over into Port A). This was back when I used to live in Ingleside," she explains between bites.

"Is that where you know Matt and Jen from? Because I know the church we went to the other day is close to Ingleside."

"Correct, yes, it is. Anyway, I spotted a dolphin that was stranded in the shallows in Redfish Bay, the tide was really low, and I knew the ARK would help with this kind of thing. I Googled their phone number and was surprised to get Tony Amos himself on the phone. I knew who he was from the local news, but didn't realize how hands on he was, how much he took a personal approach. Anyway, he sent a team out and they helped the dolphin back to deeper water. I called back the next day to see what happened, and Tony himself explained it to me. Turns out they don't always rescue them, many times they determine they'll be ok until the tide comes back in, and then the dolphin simply swims off. I asked him more about what they do down there (at the ARK) and he took the time to fill me in. That was the day I fell in love with helping sea life, and decided I wanted to be a part of it."

Thinking about what she'd said, I reply, "All I know is how they'll rescue Kemp's Ridley sea turtles in trouble, help them get well, and let them go again."

"Over the years," Sarah responds, "they've helped over five-thousand turtles, and fifteen-thousand birds."

"Birds too! I had no idea."

"I'm proud to say I volunteer there from time to time. It's not glamorous. I clean cages, do a lot of laundry, and even cut up fish (for feed) once in a while. But I can't tell you how much happiness comes from helping one of the rescues get back to health, and then seeing them released back into the wild." A look of joy comes over her face, and I can sense just how much it all means to her.

"That's why I started crying last night. If we lose Tony, it will be such a huge loss. He's one in a million."

Gathering up our trays, we head for the trash can, and then the door.

Walking outside, Sarah reaches into her bag and brings out some suntan lotion, SPF 100. Handing it to me she says, "You're going to need this today."

"No sh--, Ah, no kidding," I reply.

Smiling she adds, "Let's take my car, I've got air-conditioning."

I grab my gear from the jeep and load it into her backseat.

Driving several miles east on SPID we then turn left onto Hwy 361; the road that runs down the center of the narrow island.

"I was expecting to see a roadblock of some

kind," I comment.

"They removed those yesterday," Sarah replies. "But there's still a curfew in Port A from 8 pm to 6:30 am. They're threatening to arrest anyone out at night."

We pass electrical poles either leaning over or completely on the ground. This goes on for miles. Besides a few subdivisions with ten to fifteen houses in them, there's nothing out here between the turnoff, and the center of town twenty minutes away. Birds are in many of the ponds and drainage ditches we pass; herons, egrets, all kinds of shore birds. They seem to be doing just fine.

"Wow it's good to feel AC again, it's almost too cold. I think I've gotten used to the heat," I exclaim.

As we get closer to Port Aransas, Sarah says, "Before we connect with the church groups, I want to go by the Institute. The ARK is right next door."

Passing the golf course on the right, I know we're getting close to town. It's not big; Port Aransas has a normal population of just over thirty-five hundred. You can drive from one end of it to the other in about fifteen minutes. But it blossoms up to one hundred thousand for spring break, and other holidays like the Fourth of July. Besides that, it's a nice, somewhat undiscovered beach haven. I love it here. That's why my heart is breaking as we pass by businesses, destroyed by water and wind. Many have piles of debris stacked up along the roadway from people working to clean up a titanic mess, others are simply rubble.

Large windows have been blown out of stores that once sold towels and swimsuits. Glass is everywhere. Boats lay on their sides in a couple of parking lots, nowhere near where they were originally moored. "Unbelievable," is all I can think to say. Looking over at Sarah, I can tell it's bringing her down too.

Hwy 361 dead ends in town at Cotter Ave. where we turn right, then we go left onto Station Street, then right again on Channel View. The older homes are in shambles; from shingles missing to entire walls gone. Others, nothing left but the poles they stood on, with lumber, furniture and belongings strewn about. Many homes were built ten to fourteen feet in the air on wooden pillars, designed to survive the seven to ten-foot storm surge a hurricane would bring, but it didn't seem to help much. If the storm surge didn't get them, the hurricane force winds did.

As we near the UT Marine Science Institute, Sarah seems in shock. She drives slowly through the area, observing the large openings in the front of the Institute where windows used to be. The destruction that Harvey wreaked on the campus is overwhelming; I understand better now why it will be months before it can be rebuilt and open again.

"I don't even want to get out of the car." She states. "Let's go see what the beach looks like."

From this point, we're only a couple hundred yards from the water. Driving slowly through the dunes we end up near the jetty, and what we see takes our breath away. The jetty runs alongside the ship channel leading into the Gulf of Mexico. It's made up of large granite boulders brought in many years ago to establish it and quickly became a favorite for fisherman and bird watchers alike. Normally, you can drive up next to the stone wall and park, where you then climb up and walk its length, all several hundred yards of it. But before us today, where there *were* several acres of parking available, it's all been washed away, leaving only standing water. No, more like a lagoon. Too deep to attempt to try to get close to the jetty. It blows me away thinking about what other parts of the beach might look like now. Are any of the piers still standing I wonder?

Sarah parks where we sit, as we blankly take in the waves crashing before us on the beach—the gulls and terns sitting in the sand nearby as if nothing is wrong. If it wasn't for the devastation, you'd think it was just another beautiful sun filled day in paradise. There's no words of encouragement, nothing that will make this all better. We turn around and go back the way we came.

Setting out in search of our cleanup destination, Sarah has the address, and fortunately I happen to know most of the streets by heart (I've worked in Port A before). Five minutes later we locate the RV park we're searching for, and see row upon row of RV's torn apart, moved around, or simply laying on their sides. I've spotted several church buses here and there around town, and I see one just ahead with Sarah's church name on it. Parking nearby, we climb out of the car. Sarah finds the group leader, and after introductions, gives us our "marching orders." It's not long before we're cleaning up muck and debris. Despite the slimy mess we find ourselves in, everyone around us is positive and happy. I think it's because they're making a difference in the lives of those less fortunate; feeling needed, wanted. I find myself even more grateful for a home to go to tonight, not everyone here can say that.

Five hours later, tired and drenched in sweat, we call it a day. That may not sound like much time put in, but when it's ninety degrees, and seventy to eighty percent humidity, it feels like you've been working in a steam sauna. Fortunately, Sarah has a Styrofoam chest in her trunk with bottled water iced down. During the afternoon we drank all eight of the ones she had in there, plus the large ice waters from the restaurant. And I'm still thirsty.

Driving back down Hwy 361 towards Corpus Sarah asks, "Do you have a change of clothes in your pack?"

"I do, but there was really nowhere to change back there."

"Don't take this the wrong way Paul, but how clean are your backup clothes?"

"I've washed them at the house in the tub, so they're not too bad. Better than what I'm wearing now. Why?"

"Power and water are on at my apartment and I've got a washer and dryer there. I was thinking, if you wanted to, we could go by and get cleaned up while your clothes get some real washing."

How can I turn that down? A real shower? "That would feel like heaven right about now," I reply.

"We'll do that, then I'll get you back to your jeep at Whataburger."

"Thanks Sarah."

"No, thank *you* Paul for helping today. Not only were the people with the RV's appreciative, I know my church family was too." Pausing she adds, "So am I. And, I can't imagine what trying to work with a dislocated shoulder must have been like."

"It's getting better, I'm slowly getting used to working around this sling."

Hesitating for a moment she adds, "Normally I would never consider inviting a guy to my apartment, but I know you have no electricity, hence no running washing machine over at your house. And the fact that Matt and Jen trust you, well, that's enough for me."

"Thanks Sarah. It's greatly appreciated."

I realize I've just been put on notice in a way. If I want this relationship to go anywhere, I'd better behave. But you know what? She's worth it.

Chapter 23

We park in front of a beautiful new complex that's four stories tall. Grabbing the ice chest, my pack, and Sarah's gear we head for an elevator to take us up to the top floor. Walking down to her door, she punches in a code on the electronic lock, and we're inside. Cool, dry, refrigerated air washes over me. Looking around, I notice how spotless the place is, I'm almost afraid to sit down.

Seeing my reaction Sarah tells me, "Come, sit over here at the kitchen table. Would you like some water, or iced tea?"

Sitting down, setting my pack on the floor next to me, I respond, "Tea would be great, thanks."

Looking about I notice the rooms are painted in soft pastels of blue and coral. There's a large fish tank along one wall. Next to me are two watercolor paintings of sailfish and turtles in the ocean; the name of the painter is Guy Harvey.

"These are really nice pictures Sarah, but why do they have numbers in the bottom right hand corners?" (I don't know much about art.)

Glancing towards them as she carries two ice teas over, "Those are two of my favorites, they're limited edition prints, so they're numbered. My parents took the family to the Cayman Islands one year and Guy Harvey has a studio on the waterfront in Georgetown. I just love his work, plus, he donates part of his profits to foundations supporting sea life."

"You have a very nice apartment Sarah, it reminds me more of some of the condo's I've seen in

Port Aransas." Realizing that needs some explanation I add, "I used to help a guy with his window cleaning business a couple of years ago."

Blushing, Sarah replies, "I have to confess Paul, it *is* a condo. I tell people I live in an apartment because they treat you differently if they think you have money. Actually, it's my parents' condo. My dad decided to buy it while I was in school down here; he thought it would be a good investment. That it would pay for itself once I graduated and moved out. There's two bedrooms, and two baths; one's mine, the other is theirs. They come down occasionally because my dad loves to go out on the deep-sea fishing boats. My mom and I spend time on the beach and go shopping."

Hesitantly I ask, "Are your parents rich? Sorry, I guess that's none of my business."

"It's ok, no, they're not. Just well off enough to put me and my sister through college and have a few investments. Dad was a pilot for American Airlines for many years, he just retired recently. Mom is a teacher in Irving where they still live. It's close to the DFW airport so dad didn't have far to go for work."

"That's cool. My Dad worked as a manager for different restaurants in San Antonio. Mom had fibromyalgia and couldn't work much; it was just too painful, and the flairs were too sporadic for her to be able to hold down a job. Until recently, no one really believed that fibromyalgia was for real. They all treated mom like she was a hypochondriac or something."

Looking at the clock, Sarah says, "It's 3 o'clock. Why don't you get a shower in the hallway bathroom? I'll drop a robe off in front of the door, you set your dirty clothes outside, and I'll throw them all in the washer with what you've got in your pack."

"Are you sure? I feel weird letting you do that."

"No worries, I used to do all the laundry at our house as a teenager. Washing my dad's clothes was no big deal."

"Okie-Dokie." I reply awkwardly. "The robes not going to be pink is it?" Asking with a grin.

"Brown. It belongs to my dad, and I don't think he'll care if you borrow it just this once, but don't tempt me," she replies smiling.

Wearing her dad's robe, this is going to feel strange.

Carrying my stuff into the bathroom, iced tea too, I strip down and prepare for the first real shower in a week. Setting my dirty clothes outside the door, I find the brown robe as promised. Turning on the hot water, (hot water, imagine that!) I step in and squeeze some shampoo into my hand. You just don't realize how spoiled you are until something like this changes your life. Taking a good long time to scrub down, I enjoy every moment because I don't know how much longer it'll be until we get power back on at Matt's house. Or is it Jens' house? No matter. Putting on the robe I can hear a washing machine going somewhere. Walking out into the hall and into the living room I feel strange dressed in only a robe; being in Sarah's place and all.

Sitting back down at the kitchen table I'm drawn to the fish tank. The beauty of the colorful fish is matched only by the different types of sea plants growing from the bottom. There's coral too. A "treasure chest" occasionally opens its lid to release air bubbles, but it's probably just for show because I see a stream of micro-bubbles being released in a corner.

The sound of a doorbell snaps me back to reality. Looking around, I decide I really don't want to answer it, but Sarah's back in her room somewhere. Walking to the hallway I shout, "Someone's at the door Sarah," facing her bedroom.

"Can you get it Paul? I'm just finishing up with my hair."

"Um, sure, ok." It's probably a delivery of some kind, anyway. There won't be anyone there I reason.

Opening the door, I find an older couple staring at me, suitcases in hand, with their mouths hanging open.

The woman finds her voice first and shouts at me, "Who are you? And why are you in Sarah's condo!?"

Right on her heels the man says, in a very unfriendly voice, "And what are you doing in my robe?"

Sputtering I attempt to answer, "I, I, I'm Paul, a friend of Sarah's---"

Before I can finish I hear raucous laughter filling the hallway behind me. Turning around, I find Sarah, bent over, yucking it up.

Then, there's laughter back in front of me. Turning to face the people in the doorway, the woman says, "I'm Samantha Connors, and this is my husband Mitch," nodding back in his direction.

Realizing I'd been had, I reply, "You mean, you knew in advance I was going to be here?"

"Yeah, sorry Paul. Sarah thought it would be fun to make you squirm a bit," Mitch replies between chortles. "I guess you didn't know what a prankster she can be."

Looking at Sarah, who's now entering the room, I slowly reply, "I-had-no-idea."

"Paybacks," I say to Sarah as she comes close, "there'll be paybacks."

"Ooooh, I'm worried now," She replies grinning.

"Besides, I think the robe looks good on you," Mitch kids me to relieve the tension. Another round of laughs assails me.

Entering they take their bags back to their room, then we all reconnect in the kitchen, Sarah pours iced tea for her parents.

Samantha, or 'Sam' as she likes to be called, and Mitch turn out to be super nice. I discover that Sarah had spoken to them by phone while I was in the shower. She explained the dirty work we did today, and the fact I have nowhere else right now to get a decent shower. So, fortunately, they weren't upset.

The conversation turns to work, and it comes around to Sarah's dad; speaking to his career as a pilot, "My favorite route was from Dallas to Hong Kong. It was at least sixteen hours, one way, so I only had to fly three or four times a month."

"I've always wanted to learn how to fly, it looks like a lot of fun." I respond.

"Right you are Paul, I still enjoy getting in a Cessna and playing around a little."

Looking at the wall clock, Sam says, "It's almost five, shouldn't we be thinking about dinner?"

"Yes, I think so." Looking at Sarah and I, Mitch says, "Do you two have time for a meal? I mean, your clothes aren't even out of the dryer yet Paul."

Feeling like a third wheel here, I reply, "Thanks,

but it's up to you all. I feel like I've imposed enough already. I'm sure you'd like to spend time with Sarah as a family."

Looking at me with that take-charge attitude Texas women can have, Sarah says, "That would be great, Dad, we'd like that."

"Well, ok then," I think to myself. Staying for supper it is.

"Great," Mitch replies. "It gives me a chance to try out this app, anyway. There's a service in Irving where you have someone pick up food from just about any restaurant and then delivers it to you. I want to see if they do the same here in Corpus Christi."

"So how long will you all be here Dad?" Sarah asks.

"The plan is to stay through Monday. It is Labor Day weekend."

"You know, I didn't even think about that," Sarah responds. "Labor Day already! With the hurricane and all, it slipped my mind. I guess that's one more reason the university won't reopen until Tuesday. So how are you Mom?"

Looking at each other, Sarah's mom replies, "Good Sarah, as a matter of fact, I don't think we've told you yet—I've decided to retire. I just don't feel like dealing with another classroom full of kids anymore. Twenty-five years is enough," she says with a smile.

"Congratulations, Mom, that's great!!" Sarah responds. "I'm so happy for you. That means you all can come down anytime and we can do things together."

"I'm looking forward to that, I really am."

Working the app on his cell Mitch says, "That

reminds me Sarah, when are you going to come up to Dallas, so we can ride that new roller coaster at Six Flags?"

"Maybe over the Thanksgiving Holidays Dad, weather permitting."

My ears perk up, "Six Flags?" I ask.

Looking my direction Sarah says, "Yeah, it's a tradition that we ride the roller coasters together, especially the new ones when they open. We've been doing it since I was a little girl."

"The funny thing about Sarah," Sam adds, "Is that no matter what they come out with, her favorite has always been the 'Runaway Mine Train.'"

My heart skips a beat. This is like Déjà vu or something. We both love the same "old as the hills" silly little coaster.

"The Runaway Mine Train, huh? So, where do you like to ride Sarah, at the front of the cars or the back?" I ask.

"At the back of course, so when you go through the Saloon at the end, you get whipped over the top as the front of the coaster drops, and you feel like you might hit the wall at the back of the room," she says smiling.

"Me too!" Is all I can think to say. This could be love.

"Did you know you can do a virtual ride on YouTube? They've recorded it from the front car." Sarah adds.

"I never thought to even look that up, I'll have to do that when I get internet back. Thanks Sarah." I feel silly talking about such a childish thing, but I do love that old coaster.

An hour later, I'm back in my now 'super clean' clothes, and we are all eating some excellent Italian food. With all the talking and laughing, I'm really feeling the loss of my parents. For the first time in months, I'm not mad at them for dying anymore. Now, I just wish they were here.

It's almost eight when I arrive home, candlelight in the windows. Still very hot and humid, but I don't mind so much. The joy of meeting Sarah's parents and being around her for a whole day makes it all seem bearable.

Walking in the front door, Mindy pops her head up from the doggie bed she was laying on and comes over to me. Dropping my pack on the floor I gently pick her up, and scratch behind her ears.

"A long day!" Jen proclaims, "You two must have worked hard!"

"We only put in about five hours Jen, but it was enough to really wear me out, not to mention give me a class 'A' sunburn."

"You should have worn sunscreen then," she replies.

"I did. Remember, this is *Texas* sun," Replying with a smirk.

"So, what was it like over there?" Jen asks.

"It's sad, Jen. Really sad. So much destruction. I can see now why they say it'll take a long time to rebuild Port Aransas. It's almost impossible to describe, you'd just have to see it for yourself. The thing that hit me hard is how people's lives are completely upended. We helped in an RV park today, and up to now, I always thought it was just rich people with their play toys who stayed there. Turns out there's a lot of 'average joes' who were living out of their campers, with everything they own inside. More than once we assisted in climbing on the top of a trailer, which used to be the 'side' before it was blown over. And then opening the door to climb down inside and hand out their belongings piece by piece. Those were the lucky ones."

"Lucky ones, what do you mean?"

"Some campers were completely destroyed; clothes, bedding, you name it, strewn all over the place. Soaked in smelly sea water and covered in slime and mud. The ones I felt sorry for the most, were the young couples; some with babies, searching for anything salvageable. I count myself fortunate I was able to go to my old apartment and retrieve things precious to me, like picture albums and personal belongings. This trip to Port A showed me just how blessed I really am. I didn't think so until now."

Noticing I've got Mindy laying in my lap, stroking her head with the good hand, Jen says, "By the way, I took Mindy into the clinic today. First, the bone was set correctly, and she's healing nicely. One of the veterinarians looked at her and says she's about three years old and weighs a little over nine pounds, making her a miniature. She does *not* have a microchip, and the number we have on file with her Rabies tag is the same one we tried calling when we first found her. There's still no answer."

"So, what's the plan," I ask, concern in my voice.

"We'll keep her for a while, so she can heal, and then try to find her a good home."

Upset by what she said, but not sure how to respond, I choose to change the subject for now. "So how was your day Jen?"

"Good," She replies. "Once we get power consistently back on at the clinic, we should be able to open. The veterinarians are doing limited house calls until then."

"And Matt?"

"It'll take a while for them to reopen down at the lumber store. There was some roof damage, but I think they'll work around it somehow. Shouldn't be more than a week."

Yawning, I tell Jen, "Well, I'm working eight to four-thirty tomorrow. I'm going to hit the hay, goodnight."

"Goodnight Paul."

Carrying Mindy out the front door so she can do her business, I'm struck by how dark it is. I can't see fifty feet in front of me. Fortunately, it seems that all the mosquitos have gone to bed because I'm not being attacked. It's either that, or they can't find me in the dark, I chuckle to myself. She comes back up to me and paws at my leg, so I pick her up, and we head inside to my bedroom. Using my cell phone for light, I arrange some of my stuff on the floor, so Mindy can climb up on my bed if she wants to. Or back down for that matter. Stripping down to a t-shirt and shorts I turn on the fan Sarah gave me and lie on the bed next to the pup. She crawls under the sheet and we fall asleep together. Mindy's definitely growing on me.

Chapter 24

Friday, September 1st, 2017

My cell phone wakes me up—it's six-thirty. The forecast says the high will be ninety-three degrees today, the humidity in the eighties. I must be a glutton for punishment, without AC, it's gonna' be miserable. Turning the fan off, I slip out of bed and head to the bathroom. I should buy some more batteries today, just to be safe, that fan makes all the difference at night.

Walking into the kitchen I find Eli sitting at the table, the percolator sitting on a hot pad, and an empty cup waiting for me.

"Thanks Eli, I assume that's for me."

"Yep." He replies.

"You're always up early, I noticed." I set Mindy on the floor, so I can pour myself a cup of coffee.

As I sit down across from him, Eli replies, "Habit. When you live on the street, you wake up with the dawn. Then it's time to pack up and move before anyone realizes you were there to begin with."

Not quite sure what to say, I respond with, "Well, I'm glad you're here. I know Matt and Jen would be happy if you hung around for a while."

"They've been mighty nice to me, but the walls are startin' to close in again." With that, he gets up with his mug and heads out the door.

Fixing a peanut butter and jelly sandwich for breakfast I go back to the bedroom to get ready for work. I'll be glad when the refrigerator's working again so we can start keeping bacon and eggs once more. Not having refrigerated foods or a microwave to cook them with is getting old. But, it is what it is. Like Eli said, things could be worse. Making sure Mindy has some kibble and a fresh pan of water, I finish getting dressed.

Driving down the street I see the junk piles are growing outside the homes and businesses. Next to them are refrigerators, something I hadn't noticed before. I'll have to find out why people are getting rid of those too. Once I get to town, I happily discover that the portable stop signs used in the intersections are now gone as most of the streetlights are now working again! Traffic has picked up a little, but nowhere near normal. Pulling into the stores' parking lot I find the port-a-potties gone, but the mobile kitchen, and the refrigerated truck with the free bags of ice are still present. A smile crosses my face as I spot 'one legged Willie,' checking out the remains of someone's meal on the ground.

Excitement! I feel genuine excitement as I walk through the lot, seeing cars belonging to customers, realizing the store is open once again. Walking through the automatic doors, cool air assails me, and the lights are shining inside. Something in my life is back to normal, and it's a great feeling.

Clocking in I find a head clerk and am assigned a till. It's funny how something I used to see as drudgery, now makes me happy. I realize my job is my second home, and it's good to be here.

"How are you feeling today?" Mrs. Henry says, as she comes through my line.

"Much better, thanks. And how are you and your husband?" I reply.

"Doing fine Paul, we have a generator at home now. We use it to keep the fridge cold and run the little window AC unit when it gets unbearably hot. The people at AEP tell us it's going to be a few more days until they can get to us where we live."

That means the same for me—not being very far from her. Even though we're only three miles from town, we're "in the sticks" some might say.

Totaling up her purchase, I remind her, "Don't forget to get your two free bags of ice on the way out."

"Thanks, Paul. But we'll leave those for someone else who's in worse shape than we are. God bless you. I'm glad you're feeling better."

"Thank you, Mrs. Henry."

The day passes slowly, not many customers are back in the area yet. And then I remember, the situation's even worse because there are usually lots of tourists loading up here before they head to Port Aransas. It saddens me to know that this is going to be the new normal for a while.

Going outside at lunchtime, I see men in hardhats walking around the large curved sheets of metal that was once the water tower across the street. Then I begin to wonder, if we're getting water already, where's it coming from? There must have been a backup plan, I decide. Getting in line at the kitchen on wheels, I feel a little guilty. I think I'll bring my lunch from now on, taking what Mrs. Henry said to heart; save this food for those who have lost their jobs, their homes.

With lunch over I finish my shift and do a little shopping. Purchasing some of the same things we've been eating, I add some snacks that don't need refrigeration, hoping everyone at home likes chocolate cake. There's even some chew treats for Mindy, and more coffee, I can't forget that.

Arriving on Armstrong Road I see a bonfire blazing in the yard of a home, just a couple of lots down from mine. Wow, now I'm starting to think of Matts' and Jens' house as "my home." Nearing the fire, I recognize Matt and Eli standing close by, and surmise this must be the remnants of the barn roof. I guess that's the easy way to get rid of the problem, burn it to ash. Just down the road I pass a mailbox cluster for all the homes in the area, and it reminds me I need to check and see if I have any mail back at the apartment complex. I wonder if they're even delivering? Shaking my head, I realize, there's just so much we take for granted. It's been a week now since Harvey roared through with no cable, no video games, no CBC coffee. It sucks. Then I have to remind myself to focus on the good things around me, it could definitely be worse.

Pulling up to the house I see Jen cooking with a large iron skillet, using the Coleman stove on the table out front. Brian's sitting in a plastic chair nearby, and the aroma that assails my nostrils is like nothing I've ever smelled before. Fish like—kind of.

Carrying the grocery bags up to the porch I ask Jen, "What's for dinner?"

"A Louisiana favorite," she replies with a laugh. "Alligator tail. Brian brought it over and suggested we all share a meal tonight."

"Alrighty-then," I reply half-heartedly. "I hope it goes with chocolate cake," I reply, holding it up for all to see.

"I guess we'll find out," Brian says chuckling.

Walking through the front door and into the kitchen, my new best friend comes trotting over, seemingly better on her new cast.

"Hi Mindy," I tell her as I set the bags on the counter. "I've got a treat for you." Fishing through one of the bags I find what I'm looking for and take a skinny rawhide 'bone' out of the package and hold it down to her. She must recognize what it is because she quickly snatches it out of my hand and returns to the doggie bed. Max and Molly come running into the kitchen. They must smell the treat I gave Mindy, so I give them each one too, and back to their bedroom they fly. I can only hope they don't chew them up on Matt and Jen's bed.

After putting the food away, I check my phone for messages. Friends wanting to know when I'll be back online in the gaming world. Others asking how things are, if everything's back to normal. I actually laugh out loud. If you look at the news, it's all about Houston now, the assumption being the rest of us are fine, since there are no more updates about Aransas Pass, Rockport or Port Aransas. Responding to the posts, I realize that this destruction is the "new reality." The rumor is it will be weeks or months before Walmart and Lowe's in Aransas Pass are back open. Other businesses will not reopen at all. The power may be back on in town, but it's not out here. The curfew is still in effect, from 10pm to 6am. Hundreds have lost their homes and may never come back. Many others will probably move because their jobs are gone even though their homes survived. I'm not sure what normal is anymore. All I know is that in the future, I'm going to prepare better for the "hurricanes" of life.

The front door opens, and I hear Jen say, "Dinner's ready Paul."

Putting on mosquito spray (mornings and evenings are the worst times for mosquitos) I join the group outside on the front porch. Matt and Eli are now back. Three more white plastic chairs have appeared on the porch and a large fan is blowing air our way. I see an orange extension cord running from the fan to Matt's truck where it runs inside the driver's side door.

Noticing my gaze, Matt explains, "I've got an inverter plugged into the 12-volt power outlet, so as long as we don't run it too long, we've got a breeze while we eat."

"Great idea! I didn't know they made things like that," I exclaim.

Dinner is laid out on the table, and while alligator tail doesn't look exactly appetizing, I'm not going to say a word. I load up my plate with some and mixed canned vegetables, there's a pan of rice too. My chocolate cake is at the end, covered until it's time to slice. Collecting a fork, knife, and a large glass of iced tea, I find an empty chair.

As I sit down I'm startled to hear Matt say, "Paul, would mind saying grace?"

Everyone's already looking down, eyes closed, so it's hard to back out. I hesitate for a moment before I find my courage, then say, "Thank you God, if you're listening, for this food and these nice people. Please help all those that I've seen in the last few days who are hurting." Thinking to myself, if you're as big as everyone says you are, that shouldn't be too hard. Fumbling for something else to say, I finish with, "Amen."

A chorus of 'amens' comes back at me. Looking up, I spot Eli looking my way. I swear, with that long silver hair, beard and mustache, all he needs is a cowboy hat and he could be a movie star.

He tells me, "Good prayer kid."

In TV shows and movies, the running joke is that every mystery dish tastes like chicken. I hate to add to the cliché, but so does alligator. Well, it *smells* like fish, but it *tastes* like chicken. I don't know if I would ever order this in a restaurant, assuming it might be on a menu somewhere, but's it's not as bad as I thought it would be.

While we eat, Brian and Eli regale us with stories of being in the military, playing off each other as if they had soldiered side by side. From the heart-breaking accounts of death and sacrifice, to the tales that have you rolling around on the floor laughing, I find myself enjoying this group of people more than I ever thought I would. Some would say I'm just a youngster in an adult world, playing video games and surfing for my entertainment. And they would be right. But I think I might have grown up a little in the last few days, and it's feeling good.

Brian gets up, and addresses Matt and Jen, "Well, I'd better be getting home before it gets too dark. I don't want to step on any snakes."

"Snakes?" I ask surprised.

"Sure kid," Eli jumps in. "Matt and I killed two water moccasins today that came out from under the old barn roof we set on fire."

"And I killed a copperhead in my yard yesterday," Brian adds.

Sitting there stunned, I ask, "So, you're telling

me, that when I helped with the horses, and then rounded up the alligator the other day, sloshing around in all that water, there were snakes in there too!?"

"Yep," Eli says confidently, "But if you ever get bit, just do what I do."

Looking over at him I reply, "What's that?"

Looking at me all serious he says, "Bite em' back."

Everyone starts laughing, and I realize I've been had.

Brian ambles toward home, and I start rounding up plates, bringing everything back inside the house—I help Matt wash and dry the dishes. Noticing his clothes look cleaner than normal I ask, "What technique are you using to get your clothes so clean, Matt?"

"Paul, I have to admit that Jen and I are cheating. She got permission to use the washer and dryer at the veterinarian clinic while it's still closed. So, as she's going down to help prepare the place for reopening, she's taking a load of clothes with her."

"I thought the power was off there?"

"It came back on yesterday morning. They've been cleaning, checking out the equipment and computer system; Jen says they'll open on Monday."

"That's great!" I respond. "Maybe I can find an open laundromat somewhere close by."

Changing the subject, Matt says, "If you're not working on Sunday Paul, you're welcome to come to church with us."

"Thanks, I'm not quite sure what I'm working, we were all told this morning a new schedule would be posted soon. Hours were going to be shortened now that we're up and running again, and not much business has returned yet."

"Well, I'm sure something will work out. I'll be watching for opportunities for you."

"Thanks Matt."

Mindy starts scratching at the front door, and this time I escort her outside to be sure she doesn't run into any "critters," snakes or otherwise. She needs a protector I decide. And I'm happy to do it. Matt and Jen have taken me under their wing, so I'll take her under mine.

Returning inside, Mindy trots in and gets a drink of water, then heads off down the hall. Eli is sitting alone at the kitchen table reading by candle light now that the sun light's just about gone. I notice he winces in pain as he holds his stomach.

"You ok Eli?" I ask, looking his way.

"It's nothin' kid. Just a little pain that comes and goes, I've had it for a while now. It's probably just the alligator gettin' even with me," he says with a grimace. "And about the snakes out here—just be cautious. They don't like you any more than you like them. Just give em' a lot of room, you'll be fine."

"Thanks for that Eli. The wildlife out here is a little scary sometimes."

"Not as scary as the two-legged creatures callin' themselves politicians."

By the look on his face, I could tell he was serious this time. "Goodnight Eli."

"Goodnight kid."

Chapter 25

Saturday, September 2nd, 2017

This morning I wake up on my own because my phone is dead. Crap. Sliding out of bed, leaving Mindy under the covers I throw on some pants, grab my phone, and head for the kitchen.

Seeing Jen at the kitchen table I ask, "Good morning, do you know what time it is?"

Checking her watch, she replies, "Seven-thirty."

I can make it to work on time (eight o'clock) if I skip breakfast. "Thanks Jen."

Hustling back to my room, I get dressed and then carry Mindy outside. After plugging my phone into the charger in the jeep, I then pull the tarp off, thankful I've been using it. As I was parked under the tree, it's now covered in bird poop. I need to find a new roof; the whole tarp thing is getting old. Spotting Matt in the horse enclosure I wave good morning to him—he waves back. It doesn't feel as humid today, and I'm grateful.

Finding Mindy sniffing at something dead, I pick her back up and return her to the house. Then, wishing Jen a great day I return to the jeep and drive off to work. As I near Wheeler, I see a couple of repair trucks working on the electrical poles. They're still two miles from the house, but I can't help being encouraged.

"Good morning Paul," Alex greets me as I head for the timeclock.

"How's it going Alex?" I reply as I punch in my numbers.

"Not bad, not bad. I need you to check out the new schedule, and just to let you know, if today is as slow as yesterday, you'll be off by noon."

Concerned doesn't begin to cover the way I feel, I need my hours if I'm ever going to get back out on my own. Trying to be positive I reply, "I understand, so, how does it look for the next few weeks?"

"We're trying to get everyone at least twenty hours. Even with all the people who haven't come back to the area yet, we're still heavy with employees. If you're willing to go to Corpus, we may be able to squeeze you in for some extra time there, Paul."

"Thanks Alex, anything you can do will help."

Sure enough, I'm off at noon—four hours is better than nothing. Arriving back at the house, Jen, Eli and Matt are having lunch.

"If you haven't eaten yet Paul, you're welcome to join us," Jen offers.

"Thanks Jen, I didn't have a chance to eat anything today, and I have a headache now to boot."

"Did you have any coffee this morning?" Matt inquires.

"No time," I reply.

"What you need is some coffee kid." Eli states.

"Why's that," I reply.

Matt jumps in, "You're having caffeine withdrawals Paul. Have some coffee, it's cold by now, but it'll get rid of that headache." He gets up and pours some from the percolator into a fresh mug, and hands it to me.

"I don't know what I'd do without you guys,

thanks."

Joining the trio, I make myself a sandwich with an open can of tuna, and some mayo hiding in the ice chest on the kitchen counter, chips round out this gourmet meal. All kidding aside, it tastes good.

"Is it just me, or does this taste extra special today?" I direct at no one.

"Hunger makes the best sauce," Eli answers.

"Yeah, I guess it does." I reply.

"Well guys, if you all know of anyone who needs a part-time employee, I just found out today I'm only going to get twenty hours a week for a while."

"We'll keep our eyes and ears open Paul, I'm sure the Lord will provide something." Matt says.

"Thanks, I'm willing to do just about anything. I want to start paying you all rent."

"No rush, it's all going to work out." Jen says. You've got to love the optimism of these people.

My phone chimes, letting me know there's a new text message. It's from Sarah. She wants to know if all of us; Matt, Jen, Eli and myself would like to join them for dinner tonight. I share the message with everyone, and they all agree to go.

"It'll be nice to get out of the house and eat somewhere cool for a change. Not to mention, no one here will have to cook." Jen says.

"We'd love to," I reply to Sarah's text. "Just let us know when and where."

"Do you all know Sarah's parents?" I ask the trio.

"Matt and I do. They come to church with Sarah sometimes when they're in town," Jen responds. "Very nice people."

Part of what I spend the afternoon doing, is refilling water buckets. The barrels are getting low, now that there's been little to no rain lately. I hope they get the power back on soon. Next, I drive down to my old apartment; find the mailbox and retrieve the contents. There're bills and advertisements, but as far as I can tell, nothing new since the date of the hurricane. I look through my stuff one more time in the apartment and decide I need to figure out what I'll do with what's left. I know some people will simply abandon their belongings, but I feel obligated to at least haul it to the street where it can be picked up later. Some of my old neighbors are there as well, digging through what's now destined for the landfill. We greet each other, but there's not much to say. I find myself wishing my surf board was still here; fall's a good time to hit the waves, and it'll be awhile before I can afford a new one. Maybe I can sell my Xbox. Wow, did I just really think that? Maybe it *is* time to let some of my old habits go. I think I'd rather spend time with Sarah on the beach, then sitting in a dark room pretending to be some super soldier on the screen.

Later, we all drive into Corpus Christi in Jens' truck, enjoying the AC. Locating the restaurant on Staples takes no time at all, and we walk inside to find Sarah, with her parents sitting at a nice table near a window. Sarah's wearing a beautiful dress, making me feel shabby in what I've got on. Time to buy some new clothes I decide. She's worth it.

There are greetings all around as Matt introduces Eli to Mitch and Sam, informing them he's a navy veteran. That's what I like about Matt, always looking for the positive; never mentioning Eli's homeless—well at least he was.

Mitch firmly shakes his hand and says, "Thank you for your service Eli. We're proud to have you dine with us tonight."

This is the first time I think I've ever seen Eli caught off guard, "You're welcome," He quietly replies, pride showing in his face.

Sitting down at the table we peruse the menu. A moment later a server appears with two bottles of red wine, and seven glasses. Walking around the table she checks mine and Sarah's I.D., then serves each of us a half glass until she gets to Eli.

"If it's all the same to you folks, I'd rather have a beer," he states.

Mitch chuckles and directs the server to bring him whatever he wants. To my surprise Matt and Jen take a sip and seem to enjoy the flavor.

"I thought you didn't drink?" I ask Matt. Then realizing it's not really any of my business I add, "Sorry."

"No, it's ok Paul. My personal understanding is that the bible doesn't say anywhere we can't drink, but it does admonish us not to get drunk. Jen and I rarely drink because we don't want to set a bad example for those in our bible study group."

Huh, I learned something new today.

This restaurant specializes in steak, and so I order a New York strip with all the fixins'. Once everyone orders, the conversation turns to the destruction left by the hurricane, and what it'll take to fix it. We all conclude that some will be rebuilt and some demolished, or something new will take its place. But it'll never be exactly the same way again. Looking on the bright side Sarah points out it could all come back even better than before. A chance to start fresh, a new beginning. I decide then and there to embrace her attitude—to try to find the positive in every situation. To look for ways to improve upon what's now destroyed, instead of mourning what's been lost. One more reason I feel drawn to her.

At the end of the meal there's the usual fight over the check. Matt wants to cover the tab while Mitch insists he pay since it was he who invited us. In the end, Mitch wins out, and Matt rebels by leaving the tip. We all get up from the table except for Eli, who appears nauseous, and is holding his gut again.

Jen puts her hand on his shoulder and says, "Are you ok?"

Not responding, she puts her other hand on his forehead, and finds him feverish.

"Tell me the truth Eli, how bad is it?" She looks him in the eye, daring him to try to lie his way out of it.

"It's bad Jen." He answers.

"Matt, I think it's time to get him to a hospital."

When Eli doesn't argue I conclude it *must be bad*.

"Do you want me to come with you all?" Sarah offers.

"No, we'll call you when we know something." Jen responds. "Please pray that this isn't something serious."

"Consider it done." Sam answers, speaking for everyone.

Matt and I half carry Eli out to the truck, and then drive into downtown Corpus Christi, towards

Christus Spohn Memorial.

Arriving at the emergency room entrance Jen parks and instructs me to go inside and find a wheel chair. Coming back out with one, Eli looks absolutely green, and still doubled over in pain. Matt and I help him into it, then roll him inside while Jen leaves to park the truck. Maneuvering his chair next to a row of seats in the waiting room, Matt then quickly walks over to a sign that says "Admitting," as I sit down in a chair next to Eli. Returning with a clipboard, Matt queries Eli as he attempts to complete the paperwork, but he's not able to respond to many questions. Returning to the front, I can tell Matt is adamant that Eli be seen ASAP, describing the symptoms to the receptionist. Jen walks in and sits across from us, then she closes her eyes and begins to pray quietly. They must have taken Matt at his word, because five minutes later, an orderly comes out to retrieve Eli and rolls him through the double doors.

Not knowing what else to do, we huddle in the waiting room. Getting my phone out I text Sarah and update her on the situation, she responds with a promise to pray for Eli. Matt gets on his own phone, and I overhear something about calling the 'prayer chain'; getting everyone on their knees for our friend, I just hope it helps. "If you're listening God, please heal him," I ask quietly. I've come to like Eli; I don't want to lose him.

Two hours later, a middle-aged doctor with a dark complexion and black hair approaches us.

"Are you Matthew Murchison?" He inquires, looking towards Matt.

"Yes I am."

"I'm Doctor Patel. Are you relatives of Eliot Samuels?"

"No," Matt replies, "As far as we know, he has a family, but we don't know where they are. Eli is a homeless man we took in just before the hurricane hit; he's been staying with us since then," nodding towards Jen and me.

"Mr. Samuels indicated on the paperwork that the hospital can share any information with you, so it is not a problem. We have another test to run but we're reasonably sure he has diverticulitis."

Looking around at all of us, Matt asks, "I'm not sure what that is."

"Diverticulitis is a condition where small pockets have formed in the walls of the colon. They can retain food particles and cause pain as well as nausea and vomiting. It's not uncommon in someone of Mr. Samuels age."

"So, what's the prognosis Doctor?"

"If it turns out to be diverticulitis, as we suspect, there are two methods of treatment. If the pockets have not ruptured, we can administer antibiotics and send him home in a day or two, with a strict diet to follow. If they have ruptured, we will schedule surgery as soon as possible."

"It sounds serious," Jen comments.

"It can be," Dr. Patel responds. "If it is what we suspect, and the pockets have ruptured, what's called peritonitis, then there is a very high possibility that the contents of these pockets have spilled into the abdominal cavity and have caused him to become septic."

"That can't be good." Pausing, "How dangerous

is the surgery?" Jen asks.

"I'm sorry, but I can't tell you anymore until we know for sure what is going on. I have told you too much already. But be assured he is in good care here. If it is required, he is in good hands; we perform this type of surgery frequently. I suggest you go home and rest, I will have someone call you when we confirm the diagnosis."

Shaking hands with Matt, the doctor turns on his heel and leaves. Moments later we all walk out into the hot, steamy darkness that thrives in Corpus Christi during summer nights. The bay water must be close.

Driving back home, everyone's quiet for a while. Then Jen speaks up, "Matt, do you remember Eli talking about a daughter somewhere? Any idea if he's got any family we can reach?"

Taking a moment to reflect, he says, "I think there's a daughter here in Texas, although I'm not sure. But, we do live in the age of Google and social media; if we can get a name, I'll bet we can track her down."

"Good idea. I'll check his things when we get home and see if it's written down somewhere. I know he'll be mad, but in this case, he'll just have to deal with it."

"That's my wife, tough as nails and not easy to discourage," Matt says.

As we've been driving I find info about diverticulitis using my smart phone. "Hey guys, I've got some information here I think you all should know."

"Go ahead Paul." Matt replies.

"Depending on the seriousness of the diverticulitis, and assuming he's septic, his chances of surviving range from one in two, to one in five."

"Let me see that," Jen reaches into the backseat for my phone.

Handing it to her, Matt tries to glance over to see, but the print's too small. Besides, Jen turns it sideways forcing him to watch the road.

With a tone in her voice I've never heard before, Jen says, "Pauls' right. This just means we'll be praying and trusting God even more." She sounds as if she could convince the big man upstairs to heal him all by herself.

Arriving home, still hoping to hear something tonight, we all prepare for bed. Laying down I stroke Mindy's back as she lays with her head across my chest. Just before 11 pm a phone rings in Matt's bedroom and I can hear muffled speech. A moment later he walks to the doorway of my room and lightly knocks.

"I'm awake," I answer, "What's the news?"

Pressing the door inward a few inches, he says, "It's confirmed, it's diverticulitis. Eli's scheduled for surgery tomorrow morning at seven-thirty. Jen and I will be going down early; to be there for him. You're welcome to join us if you like."

Choking back the emotions welling up within me, "After the schedule changes today, it turns out I'm off tomorrow, so I'll go with you. Thanks Matt."

"I'll wake you up early then, get some sleep. Goodnight Paul."

"Good night Matt."

Thinking about Eli I begin to feel really sad. Wait, what's wrong with me? He's just some homeless guy, right? But deep down I realize what a friend he has become to me in such a short time. He's a man tough enough to kill alligators, and strong enough to remove the log that's laying across your jeep with a chainsaw. Yet, cooks you breakfast without ever expecting any thanks and plays with little Mindy when he thinks no one's looking. Eli's a marshmallow wrapped in barbed wire. But I don't have the guts to ever tell that to his face. If you're listening God, please let him live.

Chapter 26

Sunday, September 3rd, 2017

Matt wakes me up at six, informing me we'll be leaving in half an hour. I'm hustling so I can try to squeeze in a cup of coffee. Fortunately, the pot's out front on the stove; an empty cup sitting on the table as I take Mindy out front to do her thing, so I don't have to rush so much after all. It's the little things that make life a little more bearable. Whatever old person who said that was right.

Putting on my cleanest jeans and a button-down shirt, I then find some socks and put my shoes on. As I'm leaving my room I find Jen and Matt heading from the kitchen to the front door.

"Perfect timing," Matt says.

They're both in nice clothes, as if headed for church. I feel a little under-dressed, but if they notice, they don't say anything. Driving towards Corpus we cross over the bay just before the Harbor Bridge. The sun is just coming up over the water—a beautiful sight.

"So, how are things between you and Sarah, Paul?" Jen inquires.

"Good, I really like Sarah. She's not like any other girl I've ever met. But then, I've never really known any college students besides her. She loves the water, and so do I."

Cresting the top of the bridge, it's hard to deny the beauty of the area; broken orange-pink clouds along the horizon, turquoise water below us, even some boats out past the marina. I have to remind myself we're going to visit a man who's about to have major surgery. Taking an exit, a little way past the bridge, we weave our way through downtown and eventually to the parking lot of Eli's hospital. Getting out of the truck we go through the main entrance and stop at the information desk. Five minutes later, we enter his room to find he's asleep.

"Shouldn't they be prepping him for surgery?" Jen whispers to Matt.

"Let's go see what's going on." Matt replies as we march back to the nurses' desk.

"Mr. Samuels, Mr. Samuels," the station nurse repeats as she looks through the computerized listings. "Yes, here he is. His surgery has been postponed one hour, but we'd be waking him up soon, anyway. You have a few minutes before we'll have to ask you to leave."

Walking back towards the room I find two others have joined us to show support for Eli this morning; Pastor Weaver and Sarah. There are handshakes between the men, and warm hugs from the ladies. Together we enter his room.

"Eli, it's time to wake up." A nurse shakes his shoulder, "Eli, there are some people here to see you."

His eyelids flutter open, staring straight up. He mutters, "Where the hell am I?"

Hearing us chuckle he turns his head to the left—spotting us he says, "I sure hope you're here to take me home."

"No can do my friend, you need a little work done on your pipes, *then* you can come home and be an ornery old cuss." Matt says with a smile.

Jen and Sarah walk over to one side of his bed, the pastor, Matt and I to the other.

"It feels like you're here to carry my casket," Eli announces, to the laughter of us all.

"We're just here to let you know you're loved, and we want to pray for you, and wish you a speedy recovery." Jen says, her voice cracking.

"I'm too mean to die. Besides, God doesn't want me in heaven yet, I gotta' get a shower first."

More laughter. Then, "Alright Eli," Pastor weaver says. "We're going to pray for you now."

Everyone holds their hands out, so I take one on either side of me as we ring the bed. The Pastor leads off asking the Lord to guide the surgeon's hands, with Matt and Jen right behind asking for a quick recovery. Even Sarah says some words for him. Finding it's my turn, I add, "Dear God, don't take him yet. He's one of the few real friends I have."

Looking up, we find a respectful nurse standing in the doorway. Seeing we've concluded our little prayer session she lets us know it's time to leave. Matt addresses her by saying, "How long does a surgery like this usually last?"

"I've seen them go anywhere from three to seven hours depending on what they find."

Matt thanks her and we walk out into the hallway towards the elevator.

Exiting on the first floor Matt suggests we all go to breakfast together. "Eli's in good hands, so we may as well get something to eat instead of wringing our hands in a cold little waiting room."

Finding an IHOP, we walk inside and wait for a

large table to open, which doesn't take long. When we arrive at our table, somehow, Jen manages to make sure Sarah and I are seated next to each other. But who's complaining?

As the moments go by, everyone seems happy; chatting about the weather, what people are doing to rebuild their lives, anything but the surgery happening as we speak. Inside of me, emotions are churning, I can't help but worry about Eli and I begin to get angry; like I did about Matt's "God loves you" comment and my parents dying.

Noticing my reticence, Sarah quietly asks me, "What's wrong Paul?"

"Well, don't take this wrong, but everybody seems to not care about Eli all of a sudden. I mean, I feel like I'm the only here one worried about him."

Concern over what's going on between Sarah and I, Pastor Weaver asks—"Is everything ok?"

Feeling embarrassed, I clam up. Sarah looks at me, saying, "It's ok, please tell them what you told me."

She says it in such a way that I trust her, and it gives me the courage to continue.

Responding to everyone who is now focused on me, "Well, I know you all are Christians, and I'm not. And I don't mean to offend anyone here, but how can you all talk about anything and everything and not seem to care about Eli's surgery right now?" It's difficult keeping my anger in check.

"Paul," Pastor Weaver begins, "It's not that we don't care, it's a matter of differing perspectives." Seeing my lack of understanding he continues, "As Christians; having prayed over Eli, we know one of two things will happen. He will either come through the surgery and be fine, or the Lord will take him home, and he'll never suffer pain again. As a matter of fact, he'll be in a place where he'll be truly free and at peace. A place of joy and happiness."

Jen, seeing I'm still upset and not convinced, adds, "What he's trying to say, Paul, is that from our perspective, we've turned this all over to God. We have complete faith it will all work out, either way. healed, or in Heaven. By praying about this, and turning this over to Him, (she points up), He takes the worries and concerns in our hearts and replaces them with a peace that passes all understanding."

I've heard that somewhere before, I think.

Sarah looks at me with a softness in her eyes that dissolves my frustration. I can tell that she senses the depth of my anguish for what Eli must be going through. Pausing, she adds, "Paul, we don't know what the future holds, but we know who holds the future."

Chapter 27

Having finished breakfast, we go in two directions; Pastor Weaver heads to his church with Matt and Jen following, as Matt has a Sunday school class to lead. Sarah offers to spend a little time with me, as we wait for the news from the hospital, so we get in her car, and head for the beach—just fifteen minutes away. Parking next to Bob Hall pier, she invites me to take a walk with her, so we remove our shoes and socks and amble towards the water. It's already hot, the temperature in the eighties, but I just don't care. It actually feels good to walk through the sand down to the waves, and there's a light breeze coming off the surf. The breakfast conversation runs over and over through my head, and I can almost see their side of things. They all seem to be of the same mind—even Sarah. Is it possible that this whole thing about believing in a supreme being isn't just some mass delusion as I always thought it to be? I just don't know anymore.

Looking at Sarah, as we walk along the water's edge, I say, "Thank you for caring about me. It's been a while since I've met someone who seemed to consider what I was feeling might be important too."

Taking a chance, I hold out my hand. She takes it in hers, and replies, "You're welcome Paul." Just walking hand in hand, makes me feel better than I have in a long time. A closeness that, until now, I didn't realize how much I'd missed. Picking up colorful seashells as we go takes my mind off things a bit, and it's fun.

After a mile, we turn around and go back. Arriving at her car, we grab some bottled water from the trunk, and find some shade from the pier and sit in the sand. Sarah then describes the birds on the beach in detail to me, where the seaweed comes from, and the names for the different types of seashells we collected along our stroll. Her passion for all things "of the sea" is intoxicating. I find myself wanting to take up oceanography too. I was mostly interested in surfing on the top of the waves before—now she's teaching me about the world beneath them. As the morning becomes afternoon, I come to sense some of the peace Sarah seems to have, And I find myself wanting it as well.

Both of our phones alert us at the same time; there are text messages letting us know Eli is out of surgery, and to all meet back at the hospital. After replying, we pack up the empty water bottles, and climb into the car. The shells go into a grocery bag from the trunk-- I have a plan for them.

It's almost two o'clock when we arrive, Jen's truck is already in the lot. Finding the waiting room, we cross to where Matt and Jen are seated and say hello.

"We just got here ourselves," Matt tells us. "The doctor should be out to speak to us soon."

Seconds later I spot Dr. Patel walking in our direction, and over the next five minutes he goes into detail about Eli's surgery. I don't understand all the big words, but the three things that stand out to me is— 1) They removed part of his colon and cleaned out the abdominal cavity. 2) Eli came very close to having a colostomy, (I'll have to Google that one later) and, 3) It will be touch and go for a couple of days—but the prognosis is good. He's sedated and in the recovery room, so it was advised that we go home and come back tomorrow for a visit.

Sitting together, trying to absorb what we've just been told, Sarah speaks up, "Doesn't Eli have a daughter somewhere?"

"He talked about her one time in one of our bible studies," Jen responds, "If I remember right, her name is Shelby, Shelby Samuels. Why? What are you thinking?"

"I just thought she should know her dad is in the hospital." Sarah replies.

"Well, as far as I know, they haven't spoken in a long time. They had a nasty argument, probably several, when Eli was drinking heavily years ago, and she swore him off for good," Jen adds. "At least that's what he told me."

"I understand," Sarah replies, "It was just a thought. So, what are you all going to do for the rest of the day?"

"Matt and I have to get ready for work tomorrow. And there are still things like feeding the horses, and dinner to prepare."

"So, you ready to head home Paul?" Matt asks.

Sarah jumps in, "We still have a project to finish, something Pauls' helping me with. But I'll bring him home in time for supper."

"Oh, ok." Jen and Matt glance at each other, surprised. "Well, we'll see you two later then," Matt says, as they turn and head for the door.

Looking at Sarah, I whisper, "What project?"

With a sneaky smile, she replies, "You'll see."

Loading up in her car, then driving down the freeway, it's not long before we reach her condo; walking inside I expect to see her parents here.

"Where's your mom and dad?" I inquire, looking around.

"They're visiting some friends in Kings Crossing, they'll be back later this evening."

"So, what's the big 'project?'"

Bringing her laptop over to the kitchen table, she replies, "You and I are going to try to find Eli's daughter. She may not care to see him, but then again, she might. All I know is, I want to at least try-- for the both of them. I figure between the power of social media, and all the search engines out there, we might find her pretty quick."

And you know what, Sarah was right. Fifteen minutes later we have a full name: Shelby Marie Samuels. She's thirty-three years old, divorced and has two daughters. Her current address is in Austin. Any more detail than that will cost us some money.

The next step we take is locating her on a social media website, and then sending an IM, or instant message. It reads, "Hello, my name is Sarah Connors. If you are the daughter of Eliot Samuels, I want you to know your father's in the hospital in Corpus Christi. If you care to see him, or want more information, you can reach me at 361--------."

Fifteen minutes later, Sarah's phone rings. Recognizing it's an Austin number, she put's in on speaker, "Hello, is this Shelby?"

"Yes, it is, is this Sarah?" Children are making a noise in the background.

"Hi Shelby, I'm glad you called. My friend, Paul

and I thought you might want to know that Eli's in the hospital," . . . struggling for something else to say, she pauses.

"Well Sarah, thank you for finding me. This is an answer to prayer, I've been looking for my dad for a long time now," emotion filling her voice.

The satisfaction on Sarah's face speaks volumes. "I'm so happy to hear that Shelby, Eli's a wonderful man. I heard he used to drink a lot, but he's been sober for several years now," a tear rolls down her cheek.

"Well, I haven't been able to locate him; he's homeless I think, and that makes it next to impossible to track him down." Hesitating, Shelby asks, "Do you really think he wants to see me? I mean, I'd love to bring the girls down, and visit, but I don't know---"

"Shelby, I can't say for sure, but knowing Eli, I think he might miss you as much as you obviously miss him."

They talk for a few more minutes and Shelby promises to think about it. Hanging up, Sarah goes to the kitchen and grabs a tissue. Her eyes are wet; and I can see the happiness, the glow from here.

"You did a really good thing Sarah. I think that was awesome."

"*We*, did a really good thing, and I just hope Eli feels the same way." Pensively she asks, "Do you think she'll come?"

"I don't know, but the ball is in her court. If she doesn't reach out now, he might disappear again."

"Then we need to take this to a higher authority." Sitting back down at the table, she takes my hand, bows her head, and begins to pray.

Later, as we drive back to Aransas Pass, a

pelican once again flanks us for a minute as we cross the bridge leading into Rockport. It always amazes me how they can fly so elegantly. Can you say that about a pelican? Elegant? No matter.

Grabbing my phone, I check out the "gallery" where the pictures are stored and find the one of my schedule. I took it yesterday after it was posted.

"I'm working eight to noon tomorrow Sarah. Would you like to meet at the hospital about one o'clock? Unless you've got previous plans of course."

"My parents are heading back to Irving in the morning. Dads' favorite fishing boat is not running this weekend; it was damaged in the storm. So, yeah, that sounds like a plan."

Driving past homes as we near our destination, I point out all the refrigerators sitting next to the debris piles along the street.

"Why do you think they're getting rid of them Sarah? I can't imagine they were broken because of the hurricane."

"Think about it Paul; you leave for a week, then come back. Without power, what do you think you'll find when you open it up?"

"A huge, smelly mess?" I reply.

"Not to mention mold. Then comes the cleaning. I think some people just opted to buy a new one; maybe it was time anyway."

Contemplating, I reply, "You know, if I had a trailer, and somewhere to store them, I could clean them up and make a little money."

Laughing, Sarah says, "Not a bad idea. A disgusting, smelly idea, but not a bad one."

Arriving back at the house, we walk in and find

Jen and Matt sipping iced tea on the couch. Mindy's asleep, wedged between the labs laying on the floor.

"So, what's the 'secret project?'" Jen asks looking our way.

"It's a surprise. You'll find out all about it really soon," Sarah replies. Changing the subject, "FYI, Paul and I are planning on meeting at the hospital tomorrow at one, would you like to join us?" Pausing, "But then if you're working---I guess that's not such a good idea after all."

Laughing, Matt responds, "We thought we were, until we realized on the way home from the hospital, tomorrow is Labor Day. So, yes, we'll join you." Then looking at me, "Are you working tomorrow Paul?"

"From eight to noon." I reply.

"So, why don't you swing by the house afterwards, and we'll go together."

"That'll be great Matt, thanks."

Walking Sarah back out to her Subaru, I tell her, "Thanks for a really good day. I learned tons about the ocean, it was fun." Looking into her dark brown eyes I add, "And it was nice spending time with you."

"You're welcome, but don't forget, you still owe me dinner," she replies with a grin.

Grabbing the bag of seashells out of the back-seat floor, Sarah looks at it and asks, "What are you going to do with those?"

"I've got a surprise coming too," replying with a grin of my own.

Sarah drives away, and I find myself missing her already. It occurs to me just how caring she is, always thinking of others. Like the fans she gave to me, Matt, Jen and Eli, then, wanting to find Eli's daughter. Also taking me to the beach when she knew I was upset—It makes me appreciate her all the more.

Walking back inside, I announce, "I'm going to get a shower while the mosquitos are asleep. And I'll fill up a few buckets while I'm out there."

"Thanks Paul," Matt responds. "By the way, I've noticed that you and Sarah are spending a lot of time together. How are things going between you two?"

Jen sits forward on the couch, all ears.

Stopping just before the hallway entrance, I reply, "Really good. She's pretty and super smart; she amazes me with how much she knows about the ocean. I'm afraid she's way out of my league though, I'm a nobody compared to her. But I've enjoyed getting to know her these last few days."

"Don't be so hard on yourself Paul, you have a lot to offer as well," Jen replies.

"Maybe, but does Sarah think so?" Is my retort.

"That's the question, isn't it?" Matt concludes.

Chapter 28

Monday, September 4th, 2017— Labor Day

The screech of a bird, a hawk I think, wakes me up. It's time to get up and prepare for another day. Turning the fan off, I look down at Mindy, saying, "How can you be so little, and be such a bed hog? Huh?"

Pressed up against my side she looks up at me tiredly and yawns.

Sighing— "Yeah, me too Mindy, me too."

I'm going to have to find a way to get Jen to let me keep this little girl, not wanting to give her away. I look forward to seeing her when I get home now; she's becoming my 'bud.'

Checking the bathroom mirror, I find that with eleven days growth, my beard's really starting to stand out. It does look rather strange; its red and my hair is brown. Time to shave. I'm sure it wasn't going to be long before I had to cut it off for work anyway. Deciding to forgo the sling, I carefully lift the bucket with my good arm, pour some into the sink, and replace the water in the toilet tank that was just used. Finding a razor behind the mirror in front of me, I get started, discovering quickly why you don't wait this long to cut it off. A razor's ok for stubble, but a pain in the rear for a beard. I'm glad to get this over with.

Glancing at the weather forecast it looks like a

high of eighty-eight, and more clouds than yesterday. It's not much of an improvement, but we'll take it. Feeding Mindy, and checking her water, I find some Oreos in the cabinet and head to work, hoping there will be coffee in the break room. To my good fortune, there is. Sugar and caffeine, what else does a person need, right?

It's busier today and I'm grateful. Although the day goes by quickly with the shorter shifts, I'm hoping the hours will be bumped up soon. Five, four-hour shifts doesn't go very far-- pay wise.

After clocking out, I do a little shopping of my own, loading up bottled water and some basic food items. I also add paraffin, white cotton shoe strings and two medium-size heavy glass vases—about six inches tall--part of my surprise for Sarah.

Arriving home, I put away the stuff I've purchased and go looking for Mindy, needing to be sure she's gone to the bathroom before we head to the hospital. After checking the kitchen and living room, I walk down the hall and spot her outside through the sliding glass doors in the room to my left, playing in the back yard with the labs.

"How did she get outside?" I ask Jen as she passes by.

Stopping, then spotting Mindy she says, "She must be using the doggie door in our bedroom. Matt installed one through the wall last year," Then continues on.

"What a little brat," I think to myself. And all this time I've been letting her in and out the front door. She probably does it for attention, I conclude laughing inside. She's a smart little thing.

Later, we all load up in Matt's truck and drive down to the hospital.

Making conversation, from the back seat I ask, "So, I'm curious, If Eli was in the Navy, how did he end up in Aransas Pass?"

Matt answers, "I only know part of the story, but the short version is that he got out in 2009 when there was a naval base in Ingleside, just down the road."

"Really?" I respond, "I know Kiewit in Ingleside builds those oil rig platforms for drilling in the ocean floor, but I never knew we had a naval base close by too."

"Well, not anymore. The base closed in 2010 due to budget cuts. Eli saw the hand writing on the wall and decided to get out. If I remember right, he'd been in twenty-seven years—used to be a Master Chief."

"Any idea what type of ship he was on?"

Jen replies this time, "He served aboard a mine hunter. They clear mines from shipping channels, a lot of times in the middle east."

"Sounds dangerous," is my response.

"It is," Matt answers, "Their motto is, '*Iron men in wooden ships.*'"

"I don't understand Matt."

"Most of the mines they deal with, are magnetic and drawn towards a steel hull where they attach themselves, or get close by anyway, and then blow themselves up."

"Wow." I reply.

"So, the ships the Navy uses have either wooden hulls, or GRP hulls (glass reinforced plastic) to prevent that from happening. They locate these things, then disarm them or blow them up from a distance."

"Ok, I get it. They had to be fearless to deal with explosives and then use boats that wouldn't attract the magnetic mines; "Iron men in wooden ships,' Eli's even gutsier than I thought."

Jen adds, "He said he would rather do that, than the work he did before on a destroyer. He just couldn't handle the bombing they did off the coast of foreign countries."

"The whole killing civilians by accident thing," I add.

Matt responds, "Yep. Only now they euphemistically call it *'collateral damage.'* Eli knew it was war, and that these things could happen, but it became a thorn in his side (or his mind) that he just couldn't remove. He asked for a transfer and got it."

"No wonder snakes and alligators are no big deal to him," I exclaim.

Matt continues, "His biggest enemy is alcohol; it destroyed his marriage and his life. He's been sober for some time now, but once an alcoholic, always an alcoholic. I was worried when he had that beer at dinner, but he never got a chance to order a second. And I don't blame Mitch, there was no way for him to know."

"Thanks for telling me all that. I'll know in the future not to encourage him if there's alcohol around."

Pulling into the parking lot I spy Sarah's car close by, glad she's already here. Walking into the hospital the cold air assails me. Why is it always so cold in a hospital, anyway? Instead of complaining, I decide to enjoy it while it lasts. Especially since we have no AC at home still, for a few more days, anyway.

Matt quickly discovers Eli's room number at the

information desk, and we head up the elevator. Walking into his room I spot Sarah, along with a woman and two girls I've never seen before. They're sitting alongside his bed, with Eli holding hands with one of the kids. He looks exhausted, but happy.

Spotting us, Sarah stands up and introduces everyone--"Matt, Jen, Paul," nodding towards each of us in turn, "I'd like you to meet Shelby Samuels and her daughters; Amy who's nine and Lindsay who's seven. Shelby is Eli's daughter."

Stunned, Matt and Jen quickly gather their wits, then reach out to shake hands with her, trading hellos.

"And Paul," Eli shouts, "I'm gonna' kick your butt for what you and Sarah did," then softening his tone, "but then I'm gonna' give you a hug," he concludes with a tired smile.

"What did he and Sarah do?" Jen asks.

"They went online and found Shelby and the girls, then the family drove all the way down from Austin this morning to see me." Pride filling his voice. "I couldn't be happier," he says, looking at the kids.

Shelby jumps in, "I've been looking for dad ever since my mother passed away three years ago. I didn't know if he was still alive, or if he even wanted to see me again. I'm so glad Sarah and Paul went looking for me online, because I may have never found him on my own," beaming a great big smile at us.

"Well, now that your friends are here, the girls and I should be on our way. It's two-and-a-half hours back home, and we've got school tomorrow, don't we girls," she says looking down at them.

"Please . . . don't leave because of us," Matt replies.

"No, it's ok. We've been here since eleven this morning and the kids are hungry, anyway. I think the nurse kindly ignored us when she found out who we were. Following the visiting rules, they should have kicked us out a while ago."

Shelby takes Eli's hand in hers, and says, "You've got my number now, please call me once in a while. Remember, you're always welcome to come visit too. And if you can't get to us, we'll come down and see you, Dad."

"I'd like that—very much. Thanks for coming Shelby..." tears threatening to roll down those rugged cheeks.

"Just say that you won't be living on the street anymore, that you'll find a place to stay where we can be sure you're safe, maybe you can continue to stay with Matt and Jen here," eyes tearing up.

"No promises, but I'll try." Eli responds. "You've given me three good reasons to do that."

Shaking Matt and Jen's hands, she says, "Thanks for looking after Eli. I know he's in good hands with you two."

Shelby approaches Sarah, giving her a big hug, "And thanks again for reaching out to me yesterday."

"You're welcome," Sarah replies, "I'm just glad you could make it down, it was wonderful to meet you all. Goodbye girls," She adds, waving at the kids.

"Girls, tell grandpa goodbye. We need to go." Shelby states.

"Goodbye grandpa," they sing out in unison.

As they head for the door Eli calls out, "Goodbye ya'll, see you soon. Or maybe Skype if Jen will show me how."

Turning back around, Shelby says smiling, "We'd enjoy that."

After they're gone, Jen looks at Sarah and I, "So, was this your big secret? Seeing how happy Eli is, I think that was a wonderful thing to do. Well done."

Looking at Eli, Matt asks, "So, how are you getting along this morning?"

"I'm in a world of hurt Matt, this is worse than being married," Eli snickers, then grimaces as he holds his stomach, "But the meds they have here are top notch. They say I'll have to be here three or four days at least to be sure there's no more infection. That, and to be sure all the plumbin's working alright."

Opening her bag, Jen takes a couple of books out and lays them on Eli's hospital bed stand.

"Here's your latest Tom Clancy novel and your bible, I thought you might want them."

"Thanks Jen, I'm glad you brought something to read. I've got a TV in here, but the last time I watched, it's all geared for young people. And it's been a long time since I believed anything those idiots on the news have to say."

Chuckling at his last remark, Matt says, "Well, it's wonderful that you've reconnected with your daughter, Eli. She seemed happy to see you."

"I really never thought she'd want to have anything to do with me, ever again. Her mother and I had some ugly fights when I got drunk. Shelby would stick up for her, and I don't blame anyone but me. So, when she came in to see me, the first thing she wanted to know was . . . was I really sober like Sarah said. I could honestly look her in the eye and say yes. She started crying then, came over and hugged me. My sewed-up belly hurt bad when she did, but I wanted the hug more."

Matt holds out his hands, taking Jen's and Sarah's in his. "I think we should give thanks for Eli's successful surgery, and the reuniting of him with his family."

I take Sarah's hand and we all bow as Matt gives a wonderful prayer of gratitude, one of which I could heartily agree with. It struck me that some of the things he gave thanks for, were some of the things he prayed about recently. Coincidence . . . I'm sure it's just a coincidence, well maybe. We all talk for another half an hour, and then when Eli starts to nod off, we sneak out of the room.

Going down in the elevator, Matt offers, "I'm hungry, and we're not too far from Luby's. Does anyone want to join me?"

He gets two 'amens', and a "hell yeah!" Looking at me he rebukes, "No desert for you kid," in his best Eli imitation. Everyone laughs, including me. Once outside, Sarah gets in her car and heads for the Luby's Greenwood location, we follow behind in the truck.

Talking over lunch, it turns out it'll be a busy week for us all. Matt and Jen will go back to work; whether it's cleaning up or reopening the business. Sarah has classes but is sad that any of them that were in Port A, will now be moved to the main campus in Corpus Christi. I'm working twenty hours and will be begging for more. All in all, we conclude this is like no other Labor Day we've ever had before. And I hope there'll never be another one like it again, all except for the time I've spent with Sarah, but I keep that little tidbit to myself.

Arriving at the house in late afternoon, I check my schedule for tomorrow, and then see what's going on with my friends on Facebook and Snapchat. Clearing out text messages is next as I sit on my bed and pet Mindy, who's crawled up next to me by this time and gone to sleep. It's warm and humid so I turn on the fan for a bit. Looking at her closely, I notice some faint spots all over her. Checking out what this might mean on internet, it turns out to be what most people would refer to as a 'Dapple.' A few of the spots in the pictures are dark and striking, others light like hers. But it turns out it's nothing to worry about; it just means she's different. To me, it makes her even cuter.

Later, Jen, Matt and I have sandwiches and chips for dinner, with large ice waters; I've grown to love ice water lately. Afterwards, they let me know they're going to be using the shower outdoors. I stay inside out of respect because the shower curtain, which can sometimes blow around in the wind, reveals a little more than you want to. Besides, it's still hot and humid. It's not much better inside, but it's still better.

Closing out the evening, we play another round of monopoly by candle light. It was fun, and I actually won this time. But it just wasn't the same without Sarah. I hope to see her soon.

Chapter 29

Tuesday, September 5th, 2017

Driving into work, the mosquitos initially buzz me since I forgot my spray this morning, but fortunately they have trouble keeping up with the jeep. Sadly, I notice the trash piles have grown substantially in the front yards I pass by; some are now five to six feet tall. It's a tragedy to see so much going to waste, so much that'll never be used again. The water in the ditches alongside the road is now down halfway--a good thing. Passing several utility trucks on 1069, my heart leaps because it means they're getting closer to our house. Has it been eleven days now without power? Yeah, it has, and I decide it can't come back soon enough. The rain barrels are empty as of this morning, with no more precip' in the forecast, so I need to bring lots of water home this afternoon, just in case. Looking up into the sky (I have no roof, remember) it's a beautiful, although hot sunny day. The winds are out of the East this morning, which means high humidity as the moisture flows in off the gulf. See, I did pay attention in Science class. And as I drive through town, I see both my gym and the coffee shop have people working to get them reopened. As a matter of fact, I see several of the people I know from the CBC inside, and a hand painted sign out front stating, "Reopening Friday." Happy, it makes me very happy.

Work goes well, but it's slow, being the day after

a holiday. I volunteer to clean, mop, restock, 'front' the shelves—you name it. My name becomes 'gopher' again, which is ok; anything to get hours. After I get off, I buy several gallons of water, and load up. Having saved another cookie from the break room, I find 'one legged Willie' with his merry band of misfits and crumble up their treat. If there's one thing I know for sure, whatever you feed gulls will be gone before you can count to ten. And yes, I know I'm encouraging them to hang around and poop on cars, but I just can't help it where Willie's concerned. Like Mindy, I just feel a certain responsibility to take care of them, even if its self-imposed.

Arriving home, I see Jen's already here. Walking in with gallons of water, she takes them from me, admonishing me for not going easier on my bad shoulder.

"I think it's healing well, Jen," defending myself. "It mainly bothers me at night, although I don't understand why. The worst news, is that a friend of mine at work said it may be six months before it's completely healed. I hope it's not that long."

"That's how long it took for Matt a couple of years ago. Just don't lift a lot of heavy things and try to do simple stretches to keep it from becoming limited in how far you can move it around. Matt lost 40% mobility before he saw a doctor and began to work on it. If you're not sure what to do, I'll have him show you some exercises that he used."

"Thanks Jen. There's more water out there, I'll be right back."

"I'll help—whatever's left we'll get together." Jen replies walking out with me.

We retrieve the last of the groceries, and then I re-tarp the jeep. Going inside, I fill a glass with ice from the cooler and make myself some tea. Sitting down at the table I watch Jen reorganize the pantry, adding the food I brought home.

"Jen, can I ask you a question?"

"Anything."

"I'm not sure how to tell you this, you might even think it's crazy. But I had a dream I just can't shake, and Matt seems to think you have some kind of 'psychic' ability."

Grabbing a glass and making some iced tea for herself, laughing she sits at the table facing me. "I'm not psychic Paul, but there are times I feel the Lord leading me in certain directions. I don't know if I can help, but I'm happy to listen."

I take some time to describe in detail what I saw, and how vivid it was to me. The bright colors, the sureness I felt that this was my folks, and the possibility of my sister being there too. The strangeness at being at Six Flags in front of a ride, and the golden rope separating me from them.

She closes her eyes and looks down at the table; as if in prayer. Then looking up, she begins by saying, "First of all, there is a passage Paul, in the 2nd chapter of the book of Acts that tells us, in the last days that young men will see visions."

"But I'm not a Christian, how could I see a vision?"

"There's more than one story in the Bible where unbelievers have had visions and then needed them explained by someone of God. King Nebuchadnezzar is one that comes to mind."

"Ok, well, what do *you* think it means?"

"Were your parent's Christians?"

"Yes, but my sister died very young, so she couldn't have been one."

Meditating on what I've said, Jen then replies, "From what you describe, I think it's possible God allowed you to see your mom and dad, showing you as they are now; young and very much alive in Heaven. Your sister too. The rope separating you all is the symbolic boundary between you and heaven; close enough to see, yet somewhere you can't go. The park represents a place of happiness and joy for you, a small preview of what you may one day find."

Thinking about what she's said, I then ask, "But how is it possible my sister is there too?"

Jen responds, "I personally believe that babies and young children who die are instantly in Heaven with the Lord, because they never had the option to choose to follow the Lord for themselves. Once everyone reaches the age where they can understand right from wrong, they can then make their own decision."

"What about me then? I'm still not sure what to believe."

"Paul, everyone must come to their own conclusion. God has given us all free will, so it's up to you at this point. And I can sense your anger at God is waning, bringing me hope you'll decide to follow Him one day soon. The last thing I want to see, is something unexpected happening to you, and you ending up in hell."

Laughing, "Then I'll wind up in a big party with all of my friends."

"No." Jen says sternly, "No you won't. Hell is a place of darkness where you'll spend eternity alone. If you want to read it for yourself, start with the first chapter of Jude. There are many scriptures that back this up. Jesus spoke of hell more than any other person in the bible. God wants you to choose Him, but it's totally up to you."

No longer laughing, I respond, "Wow, so serious."

"I've never been more serious in my life," Jen counters.

Taken aback, I'm not sure how to respond.

Toning it down a bit, Jen adds, "Paul, we all come to the same point in our lives. Is the bible a bunch of fairy tales, or is it really the word of God? Is Jesus the personal savior we can turn to, or a lunatic from two thousand years ago?"

At the risk of angering Jen, I respond, "I just don't care that much for religion, especially pushy preachers."

Smiling at me Jen says, "So, how does it feel to have something in common with Jesus?"

Surprised, I respond, "What are you talking about?"

"Jesus frequently challenged the religious people of the day, at one point calling them snakes and vipers. It was these same people who demanded that Jesus be put to death." Pausing, "Look, Paul, when you dial it down, all the other religions of the world give you a list of do's and don'ts to get into heaven. True biblical Christianity tells us there's nothing you can do to get there on your own, except trust in, and accept the one who earned your place in heaven for you."

Trying to let it all sink in, I ask, "So, you're telling me if I become a follower of Jesus, I will one day see my mom, dad, and sister?"

"That, and you'd have the peace of knowing your sins were forgiven, and the guidance of the Holy Spirit who would come to help you in your daily life, just like me, Matt and Sarah do. Oh, and Eli too."

"I'm just not sure I want to give up being the captain of my own ship. There's still so much fun I don't won't to miss out on."

"I can't speak for you Paul, but giving control of my life to Jesus, has brought me more happiness than I ever had before I accepted Christ. And opened more doors to experiences, well, than I ever knew was possible. But like I said, it's your call."

"Let me think on it some more Jen. I may not always like what you say, but I know you and Matt are always straight with me. I've never known Christians like you all, you're different."

"I'll take that as a compliment." Changing gears, she asks, "After we get through with the tea, can I get your help feeding the horses?"

"Happy to, Jen," I reply. Going over her comments in my head, what she's said makes some sense to me, and I'm beginning to understand a little. I'll just have to keep looking for answers and go from there. Someone at work once told me, the more information you have, the more obvious the solution becomes, or in this case, decision. Why does this thought of being a Christian scare me so much? I need to figure that out.

Walking out into the afternoon sunshine, I ask Jen, "Any news on Eli?"

"Yeah, I spoke to him this morning before I went to work, he's feeling a little better. He said that he might be released as early as Thursday."

"I can only imagine how anxious he is to get out of there, knowing how much he hates being cooped up in a little room." I reply. "I'm assuming he's coming back here to stay for a while?"

"I'm sure he is Paul, since he really has no place else to go. Oh, and I just remembered, Matt says they have work for you down at the lumber store if you're interested. Some employees are not coming back, and he could use a part-time person."

"Any idea what kind of job?" I ask.

"I'm not sure, but Matt should be home by five, you can ask him then."

"Thanks Jen, you all have been very kind to me. I'm not sure how I can ever repay you."

Grabbing some feed out of the garage we proceed to the corral. Once the horses spot us they head our direction at a fast trot. Dividing up the pellets into separate pails, and setting them on the ground, they begin to feed. The ponds in the yard created by the storm still contain enough water to take care of their needs, so we don't have to fill their one-hundred-gallon black plastic trough. I'm glad to, because until the powers back, and the well pump is running, filling that thing would be a major hassle.

Walking back to the house, I ask Jen, "Do you have a double boiler?"

Looking at me strangely she replies, "Yes, why?"

"I've been researching how to make candles on the internet, and they say the best way to melt paraffin is with a double boiler."

With a grin on her face, Jen says, "This is a side of you I didn't know was there Paul. If you want to make some candles, I can give you a hand— I've made some before. Do you have all your materials?"

"I think so, I've got the glass containers, wax and some cotton shoe strings for wicks."

"I'll give you some real wicks I have; the shoe strings are ok, but the wicks I have will work better."

I grab my bag of stuff from the bedroom and Jen retrieves the pots from the kitchen. Meeting back outside, we set up the double boiler on the Coleman stove. It's hot outside on the porch, despite being under cover, but I really want to get this done. Pouring water in the bottom half, and putting the blocks of paraffin in the top, I light the stove and we sit down for a few.

"What are the shells for? To put inside the candle?" Jen asks.

"Yeah, Sarah and I picked these up on the beach the other day, and I thought I'd make a couple of candles with them."

"Sounds nice. I suspect you might be giving one of them to Sarah then?" Jen says, trying to hide a grin.

"I was thinking about it," attempting to be evasive.

"Ok, let me give you some help. For starters, when you pour the wax in, just go up an inch or so, and then place the shells along the side of the glass facing out, to make them easy to see. Most people pour the shells in and you never see them in the middle of the candle. And I can help with the placement of the wick too." An hour later we have two beautiful candles made, cooling off on the table.

"So, you've made a bunch of these I bet. Is that

what we've been using at night?" I ask Jen.

"Yes, that and I like to make special ones at Christmas for friends and family, plus a few more to sell. For me, it's a lot of fun."

"Well, thanks for your help Jen, they turned out great."

"You're welcome Paul."

As we're putting everything away, Matt pulls up in his truck. "Afternoon everyone, how are things around here?" Matt calls out.

"Great," Jen replies, "We were just making a surprise for Sarah," Jen responds with glee in her voice.

"Thanks Jen, thanks a lot!" mildly irritated for giving me away.

Laughing, she says, "It's ok Paul, Matt and I both know how much you like Sarah. Your secret isn't as big as you think it is."

Choosing to spare my dignity Matt says, "Good news, I stopped and talked to a lineman a few streets down and he told me they hope to be on Armstrong road Thursday sometime."

"Oh, thank God," Jen replies.

"That would be awesome!" I add.

"And the word on the ferries is that they've opened them up to everyone as of today, not just emergency responders and government officials. So, we can drive over this weekend and see how Port Aransas is fairing if we want."

We all walk inside the house as I consider what Matt's just said. I don't know if I can wait until Saturday, I may drive over there tomorrow after work, especially since once I arrive at the store, I'm half way to the ferry already.

The evening passes slowly; Matt works on his bible study notes for tomorrow night, Jen starts dinner outdoors on the Coleman stove, and I wash a few things in the bathtub for work. I find myself thinking about all that has happened since Hurricane Harvey, and how life has changed. Oh, sure things will get back to a somewhat normal eventually, but it's going to be weeks or months. Some homes and businesses will be repaired or rebuilt, jobs will come back, or new one's will spring up in their places. It's not so much of a getting back to normal I realize, as it will be creating a new life out of what's left, the proverbial Phoenix out of the ashes. The weather forecast is decent for the next few days, so there's no rush to get a roof on my jeep, but I need to get it done anyway. Maybe I can find a used one on an app or even a website like eBay.

I hear whimpering to my left, and I look over the side of the tub where I'm washing clothes, to find Mindy staring back at me, long floppy ears and all.

Laying my wash down, I pick her up with wet hands and ask, "Do you want a treat?" A tail wag is my answer, so we head off to my bedroom and find the stash. It couldn't hurt to let the clothes soak for a bit, I tell myself, besides, I need to get more water to rinse them anyway. Mindy goes off with her reward and I walk into the kitchen to find Jen setting the table. I ask, "Is there anything I can do Jen?"

"Sure, grab some glasses and fill them up with ice from the chest. We're almost ready to eat."

Completing my task, we all sit down at the table and begin by passing the pitcher of tea. Matt offers thanks for our food, and asks for continued healing, not only for Eli, but our State as well. Houston took a tremendous pounding not too long ago and is hurting just like we are. And we can't forget all the cities in between.

During the meal Matt asks me if I would like to work part time at his lumber store, to which I instantly agree. He gives me the details, which is basically that I'd be helping where needed until things got back to a normal operation. Work is work, and I'm glad to have it. Then, Jen mentions my dream to him, and he concurs with Jen's assessment. I'm a little embarrassed to have it be a dinner topic, but they act like this is not anything unusual, having a dream or vision and all. Not that it happens to people all the time, but that supernatural things do occur, and we tend to treat it as nothing. All I know is, I'm very happy that they were willing to take in a loud-mouthed, fire breathing agnostic when the storm came, and nice enough to put up with me for a while. After dinner, just as I'm finishing up washing my clothes, Sarah calls. With almost no juice left on my phone, I grab the mosquito spray and head to the jeep where I can plug it in to the charging cord and chat with her.

"Okay, there, now I can talk to you without fear of it shutting down on me. So how are you Sarah?"

"I'm good Paul, and you?"

"No complaints, besides the mosquitos of course. I see on the forecast we've got some winds coming out of the northeast tomorrow, and you know what that means," I tell her somewhat excitedly.

"Cooler, dryer air mainly, a beautiful day in store," she replies.

"Exactly," I answer back.

Then Sarah says, "Well, besides just wanting to

catch up, I thought I'd let you know I won't be able to make it to the bible study tomorrow night, but I would like to invite you to join me on Thursday evening, if you don't have anything else to do."

"The answer is yes, and all you have to do is tell me when and where."

A soft laugh at my instant receptibility is followed by, "There's something we do in Port Aransas on the night of a full moon. I found out about it from some people I work with at the ARK."

"Please don't tell me it involves howling," my poor attempt at humor.

"No silly, but it does involve beaches and cookies."

"Sounds fun Sarah, please go on."

"Normally we would go out to beach marker 25 along the water on the full moon, which is actually *tomorrow* night, and eat cookies as it rises up over the waves. I know it sounds corny, but we enjoy it."

"Ok, but why on Thursday now?" I ask.

"Because Port A is still under a curfew, and several of us are busy tomorrow night anyway, so we're moving it to Thursday to the beach out near Bob Hall Pier (considered to be part of Corpus Christi—no curfew). There will still be a full moon, and it should rise about 8:55 pm. So, if you don't mind staying up a little late, I'd like for you to join me."

I'm laughing inside, because just two weeks ago, that used to be early for me. Now, it's past my new *normal* bedtime. "I'd love to Sarah, what kind of cookies would you like for me to bring?"

"Surprise me," -- I can hear the smile in her voice.

We talk for a good hour and a half. It's getting dark as I unplug my half-way charged phone and go inside to find everyone's gone to bed. A single candle is left for me on the kitchen table and I use that to light my way back to my bedroom and get undressed. Turning the fan on, I push Mindy over a little way on the bed and lie down next to her. She grumbles a bit for having been moved, so I tell her, "It won't kill you to give up some room bed-hog." She grumbles again and goes back to sleep. Blowing out the candle I lay in the dark for some time, thinking about my day. A little chime alerts me to a text message has just come in. I look to see who it's from, and it's Sarah. She just found out Tony Amos passed away yesterday in a San Antonio Hospital. A sad day for the ARK, a sad day for us all.

Chapter 30

Wednesday, September 6th, 2017

The screech of the hawk wakes me for the second day in a row. Sitting up in bed I can immediately tell that the weather has changed; it's cooler and drier. The front must be coming through. Halleluiah! Maybe there is a God after all. The moment that thought crosses my mind I feel wrong for thinking it. As if I've been wrong all along about Him not being there. Were I to really think it through, I'd have to admit He's taken pretty good care of me, especially since it was *my* decision to stay in Aransas Pass when the Hurricane hit. It's a good thing the temperature has come down too because the fan died in the middle of the night, and I've already used up my spare batteries. Good news; my shoulder is feeling better, as long as I don't roll over on it in the middle of the night, and I'm able to use that arm almost normally now. I'm feeling good this morning.

"Come on sleepy head," I tell Mindy as I help her down onto the floor, wondering how much longer she'll need that little cast on. I'll have to ask Jen.

No one's up yet so I decide to fix the coffee myself. Grabbing the percolator, filling it with water, then coffee, I find some matches and head outside. Checking my phone, the temp is in the seventies, and much drier. When you're used to the eighties and nineties, seventies can feel almost cold. I'm loving it!

Before long there's bubbling going on in the little glass top, and the aroma is enticing. Once it's done, I grab the pot and go back in.

Sitting at the table with a cup of brew in my hands, I greet Matt and Jen, along with the labs entering the kitchen. "Good morning everyone, Isn't it a beautiful day?"

They mumble something polite back, and head straight for the coffee mugs, obviously in need of a caffeine fix. Together we fix a simple breakfast, and I prepare to drive into work. Giving Mindy a friendly pet on the head, I walk out the door, remove the jeep's tarp and drive towards the gate.

Have you ever had a premonition? A feeling like something is about to happen? But you're just not sure what to make of it? As I close the gate behind me, this sense of dread comes over me. I pull on to Armstrong road and turn left onto 1069. There are streets and homes on the left as I head towards town, and mostly large empty fields to the right, often times with cattle and flocks of birds in ponds. It's a great morning, so I don't know why I'm feeling on edge. Looking in the rear-view mirror I see a pickup coming up behind me fast, but I'm already five miles over the speed limit, so he'll just have to go around. To my right I see a flock of white cattle-egrets take flight, heading towards the road in front of me. For some reason, they dive down low, crossing directly into my path. Instantly I jam on the brakes, not worried about hitting just one—very worried about hitting fifteen or twenty all at the same time. The truck behind me has to swerve into the oncoming lane to avoid rear ending me, and then after he passes me, corrects back into my lane just in time to hit a feral hog that has run into the roadway—a plume of steam exploding skyward. Judging by the severity of the impact, he must be a big boy, they can weigh over a hundred and seventy-five pounds around here. I hit the brakes again, as the truck loses control and veers to the left into oncoming traffic. A dump truck, who can't stop in time, runs headlong into it; a horrible crunching sound filling the air. My adrenaline is running rampant as I pull over and park on the shoulder. Trying to steady my shaking hands, I take out my phone and dial 911. Talking to the woman on the line is like being in a dream; I barely know what I'm saying as I attempt to answer her questions, my mind reeling. She tells me to stay on the line while she dispatches emergency vehicles as I fumble about trying to unhook my seat belt. I've got to go see if the pickup driver's ok. Holding the phone to my ear, I walk slowly towards the wreck and around what's left of the slaughtered pig. There's blood everywhere. The driver of the dump truck is out and standing next to the wrecked pickup, lines of cars forming up behind us in both directions. Between striking the animal and then the dump truck, the truck's cab is mangled up. I stop thirty feet away, because from here, I can see blood splatter around the shattered windows. Something inside tells me he's dead because a second later I watch the dump truck driver turn around and retch into the drainage ditch beside him. Making the decision I don't want to see any more, I walk slowly back to the jeep and climb inside. Shaking, I hear the sirens in the distance, and moments later, they're here. My phone rings, I must have hung up on 911 by accident because she's calling back. Telling her all that I know, I hang up and just sit there for a while, watching the first responders go to work.

That could have been me, I think as I watch the firemen minutes later place a large blue tarp over the front of the vehicle. You always know someone has died when they do that. The dump truck driver is sitting on the side of the road, head down, giving a patrolman the details. Another officer walks my way and asks me if I saw anything. I tell him what I witnessed, and he gives me his card. As he's about to leave I ask, "He didn't make it, did he."

"No, and it's going to be awhile before we can get him out. It's definitely going to be a closed casket funeral." With that, he turns and walks away.

Again, it crosses my mind—*that could have been me.* If it hadn't been for that flock of birds, swooping down in front of me, I wouldn't have hit the brakes. It could have been me hitting the hog, and then the dump-truck. It could have been me they're going to have to pry out. I can hear Jen now, "Paul, that wasn't luck, that was a miracle."

Looking up into a blue sky, I say out loud, "God, if that was you, thank you."

Driving (rattled) at half the speed limit the rest of the way into work, I arrive at the store thirty minutes late. Seeing the look on my face and hearing my story, Alex obviously believes me, because he tells me to sit in the break room for a while, and when I feel up to it, clock in and come on up to the registers. Maybe I should just go home. No, I need the income too much. For the rest of my shift, all I can think about is what I saw, and how I could be dead right now. Before this, death didn't mean much. I guess I've numbed myself to the concept, because my parents died, my sister too. I also killed something or someone several times an hour in video games. So, like, big deal, right? Not anymore. Being around Matt, Jen, Sarah and Eli, has filled me with a different way of looking at my existence. Have I crossed paths with them for a reason? For the first time in my life I know for certain, that I want to live for more than the next wave to surf on, the next Xbox game to come out, the next edition of an iPhone to hit the market. If I died now, what would I leave behind? And, more importantly, if everyone is right, where would I have ended up? A good place, or a bad one?

"Are you alright Paul?" Mrs. Henry's question brings me back to reality.

"Sure, why?" I respond as I continue to scan her food.

"You seem distracted this morning."

Stopping to total her bill, I respond, "I saw a really bad accident this morning on 1069. I can't get it out of my mind."

"I heard about that on the radio. Poor man, and he was only twenty-two. So much life left, a pity."

Now I really can't stop thinking about it, he was my age. This is almost creepy. Like some dark force wanted me to be dead. No, that's being paranoid, right?

"Thanks Mrs. Henry, you have a nice day."

"You too Paul, and God bless you."

It hits me as I mumble to myself, 'I think He already has.' And then I realize this isn't the first time this has crossed my mind recently.

It's only noon when I punch out for the day, the sun high in the sky, broken clouds moving from north to south. The best part, is that I'm not sweating right now, the dry front is coming through. Finding the cookie I wrapped in a paper towel earlier, I pull it out of my pocket and crumble it in my hand as I approach one legged Willie and his band of pirates. Seeing me, he flies closer and is rewarded with the first crumbs that hit the pavement, his friends flocking to his side. Feeling like I've done my good deed for the day, I walk to the jeep, remove the tarp and sit there for the moment. I really don't feel like going home just yet, too much on my mind. Remembering I'm only a few minutes from the ferry, I pull out of the parking lot and drive due east. I would like to see Port Aransas even if everything is torn up. I guess I just need a distraction. Arriving at the landing, the line of cars waiting to cross is short, and I'm on a boat within minutes. Normally I would just sit inside the jeep for the three-minute ride across the channel, but today I stand at the rail, and am rewarded with a pod of dolphins swimming nearby. The water is a beautiful greenish blue, the ride ending way too soon.

Pulling out and onto the landing I can see from here that the big red pirate ship that's normally docked at Fins Grill and Ice House is missing. I hope it wasn't destroyed in the storm. It's a really cool boat designed to take families out for a spin in the channel where a cast of characters put on a pirate show. And then as I pass Fins I spot people working inside to get it back up and running again. I can't wait, I really like their food. Turning right onto Cutoff Road I pass Juan's, my favorite place for Mexican food. It's one of those places where the owner comes by your table just to say hi, and chat. It's closed too, but there are people cleaning up inside there as well. The businesses I pass are either destroyed or in the process of being cleaned up, large piles of debris out in front of each one. The street curves to the left, and within minutes I'm on the beach, looking out into the Gulf of Mexico. The view of the water and sand bring a certain serenity. Gulls, terns and sand pipers scour the beach and incoming waves, combing it for tidbits of food. The sound of the water sooths the anguish I feel for the man killed in the truck today, as I count myself fortunate to be alive. The sun is baking me, and I should be putting on sunscreen, but right now I just don't care. Turning the engine off, I climb out and walk down to the water's edge for a while, taking it all in, trying to forget the scene this morning. It helps, and I'm thankful for it. On a positive note, I can't help but think that somewhere along this coastline, buried treasure may have been exposed by the hurricane. I guess it's just wishful thinking, but it is true there were pirates and shipwrecks here at one time. And coins have been found. A boyish smile crosses my lips as I find myself watching the sand for something other than shells—it's fun, even if I don't find anything. After a while, I turn around and walk back towards the jeep. Climbing aboard, I drive back towards the ferry landing and get in line for the return to Aransas Pass. It's not long before I'm crossing back over, this time rewarded with two pods of dolphins off the port bow; a good day for sightseeing. Driving down the road along Redfish Bay I see shrimp boats to my right steaming out to the gulf. It brings a smile to my face that some things are back as they were.

Passing my work place, I drive through town and then onto Wheeler. There are still lots of service vehicles everywhere, and church buses from all over the state here to help. I tend to forget, some people are not as fortunate as I; having a place to sleep, something to eat, and a job. Despite all that's happened, I feel fortunate. As Jen would say, blessed. I guess I should too.

It's mid-afternoon when I arrive back at the house. Feeling tired I decide to lay down on my bed for just a few minutes, Mindy eager to cuddle up next to me. I must have been exhausted because I wake up to voices in the living room and realize it's late afternoon as Matt's leading the bible study. Oh yeah, it's Wednesday. Climbing out of bed and combing my hair, I walk out of the bedroom. There, to my surprise I see Mindy already in the lap of one of the guests— 'traitor', I think to myself. But I can't help smiling.

Seeing me walk in, Matt introduces me to those who weren't here last week. There's nine people this time, pretty much the crowd that I used to see at the coffee shop. Finding stuff to make sandwiches in the kitchen, I prepare one for myself. Grabbing the last chair left at the kitchen table I bring it over and join the group. Listening to Matt while chowing down, I discover he's in the book of Acts, talking about the conversion of Saul of Tarsus on the road to Damascus. I knew he became Paul, but I didn't know he was killing some Christians and having others imprisoned for their beliefs before he "saw the light." And I thought *I* was hard on Christians. Sitting there, I begin to feel a warmth come over me, almost a tingling sensation. A nudge telling me to share my story of what happened this morning on my way to work. The feeling grows, so when Matt opens the floor up for comments or questions, I raise my hand.

Seeing surprise in Matt's eyes, looking at me he

says, "What would you like to share Paul?"

Stumbling over my words at first, I describe everything; from the feeling something bad was about to happen when I left for work, the flock of egrets crossing my path, and then the horrible wreck in front of me—shuddering at the thought of what I saw. The words begin to flow, and I work hard to hold back the tears, I guess it's finally hitting me that someone my age died today, never to breathe again. And it could have been me.

"So, Paul, what does all this mean to you?" Matt asks.

Pensively, I respond, "I guess for the first time in my life, I realize there's more to living than surfing and playing games on my Xbox." People chuckling at me, nodding in agreement. Looking around at everyone, I add, "I know this may sound strange, but I want what you all seem to have, a peace you seem to carry with you, even when things aren't so good."

"We know exactly what you mean Paul," Jen answers for everyone. "It's a simple step if you think you're ready."

Matt looks at me with a serious expression, and says, "I'm happy Paul that you think you've decided, but I want to be sure; not trying to discourage you or anything."

Somewhat taken aback, because I assumed this is what all Christians want you to do, I ask, "What do you mean?"

"It hasn't been that long since you came into the coffee shop and confronted me, wanting to know where God was when your parents died. Now two weeks later you're ready to commit your life to that same God," Matt challenges.

Pausing to take it all in, I sense everyone is on the edge of their seats. It's so quiet, you can hear little Mindy snoring in the lap next to me. Looking him straight in the eye, I reply, "I'm not sure how to explain it Matt, but I feel something inside pulling me in this direction. Yeah, I was very angry when I yelled at you. I pretty much hated Christians then. But in the last two weeks, you, Jen and others have showed me so much kindness and love, I realized I might be wrong, well, that I am wrong. I still don't know why my parents died on that highway the way they did, but I've come to realize everyone dies, eventually. Like that guy did this morning on 1069. And it scares me. I don't want to die and miss the chance of seeing my parents once more, my sister too. I want what you have, a faith that says I'll be reunited with them one day."

Easing up on me a bit, but still somewhat stern, Matt replies, "Before you make this decision, you need to recognize it might be you one day that someone yells at, wanting to know why the world is so screwed up, and where is God in all this."

"I get what you're trying to say Matt, all I know is I'm ready to give it a chance. I need some real peace in my life. I think I've changed since the Hurricane."

Matt and Jen get up and walk over to me, placing their hands on my shoulders as a show of support. I think I see a tear in Jen's eye. "Repeat after me Paul, aloud or in your heart, either one is alright." He begins quietly, "Father, I have sinned against you, missed the mark as they say, and am ready to accept your love and forgiveness. I ask that you forgive me, wash away my transgressions and anger towards you as I'm now ready to follow you and 'The Way'. I accept Jesus and the sacrifice He made on the cross, his death for my sins, and I ask that you fill me with the Holy Spirit. In Jesus name, amen." Pausing for a moment, Matt asks me, "Did you pray along with me Paul?"

Looking up at Matt I respond, "Yes, yes I did."

There are several "amens" and "Thank you Lords" coming from the group. Looking at the faces, I see more than one person with moist eyes. It takes a moment to realize how happy they are for me.

"Paul, welcome to the family, these people here are all now your brothers and sisters in Christ," Matt says smiling.

Then he seems to get serious again and bows his head, saying, "Let us pray. Father, we thank you for Paul and ask that you guide him in the days ahead, protect him from Satan who by now must be very angry, that he no longer has control of our new brother. Wrap your arms around him Lord and keep Satan and his demons away; keep Paul safe Father, in Jesus name, amen."

What happens next takes me by surprise, Matt leads me to stand up and all the others around the coffee table stand as well. They each hug me in turn, and I can't help feeling embarrassed, but it feels good all the same. And a lightness comes over me, as if I'd taken off a backpack from one of my camping trips or put-on brand-new tennis shoes, feeling like I could run forever. It's as if a weight has been lifted from my shoulders—I don't know how else to explain it.

Sensing it's a time of celebration Jen goes to the kitchen and returns with carrot cake, a knife and some paper plates. Just as she's setting it all down on the coffee table, the light overhead blinks on, then off. Seconds later it comes back and then stays on. I hear the fan from the air conditioner running, but it's drowned out by the shouts of "Yes, Finally, and Thank you Lord!"

Jen walks over to the refrigerator, opens it up—the light on, a big grin on her face. The sink is next, where she turns on the faucet and after a few seconds, a trickle of water emerges. Returning to the living room, she finds that Matt's already cut the cake, and is serving everyone. Twelve days? I think it's been twelve days without power, and I do NOT want to go through that again. Eating my cake, I glance around and watch all the happy, chatting people, thinking how fortunate I've been to have met them only a short time ago. The world as I know it has changed since the last week of August. Some for the better, some for the worse, but I decide I wouldn't trade the last few days for anything.

Chapter 31

Thursday, September 7th, 2017

Sleeping well last night was due to an air conditioning system that put out some really cold air; I needed a light blanket for the first time in a while. Wanting to stay in bed, I force myself to turn off my phone alarm and swing my feet out over the side and onto the floor, leaving Mindy behind under the covers. Reaching toward the bathroom light switch I turn it on and off just to see if the power is still there. It is, of course, but I just had to be sure. Smiling, I flush the toilet, happy to hear water refilling the tank all by itself. Such a simple thing, yet how we take it completely for granted.

Walking into the kitchen I notice that not only is it nice and cool, it's dry too. With the AC working, we won't have to deal with the seventy percent plus humidity anymore, at least not until we walk out the front door. Jen is already up and pouring herself a cup of coffee from the carafe sitting on the kitchen counter, using the electric coffee maker, instead of the percolator. Sadly, I find myself missing it; I kind of enjoyed watching the coffee bubble up in the glass top while it 'percolated' and it tasted so good.

"Morning Paul, how did you sleep?" Jen asks.

"It was almost too cold . . . I loved it," I reply with a smile.

"Yeah, it's great to have the AC back. Good

news, we should be able to bring Eli home from the hospital today. We visited him yesterday afternoon, and he's healing well. Actually," she says with a smile, "I think the hospital wants him out almost as he wants to be."

"I can only imagine." I respond. "If he would rather live on the streets than in a house, I have no clue how much being the hospital is affecting him. It can't be good. For him or the nurses," I add laughing.

"So, how's the clinic?" I ask as I sit down at the table with my own cup of joe.

"Good, really good. We've been partially open this week, and Monday we go back to regular hours."

"How's *your* job going?" She replies, looking my way.

"Same, but I'm glad I'll be working for the lumber company when I'm not at my regular job. It looks like it will be awhile before its back the way it used to be. Matt told me I can start for him on Monday."

"Good for you. And Sarah?" She adds with a wink and a smile.

Somewhat embarrassed, (why am I embarrassed around Jen?) I say, "We have an informal date tonight, I'm meeting her and her friends at the beach in Corpus to watch the moonrise."

I instantly regret saying anything because she replies, "Sounds romantic. Don't forget to take her candle," a big grin on her face.

Picking up on my feelings, she changes the subject, "So with the power back on, would you buy some things at your store before you leave, we need to fill the refrigerator back up."

Taking the list she hands me, I glance it over and reply, "Of course."

Checking my cell phone for messages, I realize I need to find my wall charger and plug it in. It's almost dead again, and although I can still use the charger in the jeep, I no longer have to. Scrolling through the texts, I see one from Sarah. "Looking forward to tonight, and Jen says you have some kind of big announcement for me. See you at eight near Bob Hall pier, look for a fire pit, 'smiley face.'"

Texting her back, "I'm looking forward to seeing you too. And I'll be bringing you a little surprise along with the news."

Work goes well, so much so they ask me to stay two extra hours— a total of six today. With my lunch added in, I don't get off until three now, but that's fine, I'm just glad to be employed and I'll take all the hours I can get. It's funny, before all this, I would've been mad to be asked to stay longer at work; wanting to get to the gym, or to my Xbox instead. Not anymore. At lunch I see that one of the 'garage sale' apps has a soft top that would fit my jeep for sale in Corpus Christi. It must be old or something because they're not asking much. After thinking on it for a minute (realizing beggars can't be choosers) I respond back that I'll take it and pick it up this evening on my way to meet Jen. Checking my bank app, I look to be sure I've got the funds, and fortunately I do.

Clocking out, I shop for the groceries Jen requested, adding in a few things of my own. Batteries are at the top of my list just in case power goes out again. I vow to be better prepared for future emergencies-- whatever they might be. As a matter of fact, we do have tornadoes come through once in a great while, but nothing like other parts of the country. Driving home I spot a familiar couple and their baby walking by the side of the road, carrying grocery bags. Pulling over in front of them, I stop and invite them to climb aboard.

"It's Kyle and Linda, right?" I query as they get in, groceries, baby and all.

"Kyle and Lisa. But you were close," Kyle corrects with a smile.

"So, how are you guys doing?" I ask as I pull back onto the roadway.

"A lot better now that the powers back on." Kyle replies. "You never know how good you have it, until you don't."

"Amen to that." I reply.

"And you Paul?" Lisa asks.

"Same. I thought I knew what hard times were. Then Harvey blew through."

"We know what you mean. Having electricity and water back is like heaven compared to two weeks without. I don't know how the pioneers did it, seriously." Kyle adds.

"I think that's one reason they died so young." I respond.

"Ok, so I just realized, I don't know where your home is. Point me in the right direction."

"We live on Murphy road Paul, and thanks for the lift."

"My pleasure," I respond.

Driving past Armstrong, I find the next road is Murphy and turn right. Pulling up to their home, they get out and head for the door.

"Thanks for the ride Paul, and God bless you." Lisa calls out.

Repeating from before, "He already has Lisa, He already has."

Arriving a few minutes later at my own place, I see Jen's truck here, parked close to the house. It takes a second to realize that Eli's probably home too. Walking inside I find Eli propped up on the couch, eyes closed, with a light cover over him. Mindy's on his chest, asleep. Normally I'd call Mindy a traitor again, but I'll let it go—Eli needs the companionship.

I must have woken him up because he calls out in a raspy voice, "Hey kid, how you doin'?"

"I'm good Eli, how about you?"

"The Doc's say I'll be fine in a few days, but I never wanna' go through that again," holding his stomach with both hands. "Even with this 'girdle' wrapped all the way around, it feels like all my insides could fall out any minute." He chuckles, then grimaces in pain. "I can't laugh for a while either."

"It hurts just watching you lay there." I reply.

"Would you mind refilling my coffee cup on the table?" Eli asks, pointing to a mug in front of him.

"Of course. Anything else I can get you?" As I grab the cup up and walk into the kitchen.

"Nah, that's good for now." Then adds, "Jen tells me you've got a date tonight."

It's obvious there'll be no secrets in this house. "Yep, I'm meeting Sarah on the beach in Corpus Christi this evening. But don't worry Eli, she'll be safe, there'll be other people around," I reply half joking.

"Just treat her right, I'm kinda' partial to that little filly. She's as sweet as pie," he responds.

"Apple or cherry?" I reply with a smirk.

Giving me the stink eye, Eli responds, "Both, smart ass." Then it's all he can do not to start chuckling again and bring the stomach pain back.

Setting his coffee back down on the table, I respond, "I think she's pretty special too Eli. I promise to treat her right."

Looking my way, trying to keep a straight face he points two fingers towards himself and then at me as if to say, "I'll be watching you."

"Oh, and Mindy's only on loan." I tell him, "So don't go and get too attached."

Looking down at her sleeping in his lap, he replies, "I didn't know you'd called first dibs." He responds with a grin.

Jen joins us in the living room, and we spend time chatting. It feels more and more like a family every day that I'm here. I'm a happy man.

Chapter 32

It's about six o'clock as I exit my room and prepare to drive to Corpus. Eli must have gone to bed because Jen's alone at the kitchen table reading. I walk over and ask, "Hey Jen, do you think it would be a good idea to take Mindy to the beach tonight?"

Pausing with her thoughts, "I don't see why not, just be sure to take a bowl and some water with you. And a leash. I'm sure they're going to have leash laws in force down there."

"Yeah, I thought it might be fun to bring her with me, I hope Sarah doesn't mind."

"You could always text her."

"Good idea. By the way, can I use the carrier?"

"Sure, anytime," She replies with a smile.

"I appreciate it Jen, thanks."

"It's in the den down the hall on the shelf."

Texting Sarah, I finish getting ready, putting her candle in a handle bag with some tissue paper, the way I'd seen my mother do, for birthdays and Christmas. It makes me happy and sad all at the same time.

Finding the carrier, I load it into the jeep, strapping it down securely.

Back inside I find an old bowl and grab a gallon of water, adding it to the gift bag and the ice chest I've prepared for the evening. Loading the jeep I put a small blanket in the carrier and hunt Mindy down for her first ride with me. She seems anxious to go—I'm guessing this is nothing new to her.

"You and Matt have a nice evening Jen," I say as

I'm walking out the door, last minute items in hand.

"You too Paul, tell Sarah hi for us," Jen replies.

Driving down the road I'm grateful Mindy's inside some protection, the wind is swirling through the jeep, but she's ok. I can't wait to meet this guy and buy this top, assuming it's in decent condition. Passing through Portland and then over the Nueces Bay bridge, the setting sun is casting a warm glow over the area. What I refer to as 'bird island' on my right is covered with brown pelicans, spoonbills and gulls; I enjoy watching for them each time I pass by. A moment later, as I reach the top of the Harbor Bridge, I'm lucky enough to have an oil tanker pass right below me-- a fun sight for a guy like me. I always marvel at the four hundred-foot boats and the enormity of their size. It's even more fun to watch them as they pass through the channel near Port Aransas and see dolphins leap from the wake at their bow. Driving down through town, I take the ramp onto SPID and head towards the beach, twenty-five minutes away. Taking the off ramp for Rodd Field Road, I then turn left onto another street and follow the directions Steve gave me. Finding the right house number in a small subdivision, I spot a red jeep out front. Parking beneath the shade of a tree along the street, I turn off the key and head for the door. He must have seen me coming because he's already coming out.

Hand extended he says, "Are you Paul?"

Shaking it I reply, "Yes, and you must be Steve."

After we talk for a couple of minutes, he then opens the garage door and brings the top out, then helps me put it on, making sure it's a good fit. It's a tan color and my jeep's white, but you know what, I think it'll work out just fine.

Paying him in cash, "Thanks Steve, I'm going to enjoy having a roof again." I say smiling.

"De nada mi amigo," he answers. "Adios."

"Adios," I reply.

After checking to see if Mindy needs water, we get back onto the road. Turning on the air conditioning, I feel relieved to be able to use it, without it all going out the open roof. A moment later we're back on SPID and it's close to twilight. In less than fifteen minutes we turn left on Access Road 6, which puts us out on the beach just south of the pier. Sure enough, fifty yards away I see a small fire on the beach sand with about ten people surrounding it. First, I remove my shoes and socks, then, knowing it'll be dark soon I grab the flashlight from the bag I brought and grab Mindy's carrier. Walking over I spot Sarah, who's getting up to meet me.

"Thanks for coming!" Sarah calls out above the surf and light wind. "I'm glad you brought Mindy with you."

"Thanks for inviting me," walking up to her, "This looks great."

"Do you have more stuff in the jeep? Oh wow, you have a new top on it." She says, eyeballing the tan cover.

"The answer is yes, and no. There's more stuff to grab, and the top is used, but it is new to me," I reply smiling.

"Well, it looks fine from here. I'll take Mindy back to where we're sitting, if you want to grab the rest."

"It's a deal," responding as I hand off Mindy,

turn around and go back to the jeep.

Returning to the fire pit with the ice chest and bag, I locate my friend and see that she's brought two beach chairs, one for each of us. But the short kind, where you feel like you're on a sloped lounge chair; Adirondack I think they call it. Mindy is out of her kennel, but afraid to leave Sarah's lap, watching all the surrounding activity. After setting the gear down next to my chair, I grab two bottled waters from the chest, offering one to Sarah.

"No thanks." She answers, "But I am curious what's in the bag." I can just see her cat like grin in the waning light.

"You don't have much patience, do you?" I ask with a chuckle.

"Not when there's a surprise involved," She responds with a smirk.

Reaching into the large bag, I pull out the smaller gift bag, handing it over to her. "Remember the shells we collected on the beach the other day?" I ask. "I made a something for you with them— I hope you like it."

Taking it from my hand, she peeks down inside, then removes the tissue and slowly brings the candle out. "You made this?" Pausing, "I'm impressed Paul, this is really pretty. . . thank you!" Twirling it slowly to see the shells.

"You were kind enough to bring me out here the other day, when things weren't going so well. I wanted to show my appreciation."

"I love it, it's nice."

"Can I see it?" A girl sitting next to her asks.

"Sure, Monica." Sarah hands it to her as she

realizes I haven't been introduced to anyone at the fire; then calls out all their names in turn. At the end, she concludes, "Everyone, this is my friend Paul."

In a silly kind of way, they all say as one, "Hi Paul," and all start laughing. I get the feeling this is how all new people get introduced to the group, an initiation of sorts.

I sheepishly reply, "Hi everyone."

Just then I think Mindy has spotted a sand crab getting close, bravely coming in our direction. Sarah puts her down, and she runs after it, well, as fast as a dog with a cast on its paw can go, anyway. She gets about ten yards and then realizes it has disappeared, probably in one of a hundred holes surrounding us. Realizing she might need water now, I get her bowl out and pour some in, as Mindy gives up on the crab and trots back over.

"She's really cute Paul," Sarah states, looking down at her. Everyone goes back to their conversations, the candle making the rounds with all her friends.

"I like her a lot." Replying, "She's become my 'bud' in a way since the storm, almost like a fellow survivor I guess. We have a few things in common; her leg, my shoulder. She lost a home, I lost mine."

Mindy laps up the water, and then looks up at me, wanting in my chair with me. Once up, she settles in my lap but continues to be on guard for anything that might threaten us, her little head on a swivel; I guess she thinks she's part guard dog. I can't help but scratch behind her ears.

Looking towards the ocean for a while, Sarah and I simply enjoy the waves coming in, barely visible now, darkness closing in rapidly. I subconsciously run my toes through the sand, enjoying the coolness. Looking at her cell phone, Sarah announces to everyone it's 8:35, the moon should be coming up over the water in about twenty minutes. A murmuring of thanks comes back our way, and the private conversations continue. Someone adds more wood to the small fire and faces become more visible with the growing flames.

"So, tell me about what's going on with you lately," I ask Sarah, "How are classes?"

"Good. Things are a little crazy because of the hurricane and all, but it's coming together. I'm glad to be back in school, I love learning." Looking at me, she adds, "I guess I'm weird that way."

"I wouldn't say weird, as a matter of fact I admire that about you. The way you talked about the ocean the last time we were here, well, it made me think you're one of the smartest people I know. Nothing wrong with that Sarah."

"Thanks Paul. There are a lot of guys out there who don't really care for a nerdy girl like me."

"I don't know why you say 'nerdy', that's not how I see you at all. As a matter of fact, I kind of thought you might not like a guy like me so much. I'm not really the big partier the way so many of my friends are."

Looking into my eyes, she replies, "That's one of the reasons I *do* like you. You treat me like a good friend, someone you respect. That makes me feel special, it's a very attractive quality in you." Realizing this is getting a little uncomfortable, she changes the subject by asking, "So, what's the news Jen said I could expect from you?"

Letting out a little laugh, I say, "Well, you're not going to believe it."

"Please tell me, I'd like to hear the whole thing." Sarah says taking a sip of water.

So, I begin telling my tale; beginning with the accident I witnessed, and how much it impacted me. It still does for that matter, watching someone die is horrible, knowing it could have been me was terrifying. Then I go into detail about the dream (or vision) I had, thinking it might be real, and if so, knowing I might be able to reunite with my family in heaven one day. How I've rolled around in my head all the things that had happened in the last two weeks, and that my view of Christians, and their beliefs has changed. Then ending with Matt leading me through the prayer that now makes me born-again, I see her smile, the fire light making her soft features even more beautiful.

"Ok, so I've got to know how you feel about all that Sarah?"

Before she answers she silently points to the moon peeking above the watery horizon, full and bright. Reaching into her own bag, she pulls out a couple of cookies and hands one to me. Taking a nibble, I think 'snicker doodle', Sarah has handed me a 'snicker doodle'-- I love these cookies.

Minutes go by as I listen to the crashing of the waves, the moon soon cresting the top of the water. Then, Sarah calmly whispers in my ear, "There's something I need to tell you," Sounding ominous.

Looking at her, I say, "What is it?"

"I decided a long time ago I wouldn't let myself get close to anyone unless they were a Christian too, and I was convinced I might be alone for a long time.

Then, a couple of bad relationships made me want to give up looking for "Mr. Right" all together."

My heart begins to sink, feeling like the woman I've grown very close to is about to brush me off, "So, what about me? Where do I stand?" Trying to hide the disappointment in my voice.

Looking into my eyes she says, "I want you to know I've changed my mind." Relief washes over me and I'm filled with joy as Sarah leans over and kisses me on the lips.

End of Book One

Thanks for reading about Paul, Eli and the gang, I hope you enjoyed the book! What follows is the first two chapters of Book 2 in the Paul Stevenson series.

Hurricane Harvey Aftermath, Satan's Gambit

Introduction

Following the outcome of Hurricane Harvey's initial landfall in Aransas Pass, Texas, life has been slowly improving for Paul and Sarah as they grow to know each other better. Paul is now working full-time for a lumber company on Wheeler Avenue in Aransas Pass, and Sarah has a full schedule working towards her degree in Marine Biology at Texas A&M University, Corpus Christi.

Matt and Jen (Paul's landlords) are putting their lives back together as well after the hurricane, caring for their horses, as well as helping in their church and community.

Eli is recovering from his surgery (living with Matt and Jen since the storm) and now working with the next-door neighbor Brian, who's also a war veteran like him.

Since we last connected with our group, some businesses in the area have reopened, others have not, but hopes are high that things will improve as life continues day by day and that the Lord will see them through.

As a 'baby' Christian, Paul discovers another world opening up to him; the good things that come with his new faith and the many challenges that will try him, both in the physical realm as well as the spiritual one.

Jeriah and his companion Caleb, float lightly over the field near the house on Armstrong Rd. where Paul Stevenson lives, hiding in plain sight, doing only what angels can do.

"So, it's confirmed? All we can do is stand by and watch, we can do nothing to assist him?" Caleb asks his friend.

"This comes from Michael, we can only intervene with his express permission," Jeriah's voice resolute.

Convinced that this is the Lord's command, Caleb replies, "So it must be." And with that they unfold their wings, and gently lift off, noticed only by the Red-tailed Hawk in a nearby tree.

Chapter One
8:30 am —Wednesday October 11th   2017

Have you ever reached a point in your life when you feel like things are going really well, almost too good to be true? And something tells you the bottom is just about to drop out from beneath you? Yeah, me too.

O'Brian's Lumber store hadn't been open long when I spot Mr. Roberts approaching the paint counter where I work now, and although his daughter and I parted on good terms almost a year ago (or so I thought), the flames shooting from his eyes tells me the day is about to go south, very south indeed.

"Hello Mr. Roberts, did you need some paint today? I ask cautiously as he nears my counter.

"Paul, I'm glad I came in here today, because Sharon has been looking for you, and now we know where you've been hiding, you S.O.B.!"

"Whoa, Mr. Roberts, I have no idea why you're mad…"

Interrupting me, "Don't lie to me, I know why you've been blocking her phone calls and why you changed jobs. You can't run forever."

Having this counter between us allows me the courage (and space) to let some of my building anger creep into my voice, "What are you talking about?"

Walking in my direction, my friend (boss and landlord as well) Matt, asks, "What's going on over here?" Matt's large well-muscled physique easily matching Mr. Roberts.

"Do you work here?" Mr. Roberts demands, eyeballing Matt.

"I'm one of the managers, how can I help?" He stops directly in front of the man, facing him with a strong sense of confidence--- a confidence I lack.

Acting morally superior Roberts shoots back, "Yeah, you can fire this bastard. He got my daughter pregnant three months ago and then disappeared on her."

"What the hell!?" I gasp, "I haven't seen Sharon since... since, last winter!"

Walking up behind Matt is Brian and Eli (Eli's my friend and roommate). I was expecting him, as he and Brian are working together now, repainting homes in the area, damaged by Hurricane Harvey.

"Everything OK Matt?" Eli calls out calmly as he closes the gap between us.

Without taking his eyes off Mr. Roberts, he responds, "Nothing I can't handle, Eli. Thanks anyway."

"So, are you going to do something about this piece of trash, Or not?" Mr. Roberts spits out, his cheeks beginning to glow a bright shade of red.

"No, I'm not sir. Although I have not known Paul long, I believe him, and even if what you say is true, that's between him and your daughter. So, I'm politely asking you to leave."

They say a watched pot never boils, but this one's about to explode all over me. Leaning heavily on the counter-top, he says, "I'm not leaving until Paul tells me he'll man-up and take care of this kid that's on the way."

Crossing his arms across his chest, Matt looks at him and firmly says, "I have no idea who you are, but you need to leave now. And do not come back."

Two other employees in the store have wandered over, drawn by the spectacle, taking sides by standing behind Matt, Brian and Eli. Mr. Roberts quickly realizes he's outnumbered and has little recourse, but is still scheming; I can see the wheels turning furiously in his rage filled brain.

Looking between Matt and my co-workers, he sneers, "You won't do anything to me anyway, because if you do, I'll have you fired."

Taking a step forward, Eli counters as he looks up into Robert's face, "Mister, I don't work here so your little rule won't work on me. So, if you want to walk out on your own power, while you still can--- now's the time."

Looking down at Eli sporting a well-trimmed gray beard and handlebar mustache, he chuckles, "What's an old man like you gonna do? You think that knife on your belt scares me?"

Reminding me of a cowboy about to wrangle a wayward bull, he reaches for the knife and hands it back to Brian without losing eye contact, then quietly says, "It's not the knife you need to worry about."

Brian steps forward and adds, "I've got your back Eli."

I don't know if it was the sound of steel in his voice, or the confidence of a man who's been to war, but Mr. Roberts sail begins to deflate. Hesitation overcomes him, as he blinks a couple of times, finally grasping that he's already lost this battle and can't quite say why.

Looking around, attempting to save face he blurts out, "I wouldn't want to bust up an old fool like you anyway---- you'd probably snap like dry kindling."

Eli doesn't bat an eyelash. He just calmly stares Roberts down, waiting for the inevitable outcome; for the man in front of him to tuck tail and run. Stepping away from us he shouts toward me, "Now that we know where you are Paul, you'll be hearing from us. Don't try to run again because we'll find you no matter where you go."

Eli shouts back, "Paul's not goin' anywhere. But the next time you show up, do yourself a favor and bring some 'cajones' with you."

Daaamn---- was all I could think when he said that. That was gutsy, and maybe a little stupid. At least it would have been for me.

Looking at the retreating back of Mr. Roberts exiting the store, Matt turns to Eli, "A little over the top, don't you think?"

"Yeah, but it felt good," replying with a smirk.

The other two employees wander away now that the show is over. Matt, Eli, and Brian turn to face me directly, and after glancing at one another Matt asks, "Any truth to what he just said Paul?"

Pausing to gather my thoughts, and to wrestle down all the emotions coursing through me, I answer, "No, Matt. It's been almost a year since I've seen her. Nine or ten months at least, anyway." Looking into the distance, I add, "I knew she was angry when we broke up, well, more than angry. She wanted to get married in the worst way, and I, well, I just didn't. The longer I was with her, the crazier she became; calling several times a day, texting me all the time, tons of Facebook posts. It looks like she never got over it."

Eli muses, "This wouldn't be the first time a woman tried to trap a man with the old, 'You got me pregnant line.' But why now? Why when it would be hard to prove with so much time gone by?"

Looking at me with a discerning eye, Matt says, "I believe you Paul, but I think this is a long way from being over. We all need to pray on this and be prepared for anything. I've never met your old girlfriend, but if she has her father this worked up, there's no telling how many others she's convinced of the same thing. I suspect she's just getting started."

"I agree with Matt," Eli joins in his casual southern drawl, "and I can tell you there were at least two demons whisperin' in his ear Paul. There's something goin' on in the spiritual world here. Like Matt said, we need to all be praying on this. Something tells me it's not over."

"You actually saw them Eli?" I reply.

"Yeah, Kid." Looking around at all of us, he realizes there's more explanation needed, but he chooses this moment to turn around and head for the door.

Looking at Matt, I say, "Wow, do you think he's for real?"

Glancing at Eli's retreating back, he answers, "Yes, I think he is. And what I wouldn't give for a glimpse of what he just saw."

Chapter Two
3 pm

For a funeral, the weather couldn't have been much better— as those things go, especially along the Texas coastal bend where it's usually hot and steamy this time of year. Sure, it's October, but it doesn't really seem to cool off that much until the middle of November, which makes today kind of special— overcast with temps in the seventies.

Eli and I are here today at Brian's request, to honor the passing of a homeless Viet Nam Vet, who, unfortunately had no family to attend his funeral. Since Brian is a member of the Patriot Guard Riders, it's one of his duties (he calls it an honor) to attend the ceremony of those veterans who leave this world without anyone to give them a proper goodbye. I count myself privileged to join him in that duty today.

Looking at Brian I see he has his leather vest open now that he's no longer on his Harley and intrigued by what's printed on his shirt, asking, "Brian, what does your T-shirt say?"

Holding the vest open for easier viewing, and without the need to look down at the words, he quotes, "In Memory of the 58,479 Brothers and Sisters who never returned." Letting go of the vest he continues, "The Viet Nam War lasted from 1959 to 1975— now mostly forgotten. That's one of the reasons the 'Riders' exist, to make sure all who served get the proper respect at the end."

"Just be glad there's no draft now kid," Eli throws in, "most of those who served back then didn't have a choice."

Brian looks directly at me saying, "So, how you are feeling about that little scuffle at work today?"

"I really don't want to talk about it right now Brian. Can we discuss it later?"

Seeing the look of pain in my face he decides to cut me a break. "Ok, so make me proud and hold up one of these American flags for the procession, please." He takes one from a woman holding several nearby and passes it to me, "The hearse should be here any moment now."

Taking the ten-foot pole in my hand I reply, "Proud to." I'm just glad to be off the hook to tell him the story, for now anyway. I see a line forming— from the end of the dirt road, in this; the Veterans Cemetery in Corpus Christi and walk over to join it.

Following behind, Brian coaches me on the rules associated with this honor: "Never let the flag touch the ground, keeping it straight up, even in this wind. You will hold the flag with your right hand, with the bottom of the pole braced against your right foot. And because you're a flag bearer, you do not have to place your hand over your heart as the casket passes in front of you. Got it?"

"Got it." I reply, goose bumps coming over me as I look up at the Stars and Stripes.

Finding my place at the end I spot a line of motorcycles with American flags attached to the rear of each one, coming off highway 37, turning right onto Carbon Plant Road and coming this way. The thunder grows louder as a varied mix of bikes arrives with the hearse at the tail-end. Two Texas Highway Patrol cars in escort peel off and continue down the freeway. The bikers parking along either side of the drive create an honor guard with their bikes, dismounting, and then either saluting or placing their hands over their hearts, depending on whether they had previously served or not. (Brian told me once before you do not have to be former military to join the Patriot Riders.)

After they're all in position, the hearse creeps forward stopping close to the grave site. Emotions overcome me as I look around at all the flags and people in attendance for a man who probably thought no one would show up for his passing.

Six vets in uniform come forward and remove the coffin from the back, slowing bringing the remains to the canopy covered casket stand, in front of a podium and several chairs. The flag bearers around me begin rolling up the flags and storing them away in a nearby trailer, so I follow suit.

Walking back towards a crowd of maybe sixty or seventy people I find Brian and Eli near the back as we stand in respect; offering the seats to the many 'old soldiers' who are here today. I've never been to anything like this, and I'm glad Brian invited me.

A gentleman (60-ish) with a full gray beard and a black leather jacket approaches the podium and begins speaking, "Thank you for coming today. It is always sad to hear of a veteran who has no one to care for them at the end of their life, so we are honored, very honored, the Patriot Guard Riders and I, to have you join us this afternoon." Shifting his weight as he looks towards the casket, he continues, "My name is Mark Fellows and I'm a local pastor here in Corpus Christi. We're here this afternoon to pay homage to Donna Cummings, a woman who served proudly in the Army from 1970 to 1982. Donna spent several of those years as a nurse in the field hospitals of Viet Nam."

Wow, for some reason I assumed we would be here to pay respects to a man, not that it matters, it's just that homeless vets always seem to be men is all. I stand corrected.

The pastor reads off a list of her accomplishments and ribbons Donna was awarded and then tells us what little is known of her later years once she left the military. Brian is focused on Mark and his eulogy, but I notice Eli is distracted, looking around slowly, oblivious to the speech.

Nudging him, I quietly ask, "Everything ok?"

Without turning his head, he responds, "Yeah."

Not convinced I prod him a little more, "What do you see that's so interesting?"

Pausing for a moment, Eli responds, "Kid, you wouldn't believe me if I told ya."

"We survived a hurricane together Eli, what could be more unbelievable than that?"

Hesitantly, he replies, "I see angels here kid."

Confused, I ask, "You mean like beautiful women?"

"No, I mean like eight feet tall, holding swords, facing outward protecting the crowd." The serious look on Eli's face tells me he's not joking. Then adds, "Their swords are as tall as you are."

The sound of a trumpet playing Taps (also known as Butterfield's Lullaby, something from my Civil War history class back in High School) brings me back to the funeral, forcing me to save the rest of my questions for later. Is Eli messing with me? Could he really be seeing angels here? Glancing around I see nothing at all, just people. A five-and-a-half-foot sword sounds scary. An Eight-foot-tall angel even more so.

Numbers 22:31
Then the Lord opened Balaam's eyes, and he saw the angel of the Lord standing in the roadway with a drawn sword in his hand. Balaam bowed his head and fell face down on the ground before him.

Made in the USA
Columbia, SC
26 February 2020